Soup Night

ON

Union Station

Book Seventeen of EarthCent Ambassador

Soup Night on Union Station

Foner Books

ISBN 978-1-948691-20-8

Copyright 2019 by E. M. Foner

Northampton, Massachusetts

One

"In conclusion, it is the view of Union Station Embassy that the fastest way to an alien's heart is through his or her stomach, and a successful bid for the editorship of the next edition of the All Species Cookbook will raise humanity's profile as active participants in the tunnel network ecosystem while also giving us a chance to showcase innovative recipes from our own rich culinary traditions."

"Excellent," Kelly whispered hoarsely to her Vergallian co-op student. "It took me years of practice to make it through an entire report without pausing."

"Thank you, Ambassador," Aabina replied. "Memorizing and delivering speeches was a key component of my royal training. I'm honored that you would give me the opportunity to submit your report rather than asking Associate Ambassador Cohan to do it for you."

"He thinks I'm crazy for making weekly reports when they aren't required. I believe his exact words were, 'Why give them the ammunition?' Most of the ambassadors only submit reports when something goes so wrong that the president is going to find out about it anyway."

"Shall I begin transmission?" the Stryx librarian inquired.

"Yes, Libby," the EarthCent ambassador replied in her normal tone of voice, then gave a pained look and went back to whispering. "I don't know what I was thinking this

1

afternoon at the Frunge reception when I let Czeros talk me into a duet. Human throats just aren't designed to make those creaking sounds."

"If that's everything for today, my mother is expecting me at her embassy. We're hosting a breakfast for a visiting Fleet delegation, and they're cousins of a sort, so I have to put in an appearance."

"Please, enjoy, and say 'Hi' to Samuel for me. I haven't seen him at home all week and I'll be in bed by the time he gets off work."

"Have a good weekend," Aabina said, and exited the ambassador's office.

As soon as the doors closed behind her co-op student, Kelly glanced at the ceiling and asked, "Well?"

"Your sore throat seems to have cleared up nicely," the Stryx librarian observed.

"You knew I was pretending all along, didn't you? Do you think Aabina could tell?"

"I wouldn't be surprised, but it was still a nice gesture on your part. There aren't many ambassadors who would fake an infirmity to let a co-op student from a different species make an official report to the home government."

"I don't want to lose her, Libby. Do you think I could convince Aabina to stay around until I retire? Joe suggested giving her new responsibilities to keep the job interesting, but she's so efficient that I'm running out of ideas."

"The point of the cooperative education program is to provide students with workplace experience, not to keep them permanently in low-paying jobs. And don't forget that she'll be out next Wednesday for the Open University's halfway assessment."

"Halfway!" Kelly groaned. "Has it been three months already?"

"She's been working for you almost two cycles, and four cycles is the limit for participation in the co-op program."

"Can't you make an exception?"

"Do you want me to keep Aabina registered in school against her will so you can employ her without benefits?"

"You know that's not true. I'd love to hire her full-time, but even if EarthCent goes along with it, I don't think it would be fair to offer her the job."

"You're worried about her reputation with her own people."

"Of course. Being a co-op student gives her political cover—she's working for us because the Open University assigned her here. But for a member of a Vergallian royal family and the daughter of their Union Station ambassador to take a job working directly for EarthCent…"

"Would you have a problem if Samuel accepted full-time work at the Vergallian embassy when his co-op assignment is over?"

"Of course not, if that's what he wants, though I thought he'd be returning to the Open University. I know that the Vergallians would pay him much better than I could in any case," she added ruefully.

"But you would be comfortable employing Aabina for less than she could earn working the same job in her mother's embassy."

"You're the one who told me that she doesn't need the money. I'm doing my best to pay her in experience."

"It would set a bad precedent to change the rules to accommodate a single student," the Stryx librarian mused.

"But it's not just Aabina," Kelly insisted. "Joe really enjoys working with Samuel's Horten friend, Marilla. She's a fast learner, the dogs love her, and she knows a surprising amount about running a rental fleet considering her only prior experience was cleaning returns. But I don't see how she can stay on after the co-op period is up because she's dating the Horten ambassador's son. Ortha had to bribe somebody to fake their Peace Force records so it looks like she's doing outreach work to a primitive species."

"As long as Ambassador Ortha and Joe are comfortable with the arrangement, I don't see why it couldn't continue without the Open University functioning as a middleman. The Hortens have been sending Peace Force volunteers to work with primitive species for hundreds of thousands of years. It's the other side of the piracy coin."

"What does the one have to do with the other?"

"The Hortens aren't comfortable with behavioral extremes so they push their young misfits to separate themselves from polite society. Peace Force gives them a place to send the young idealists who would otherwise be demanding change at home."

"Aabina's spoiled me, Libby. Maybe I'm just getting old, but I can't imagine going into a meeting without her briefings. Since she's started helping with my speeches I've been getting requests left and right to give keynote addresses at business conventions. We wouldn't have even known about the All Species Cookbook if she hadn't mentioned it as a possibility. I've been meaning to ask you how come it never came up before."

"Most of the cooks who have bought a new edition in the last million years have been AI. Can you guess why that is?"

Kelly bit back her first response and gave it some thought. "Artificial intelligences don't have taste buds?"

"The cookbook was originally conceived as a way to bring the species together, but it quickly became apparent that the only way to guaranty safety was to limit the ingredient list to the lowest common denominators, foods that wouldn't poison any of the tunnel network species. You've eaten Vergallian vegan?"

"I try to avoid it."

"There's a large section on Vergallian vegan, which might explain Aabina's familiarity. You know that she keeps a strict diet."

"I try to get her to eat more, but—wait. Are you saying we shouldn't be bidding for editorship of the cookbook? Blythe and Chastity both thought it was a great idea, and I assumed you would warn them if it wasn't."

"You know I can't provide that sort of competitive information. It wouldn't be fair to any other species taking part in the auction."

"That's the part I don't get," Kelly said. "From what I understand, the last major edition was published almost eighty thousand years ago. But after Aabina mentioned that the editorship was something we might want to look into, it turns out the next auction is only a few weeks away."

"The timing is controlled by the current rights owners,"

"The Hortens, I know. I have a meeting scheduled with Ortha next week. I was surprised at how quickly he was able to find me an open slot." Kelly paused again, reviewing the conversation in her mind and seeking any subtext in case the Stryx librarian was delivering hidden clues. "Will we be the only species bidding?"

"That's competitive information."

"We will, won't we," the ambassador concluded triumphantly. "But what's so bad about editing the All Species Cookbook?"

"What do you usually do when you have a question about the other species that I won't answer?" the Stryx librarian prompted.

"I ask Bork or Dring. Thank you, Libby. Dring is coming to dinner tonight so I'll start with him."

"Will you be making something from the All Species Cookbook?"

"Very funny. Dring is a vegetarian, or at least, that's all I've ever seen him eat. He and Aisha are always exchanging seeds and recipes."

"And you can eat all of his produce?"

"Of course, it's just salad ingredients." Kelly paused again and looked thoughtful. "That's not true in general, is it? I tried a taste of a Grenouthian tomato once and I had to run for the bathroom, and you stopped me that time I almost bit into a Dollnick apple at an embassy reception."

"Just because it looks like an apple and the name translates to 'apple' doesn't mean that it's an apple."

"So why can we eat all of Dring's produce? Does he get all of his seeds from Aisha?"

"You'd have to ask her."

"Do you mean you don't know or you aren't telling?"

"A Horten just entered the reception area and Donna isn't at her desk."

"She left early because it's Chastity's son's birthday and—you know that," Kelly cut herself off and rose from her desk. On second thought, she grabbed her purse and then headed out to the reception area.

"Ambassador McAllister?" the immaculately dressed alien with yellow-tinted skin inquired.

"Yes. May I help you?"

"My card," the Horten said, producing a plastic chit with a flourish.

Kelly accepted the card and studied the alien characters without success. "I'm sorry, I don't even recognize this language."

"My mistake. If you have a coin, the silvery coating with Universal Eleven rubs off."

"Like one of those instant lottery tickets the Tharks sell?" Kelly dug in her purse for a five-cred coin, and placing the plastic card on Donna's desk, carefully began rubbing off the coating. "What's Universal Eleven?"

"The eleventh attempt by linguists to come up with a written language that all of the tunnel network members can adopt for official correspondence and scientific publications."

"I've never heard of it. Was it any more successful than the previous ten?"

"The only publication to use Universal is the All Species Cookbook."

"You're with the cookbook?" She brushed away all of the little bits of silver coating the coin had rubbed off and saw a typical Horten business card, including a graphic that showed an egg of some sort being cracked on the edge of a mixing bowl.

"Ursho, the current maintenance editor. I understand that you'll be bidding."

"That's our plan. I hope you don't think we're trying to put you out of a job."

"Not at all," the editor hastened to reassure her. "My term as the caretaker has been an honor, but I'm more than ready to turn the keys over to the next species. I just stopped by to see if you needed any further information to

7

put your bid package together because I've been informed that this will be the first time EarthCent is participating in the auction process for a tunnel network monopoly."

"Monopoly?"

"Of course. You don't imagine there are two official All Species Cookbooks, do you? It may be the smallest of the monopolies but it's quite prestigious in certain circles."

"With AI cooks?"

"Well, yes," Ursho said, looking slightly deflated. "How did you know that?"

"An educated guess. I don't want to sound ignorant, but what are the other monopolies you're talking about?"

"There must have been a translation glitch," the Horten said, turning a deeper shade of yellow and backing towards the exit. "If you need anything before the auction, just ping me, or better yet, have your bid team get in touch." He turned and fled as soon as the doors slid open.

"Libby?"

"Yes, Ambassador."

"What other monopolies is he talking about?"

"You'll be late for dinner if you don't get moving."

"So tell me in the lift tube," Kelly said, picking up her purse and exiting the embassy.

"I'm not hiding anything from you," the Stryx librarian replied. "The tunnel network members are always generating new ideas for collaborative efforts and the All Species Cookbook is an early example."

"But why haven't I ever heard of these monopolies before?"

"We only grant them for low priority projects. When something affects the security and welfare of all tunnel network members, such as interstellar ice harvesting, there's a proven diplomatic process for establishing treaties and enforcement mechanisms. Less important initiatives are subcontracted to monopolies which bid for the privilege of trying their hand."

"Sounds awfully haphazard," Kelly commented, as the lift tube capsule set off without instructions. "Since you've been hiding the existence of these monopolies from us to date, I assume that there's a reason."

"It's possible that in some cases, accepting responsibility for a monopoly can have negative consequences," Libby hedged. "As Ursho told you, the All Species Cookbook is the smallest of the monopolies, so the downside financial risk is relatively limited."

"Can you give me an example of a monopoly that went wrong, or are you going to make me ask Dring?"

"Very well. Sometime back during a recycling craze, a number of tunnel network species became obsessed with finding a practical use for nail and talon clippings. Stryx Fersh on Cube Station created a monopoly to deal with the issue, and the Huktra won the management contract at auction."

"When Samuel was working in your lost-and-found, he got a big tip for returning a lost egg to a brooding Huktra mother."

"Their hatchlings are very competitive, and pushing any other eggs out of the nest is a common strategy for the firstborn. The Huktra also generate large quantities of talon clippings when living in space because they aren't wearing their claws down in a natural environment."

"So what went wrong?" Kelly asked, as she exited the lift tube capsule and headed for home.

"It was the first monopoly win for the Huktra and they wanted to make an impression. They started right off collecting nail and talon clippings from all of the stations on the tunnel network before coming up with a recycling plan. In the end, they spent a fortune on storage and shipping before giving up and dropping the lot into a black hole."

"Are you making this up?"

"Cross my heart," Libby responded.

"Crossing your fingers is more likely," Kelly muttered, but she resigned herself to waiting to ask somebody who wasn't constrained by the rules the Stryx imposed on themselves when it suited their purposes.

Joe had already set the table and was enjoying a vegetable smoothie with Dring when she entered the ice harvester and let Beowulf take her purse. The Cayl hound sniffed the handbag for signs of hidden treats or alien surveillance bugs, and then trotted off to put it on the bedroom dresser.

"Good evening, Dring," Kelly greeted the Maker. "Are all of those books for me?"

"Cookbooks. You mentioned that you're bidding on the All Species Cookbook monopoly and I thought you might want to review some previous editions."

"Real paper books? I thought it would just be distributed electronically. Libby mentioned that AI cooks were the only ones who ever bought it."

"Perhaps she meant the only ones who ever read it," Dring said diplomatically. "The first editions usually sell out their print run as coffee table books or gag gifts, no pun intended. The illustrations can be quite nice."

"But nobody actually makes the recipes?"

"I've spent many millennia in Vergallian space, and while it's not on anybody's top thousand list, academic cooks usually have one of the prior editions in their library. I had these printed up at the on-demand boutique the

10

Galactic Free Press started operating for out-of-copyright works from Earth."

"I leafed through a couple of cookbooks before you got home," Joe said. "The translations are so bad that I'd be afraid to follow a recipe for making hot chocolate with instant mix, but Dring says that's typical for Universal."

"Why is that?" Kelly asked the Maker.

"Lack of a sufficient corpus," Dring explained. "Translation technology is a combination of clever algorithms and brute force pattern recognition. Your translation implants utilize equivalency tables distilled from the nearly infinite quantity of written and spoken words each species creates, but every iteration of Universal is an arbitrary language designed by committee with no reference to previous versions or living languages. Since the only real-world application for Universal is the publication of the All Species Cookbook, it's like trying to recover a unique dead language from a single scroll. One of the reasons the cookbook is popular with AI chefs is that they enjoy the translation challenge."

"Then how do the Vergallians use it?"

"They look at the pictures and estimate the quantities."

"I don't understand. What's the point of publishing a cookbook in a universal language that nobody uses?"

"Ah, there's an interesting story behind the All Species Cookbook that one of my brothers presented at the last historical conference I attended. The Grenouthians were responsible for the first edition, which came out several million years ago, and they solicited the help of linguists from a dozen different species to construct a language that nobody could understand. They never made their reasons public, but the goal was likely to disguise the fact that they were publishing a thick book of recipes that nobody would want to eat."

"That follows the sort of twisted logic the older tunnel network species employ," Joe said. "I remember Srythlan telling me that if a Verlock doctor can't cure a disease, he'll quote an astronomical price for treatment. If by some chance the patient has that much money, the doctor will just double the price. It's the way advanced species deliver bad news and save face at the same time."

"So you're telling me that when the Grenouthians realized they couldn't actually come up with tasty recipes that all of the tunnel network species could share without poisoning themselves, they decided to make the cookbook indecipherable so nobody would actually use it?"

"They created plausible deniability," the Maker confirmed. "If anybody was to complain that they made one of the recipes and it was awful, the Grenouthians could always claim it was the fault of the translation."

"But what if somebody requested a recipe in the original language?"

"On the day they published, the Grenouthians reported that an unfortunate fire had incinerated the editorial office and all of the records were destroyed. When the Verlocks edited the cookbook, they lost the archive to volcanic activity. The Frunge editors blamed the data erasure on a hacking attack, the Dollnicks claimed that their publishing tradition insists on the destruction of all drafts in the theory that they're inferior, and so on."

"Is that really a Dollnick tradition?"

"They may have pretended it was for a few cycles after the cookbook was published."

"Are you sure you want to go ahead with the bid, Kel?" Joe asked. "I know how enthusiastic you were about finding a new project to keep Aabina busy, but it sounds more like a punishment."

"I already told Donna she could be the editor if we win. You know how much she likes trying alien recipes by substituting ingredients. Besides, we cook for aliens all the time and they wouldn't come back if they didn't like it. Now that I think of it, whenever the Gem caterers know that there will be a number of species attending an event, they mainly serve human food. That reminds me, Dring. How come we can eat all of the vegetables from your garden?"

"They're all Earth varieties."

"Even the blue tomato things that taste like peppers and the stringy black-leafed lettuce?"

"Heirloom seeds," the Maker replied. "And while we're on the subject, what's for dinner?"

"I'll ask you again later," the ambassador said, rising and heading for the kitchen. "We're having Aisha's leftovers and all I have to do is heat it up and put it out."

Two

"It all comes down to marketing in the end," Dorothy said, passing a large carton filled with individual serving-sized bags of pretzel sticks over the counter of the chandlery to her husband. "We have the best lineup of cross-species fashions on the tunnel network, but all anybody wants lately are Baa's enchanted accessories for role-playing. And do you know why?"

"I have a feeling you're going to tell me," Kevin replied. He gingerly removed a sample from the carton, taking the utmost care to prevent the biaxially oriented polypropylene bag from making any sound as he opened it. When he looked back up, both Beowulf and Alexander were on their hind legs with their front paws on the counter.

"Like father like son," the EarthCent ambassador's daughter observed. "Better give them each a bag or they'll be reenacting the Cayl invasion of Nangor."

"You really know your galactic history," Kevin said. He came around the counter, dumped a bag of pretzels into each dog's snack dish, and checked that there was plenty of water in the communal bowl. Then he grabbed the next carton from the stack and returned behind the counter.

"The emperor stayed with us once when I was a kid. He and Beowulf could chase each other around Mac's Bones for hours." Margie coughed and stretched in her sleep, causing both of her parents and the dogs to freeze. Then the baby resumed her steady breathing and the pretzel munching and conversation recommenced. "Anyway, I was going to say that everybody wants Baa's enchanted fashions because of all of the exposure they get from broadcasts of the Live Action Role Playing league."

"I assume that Jeeves is paying the LARPing federation a pretty cred for the privilege."

"He won't tell me the amount," Dorothy fumed. "How am I supposed to know what's fair to demand that he spend promoting our ballroom fashions without the proper context?"

"I'd say Jeeves is one step ahead of you there. Pass me that next carton."

"Why are you stocking up on salty snacks all of a sudden?" Dorothy asked, even as she complied with his request. "Are you planning to start selling my dad's beer?"

"Carbonized beverages don't work in Zero-G. When there's no weight, the bubbles aren't displaced by the liquid and you end up with a stomach full. Rather than burping, the bubbles pass through your digestive—"

"La, la, la, la, la," Dorothy sang, putting her fingers in her ears. "Don't want to hear where the bubbles come out."

Kevin raised his hands in a sign of submission and his wife dropped her arms. "You know that the official business launch for Tunnel Trips is next week," he continued.

"But Dad and Paul have been renting ships for months. I thought the only change was that some of the sovereign human communities with tunnel connections were opening their franchises on Monday."

"Until now, all of the rentals have been round trip because the ships had to be returned to Mac's Bones. Starting next week, renters will be able to drop the ships at any franchise location. It's going to make a big difference in demand."

"And you want to make sure they have enough pretzels?"

"And popcorn, and chips. One-way means short trips. It takes less than a half hour for a small ship to get to the tunnel entrance from Union Station, and most of the destinations are space elevator hubs or orbitals that are within an hour of tunnel access. The main part of the trip will be coasting through the tunnels at Zero-G, so snack food should be a big seller."

"Is that why you bought all of those juice boxes with the rubber seal around the straw? I thought you were expecting more family traders with children."

"It's not the seal around the straw that makes them special, it's the bladder and the box. When you suck through the straw, you're actually emptying a bladder, and there are little holes in the box that allow in air to fill the space."

"Why not just drink from squeeze tubes like we always did?"

"People prefer the boxes because they're less likely to get ruptured by accidents. Marilla said that the Frunge don't allow squeeze tubes on their rentals because it's a pain to clean up if somebody starts fooling around and squishes a tube just to see the liquid shoot out. With the juice boxes, you have to put the straw in your mouth and suck."

"How about water?"

"I've got water boxes too, and there are tea and coffee versions with integrated heating circuits. I've been cutting down on bulk orders of canned goods to make room."

"See, that's what's so unfair. You can adjust to your market just by changing what you buy the next day while I spend months developing a new fashion. By the time it's out of manufacturing and into a boutique, a half a year may have gone by."

"Do you want to compare selling prices and margins?" Kevin retorted. "If I sell the rest of the pretzels in that carton for the full retail price, I'll just about break even on what the dogs are going to mooch."

"Look, you've offended them," Dorothy said. Beowulf and Alexander sprinted off towards the training camp on the other side of the hold.

"Are there any pretzels left in their bowls?"

"All right, maybe they just finished. But the point is I spent years designing dance shoes and ball gowns, and if sales don't pick up, I'm afraid Shaina and Brinda will concentrate on the enchanted stuff while other fashion businesses eat my market."

"I thought you had a bunch of patents on the heels and those fancy gown features."

"We do, but being the best isn't good enough in fashion. You have to keep your products in front of people or they forget about you and move on to the next new thing."

"Well," Kevin said, removing a chewed tennis ball from the space below the counter where he wanted to store a box and throwing it in the general direction the dogs had taken, "I'd say that what you need are bigger balls."

"Excuse me?"

"Or more balls, it amounts to the same thing in the end."

"What are you talking about?"

"More potential customers for your shoes and gowns. I got to talking with Vivian about her competitive dancing days at our last picnic. She explained that even though the Vergallians are ballroom fanatics, they would never wear your dancing shoes because they aren't certified as competition compliant. I don't know if you ever looked into that, but—"

"We did, and they just laughed," Dorothy said. "Competition shoes can't include any active technology, so the gyroscopic stabilizers and the adaptive heel height are *prima facie* disqualifications."

"What does that mean?"

"Oh, it's the translation of some Frunge legal term I picked up from Flazint's boyfriend. He said they use it for evidence that can refute a claim on the first sight."

"I like talking with Tzachan, but sometimes my implant just translates his legal vocabulary from Frunge words I don't know into English words I don't know."

"Mom says a lot of our legal terms are actually Latin, and that it comes up a lot in diplomacy too."

"When are we chaperoning Flazint and Tzachan's next date?"

"I forgot to tell you? A week from Wednesday morning at six. Mom offered to watch Margie until she goes in to the embassy, and then Fenna can babysit until we get back."

"Do you think Fenna is old enough to watch the baby by herself?"

"Aisha doesn't leave for the studio until mid-morning, and there will be plenty of adults around in Mac's Bones, including the dogs and Dad."

"And what about Fenna's school?"

"They just started their long break, didn't you notice? You'll see a lot of her the next couple months, and probably her friend Mikey as well."

"Maybe I can hire them for something," Kevin said. "I was helping my dad trade by the time I was ten. But still, it seems funny getting up early to take my wife on a double date."

"We all agreed that it's only fair we start chaperoning half of the dates on the Frunge clock. Tzachan never would have let on, but I finally pried it out of Flazint that they've gotten up in the middle of their night on weekdays a few times to go out with us on our Friday evening."

"Can you pass me that last box?"

"It's too heavy," Dorothy said, after trying to move it with her foot. "What's in there?"

"Air fresheners. Your dad said that Marilla suggested them."

"A whole box? How many air fresheners can they need? They barely have two dozen ships available for rental."

"I'll be selling them to the renters, not to the agency. Marilla takes them out when she cleans the returns."

"Why not get them back from her and sell those?"

"Wouldn't be ethical, and besides, they don't last that long by design," Kevin said, coming back around the counter and hefting the box. "These are only good for seventy-two hours after you remove the wrapper."

"You know, Baa told me the other day that her enchantments all wear off with time."

"Does that mean that SBJ Fashions is going to get hammered with returns?"

"No, they're good for hundreds of years, and warranties on apparel and accessories never last that long. I was just surprised because I thought they were permanent. Of course, I thought that my shoes would go on selling forever too, and it turns out that they were just a fad," she concluded in a sad voice.

"They aren't a fad, Dorothy," Kevin said, storing the box of air fresheners on a lower shelf. "The fashion reporter for the Galactic Free Press described your shoes as 'Timeless classics.' You just chose to design for a market that wasn't as big as you thought. If everybody bought shoes like Chastity, you'd be richer than—"

"Richer than Chastity," Dorothy interjected. "Isn't it weird that my babysitter when I was growing up is so rich that people on the station have started using her name as a benchmark for wealth?"

"You said she's your best customer."

"Chastity's a ballroom fanatic and Marcus is a dance instructor. It's a marriage made in heaven."

"Maybe you could sponsor a series of formal dances on Stryx stations," Kevin suggested. "Then you'd have the kind of promotional opportunity that SBJ Fashions gets from the LARPing league for Baa's Bags."

"That's not a bad idea, but I doubt Jeeves would ever go for it. Between renting a venue, hiring an orchestra, and advertising, costs add up pretty quick."

"Maybe Chastity and Blythe would co-sponsor. They could buy tickets and give them to InstaSitter employees as a bonus."

Dorothy's eyes took on a dangerous gleam. "I can't believe I never thought of that."

"I'm not a complete idiot at business, you know."

"If EarthCent wins the bid for the All Species Cookbook, I'll get Mom to co-sponsor too."

"Don't make it more complicated than you have to," Kevin warned her. "Besides, I don't see the connection."

"Our fashions are cross-species," Dorothy explained. "We'll put on all-species dances and promote the All Species Cookbook for EarthCent at the same time."

"Why not put advertisements for the new rental fleet on the backs of the dresses?"

"No, that won't work," Dorothy said, missing her husband's gentle sarcasm. "Showing some skin is part of the allure."

An alien girl wearing safety-color coveralls and carrying a toolbox approached. "Morning," she whispered. "Is Margie sleeping?"

"Out like a light," Dorothy confirmed. "Do you have a minute?"

Marilla glanced around before replying, "I think so. Your father told me to meet him here."

"Joe must be planning to start on that bumboat out back," Kevin said, breaking into a wide smile.

"What's a bumboat?" Marilla asked. "It translated to something that's not very nice in Horten."

"It's kind of specialized vocabulary. Bumboats are the smallest type of ship's tender. Joe said he only learned the name himself reading Kelly's old books. Back on Earth, bumboats used to go out to ships that were anchored in rivers or just off the coast and sell supplies, mainly to the sailors."

"I don't understand," the Horten girl said. "I thought that crews were provided for by their employers."

"I don't know much about history myself, but I think the bumboats mainly sold stuff that the sailors couldn't get otherwise without going on shore. Basic provisions for the whole ship would have been bought by the captain through a chandlery."

"But you're running a chandlery," Dorothy pointed out.

"Just for the little family ships that come in and need a sack of potatoes or a few spools of twine," Kevin said. "I can take the bumboat out to the big cargo ships and colony vessels that don't enter Union Station's core."

"And what will you sell them?"

"Potatoes and twine? I don't know, I'll work that part out once I have a bumboat to reach them. Your dad was willing to let me try it with the Nova, but it would be wasteful to use a tug to deliver a pack of playing cards, and she's too big to fit in a lifeboat berth."

"Wait a minute," Dorothy said. "Do you mean to tell me that the old Sharf lifeboat out back is going to be your new bumboat?"

"It's perfect," Kevin confirmed. "They're real fuel misers, and it's almost impossible to get into an accident. And because it will fit in the standard lifeboat berth, there's no messing around with flexible airlocks or spacesuits."

"But aren't all of the lifeboat berths on cargo ships always filled?" Marilla asked.

"Ships crewed by humans are the bottom of the barrel, so there are usually a number of lifeboats missing," Kevin told the Horten girl, who turned grey with horror at the news. "Sorry."

"Morning," Joe announced himself. "Has anybody seen Beowulf? I want him to check your bumboat for coolant leaks."

"He and Alexander were here a few minutes ago, but they ran off in the direction of the training camp," Dorothy replied.

"Well, we've lost him for at least ten minutes. Thomas and Chance are starting a new kidnap avoidance class for Galactic Free Press reporters and there's always a breakfast buffet the first morning."

"What kind of repairs will we be doing?" Marilla asked. "I thought Sharf lifeboats were guaranteed for the life of the propulsion unit, and after that, the buyer is required to recycle them."

"This one sort of slipped through the cracks," Joe told her with a boyish grin. "I dug up a spare propulsion unit with a few years of life left on it that we'll be installing, and then it's mainly a reconfiguration job. The life support pods were removed by somebody else a long time ago, so I was planning on putting in a cooler and as many Zero G storage lockers as will fit. Do you have any special requests, Kevin?"

"Could you mount the lockers without welding so I can take them out if we get a special order for something that wouldn't fit otherwise?"

"I've got a couple of quick-release clamps around here so we'll work something out." Joe caught a movement in his peripheral vision and turned towards the entrance of Mac's Bones. "I see our weary co-op student is home."

Samuel noticed the gathering at his brother-in-law's chandlery and jogged over. "Is it really morning?" he asked.

"On the Human clock, it is," Marilla replied brightly. "Long day at the embassy?"

"The usual. Didn't the Open University send you an alert about the half-way thing later today? You're supposed to take the day off."

"I know, but it's not for another few hours and I wanted to get some work in," the Horten girl replied.

"I'm going to grab a nap, but I'll set my implant alarm, so if you stop by the house we can go together."

"Wait a second, Sam," Dorothy called after her brother. "Didn't you say something about wanting to get Vivian out dancing again?"

"Maybe?" the EarthCent ambassador's son replied cautiously. "Why?"

"SBJ Fashions is going to sponsor a series of fancy dress balls in cooperation with the Galactic Free Press and the All Species Cookbook. I'm thinking it would be a good idea to have some strong dancers available to help get things started."

"I know they haven't even held the auction for rights to the All Species Cookbook yet because it came up at work today. Is the part about the Galactic Free Press true?"

"It will be," Dorothy insisted. "Just mention it to Vivian and tell her I'll throw in a designer dress."

Samuel gave a noncommittal grunt and headed off for his nap. Joe led Marilla around the back of the chandlery to start working on the bumboat. Margie woke up and firmly requested her mother's immediate attention, which Dorothy provided by moving the baby from her bassinet to the stroller.

"When will you be home?" Kevin asked.

"The usual time, unless Margie interferes with everybody's work and I have to bring her home early. I'm not sure who else is even going to be in the office today, other than Baa and the Hadads."

"The who?"

"Shaina and Brinda, that's their maiden name."

"Old Peter is their father? I must have forgotten."

"Don't let them hear you call him that. And he's not much older than Dad."

"Joe's pushing seventy himself," Kevin said, but he took care to lower his voice. "I buy all of my can openers from Peter and I was going to stop in and see him about stock for the bumboat. It's the odd little gadgets that nobody knows they need that sell for a good profit."

"That certainly describes Kitchen Kitsch," Dorothy said, tucking a quilt around the baby. "Don't work too hard, and don't let my dad work too hard either." There was a scrabble of claws scratching at the smooth deck as Beowulf arrived, and he looked questioningly at Dorothy and Kevin in turn.

"Around the back," Kevin said, jerking his thumb. "They're waiting for you."

Three

"Simmer down, simmer down," barked the giant bunny, who stood at the front of the classroom alongside an even larger Verlock. "You, in the first row. Stick a tentacle in it."

"Fool me once, you're the fool," the Drazen shot back. "Do you think we've already forgotten that prank you and Grynlan pulled at orientation?"

"Here by special request," rumbled the Verlock. "Opening act."

A Dollnick princeling rose to his feet and glared at the mismatched duo. "Are you serious? On your honor?"

"On our honor," the pair intoned solemnly. Then the Grenouthian continued alone, talking at a clip that would put a used-spaceship salesman to shame. "I can understand why you wouldn't trust us. The fact is that the Open University administration recognizes this halfway checkup for cooperative education students is a waste of everybody's time, so they hired us to keep it light. We just have a three-point checklist they insisted on, and then Grynlan and I can do a little improv act we hope you'll all enjoy."

"Are you going to make fun of humans again?" Vivian demanded.

"Who, me? I got a perfect score on the sensitivity course for new Open University contractors. Grynlan and I are only doing the warm-up, so let us earn our money, and then we'll take our seats with the rest of you."

"Get it over with, then," the Drazen said, in a long-suffering voice. "What's on the checklist?"

"Performance," the Verlock declared.

"That's right, performance," the Grenouthian repeated. "How many of you feel that you're in over your head at your current assignment? We all know that your first professional job can be a bit overwhelming, especially if you happen to be working for a species that's, let's face it, better than your own. Nobody? Not even a little?"

"He's looking right at me, Sam," Vivian growled.

"Being obnoxious is his shtick," Samuel reminded his fiancée. "I thought they gave Jorb and Grude a great sendoff."

"Well, that's good news," the Grenouthian continued. "The fallback plan was to put you to work picking up trash on the park decks, but the maintenance bots and the station scouts might have made trouble. Grynlan?"

"Hours," the Verlock droned.

"Hours, that's right. We know that some of you working for alien species must be having trouble adjusting to their clocks. Any complaints about sleep deprivation? Halluci-nations? Is anybody seeing a giant white rabbit right now? We promise to use your data for the benefit of future co-op students. Who's brave enough to admit it?"

"I had a little trouble adjusting to Vergallian hours," Samuel spoke up. "It's more the length of the day than the constant mismatch with home, but napping helps a lot."

"Of course it does," the Grenouthian said. "Everybody get that? If you're having any problems at work, the Human recommends napping on the job."

"Napping," the Verlock repeated loudly, drowning out Samuel's protest that his reply was being mischaracterized.

"And last on the list," the bunny prompted his partner.

"Permanent employment," Grynlan pronounced, like he was speaking through a mouthful of gravel.

"Permanent employment. Will those of you who received—strike that—those of you who haven't received a permanent offer of employment, please raise an appendage."

Samuel and Vivian raised their hands and looked around. Aabina had her hand up, along with Wrylenth, but the four of them were it. Marilla sat on Sam's other side with her arms down, and noticing his questioning look, she whispered, "Your dad asked me this morning if I'd stay on once the co-op assignment is over."

"Two things jump out at me," the Grenouthian said. "First, one-hundred percent of our Human contingent hasn't been offered a permanent job, and second, one-hundred percent of the remaining students who haven't been asked to stay on are employed by Humans. I'm no mathematical genius, but it looks like more than random noise to me."

"Statistically significant," Grynlan concurred.

"It's because most of you are working for a family business, and the only reason you're in the co-op program is that your relatives are too cheap to pay you otherwise," Aabina said scornfully. "As an official representative of EarthCent who has sworn to do her best for humanity, I intend to file a report with the Open University questioning your suitability as an opening act for mixed species events."

"Made that part up," the Verlock ground out, and then the two large aliens performed a belly bump and dissolved in their respective versions of laughter.

"Not again," groaned the Drazen in the front row. "You swore on your honor."

"Everybody knows that oaths administered via translation don't count," the Grenouthian replied.

"All right, settle down," a tall Dollnick from admin shouted, putting an end to the legal debate about oath-breakers before it could start. He strode between the desks to the front of the classroom and glared at the comedy duo. "Sit down, you two, and if I catch you impersonating Open University employees again, I'll personally see to it that we hire you."

The Grenouthian regained his seat in a single bound, and Grynlan made it back to his chair in record time. The Dollnick nodded approvingly.

"All right, I don't have anything to hand out today, so unless somebody has a legal complaint about their employer to file, I'm going to keep this short and sweet." The admin clerk did a quick headcount of those present and then blew through a small pitch pipe before whistling a song. "Thirty-nine co-ops and peers in the hall, thirty-nine versions of ears. If one of the co-ops should answer my call, thirty-eight co-ops, no jeering at all."

"What?" a number of voices demanded.

"Hey, it's not easy to come up with something that rhymes in twelve different languages," the Dollnick said defensively. "Now who has a good work story to share? I need a minimum of five volunteers and then I can go have lunch."

Grynlan raised a hand, but the Grenouthian half of the duo was faster.

"You two are banned," the Dollnick from admin declared. "No other volunteers? Then let's start with the troublemaker," he said, pointing at Samuel.

"Me?" the EarthCent ambassador's son asked. "How am I a troublemaker?"

"First you changed majors, and then you insinuated that the Open University administration made an error in your co-op assignment. So tell us, Mr. Diplomatic Studies. Are you learning anything?"

"How to sleep on the job," somebody called out.

"I don't sleep, I power nap," Samuel insisted with dignity. "The ambassador had a cot put in my changing room."

"You have a changing room?" a Drazen female asked.

"Well, it's really a storeroom, but I needed a place for all of the formalwear and shoes the embassy provides."

"You get free shoes with work?"

"I'm on my feet for hours dancing most shifts. I go through soles in a hurry."

"So tell us about your typical day," the admin clerk said in a bored voice. "Try to include at least five action verbs."

"Since I'm working as a confidential assistant to Ambassador Aainda, I can't really talk about what I do," Samuel said apologetically. "I can say that we host a dinner most evenings for our visiting dignitaries, and—"

"Human dignitaries?" a Vergallian male interrupted incredulously.

"Vergallian dignitaries, mainly businesspeople, but some scientists and actors as well. There's usually dancing for a few hours after the meal, but some nights the ambassador hosts more intimate gatherings, and then we play parlor games, like Coronation."

"Coronation?" Vivian asked. "You've never mentioned that before."

"It's a cross between an unscripted play and a board game where you compete for the royal succession on one of the planets in the Empire of a Hundred Worlds. You have to make extemporaneous speeches to win the other players to your faction, but there are also cards and dice that let you make secret deals. I'm usually the worst player at the table and the ambassador always ends up on the throne. She can see at least five moves ahead of the rest of us."

"Good enough," the admin clerk called out. "Who's next?"

"Let's do this by degrees of separation," a Frunge student suggested. "Who's closest to the Human?"

Everybody turned and looked at Vivian.

"All right, but I changed my major course of study to Intelligence so I can't tell you where I work. I guess I can say that I'm learning a lot about surveillance methods, and I got this poison detection ring," she concluded, displaying her left hand.

"Looks like a diamond," a Drazen student commented. "Are you sure it works?"

"Oops, I guess I forgot the poison detector today," Vivian said disingenuously. "That's my engagement ring."

"You need to use more action verbs," the Dollnick from admin insisted.

"Fine," Vivian said. "I work in an organization that requires flexibility and creativity in taking the initiative and providing leadership for analytical problem solving and communication of the results."

"Excellent," the clerk said, tapping rapidly on his Open University tab. "Anybody here have a connection to Spy Girl?"

"I work for her parents," Wrylenth announced, speaking at a terrific clip for a Verlock, thanks to his months of co-oping at EarthCent Intelligence. "Wrylenth, co-op student, 4135843803."

"Is that all you're going to say?"

"Name, rank and serial number," the Verlock confirmed. "You can torture me, but I won't talk."

"You have to talk," the Dollnick clerk insisted, brandishing his tab. "There's a gaping blank space on this form that needs to be filled with five action verbs."

"Accelerated, accommodated, accomplished, achieved, acquired," Wrylenth rattled off, to the astonishment of his friends.

"Thank you," the Dollnick whistled with exaggerated politeness. "Who's connected to the walking dictionary?"

"I see him in meetings," Aabina said. "I'm working for the EarthCent embassy as an assistant to the ambassador and it seems like I learn something new every day. Last week, the ambassador had a sore throat and she let me make her weekly report to the EarthCent president's office, and I also get to help write her speeches and moderate discussions at conferences. We sponsor lots of conferences," she added. "I've been pushing my mother to have the Vergallian embassy host more of them."

"Aren't conferences expensive?" a Grenouthian asked.

"If you do it right the attendees foot the bill," Aabina explained. "Plus, if you host events frequently enough, you can get free days and discounts from the Empire Convention Center. The individual who makes the reservations accumulates points that can be spent at associated hotels on other Stryx stations."

"Don't rush off after the meeting," the Dollnick clerk told the Vergallian. "I want to pick your brain. Who's next?"

"I work for the EarthCent ambassador's husband and he just offered me a permanent job," Marilla volunteered. "I've learned more about how to keep spaceships running in the last two cycles than I did in four years of Space Engineering at the Open University."

"Second-hand junks," the princeling jeered.

"Hey, I specifically said no jeering," the clerk shouted at the Dollnick, despite their difference in rank. "Are you challenging the administration, Prince Barely-Squeaked-By-His-Competency-Tests?"

The princeling sank a little lower in his seat and didn't respond.

"Any fool can call for warranty service on a new space-ship, and the colony vessels fix themselves," Marilla continued. "In addition to second-hand ship repairs and rebuilds, my employer is launching a new rental network next week. If anybody is traveling to Open Worlds where there's a Tunnel Trips franchise, we'll meet or beat the price of any other rental agency."

"How many ships do you have available?" a serious Chert student inquired. "We did a class project on starting a new tunnel network rental agency in my Business Theory Models course, and the minimum number we came up with was eighty-seven thousand and three."

"That's exactly what's wrong with academia," Marilla said. "You sit around in armchairs trying to apply statistics to psychology and all you get is garbage. Our starting fleet across all the franchises is just over two hundred ships, and I'll bet you any amount that we're in the black before the end of the next cycle."

"A black hole, maybe," the Chert muttered, but he didn't take the Horten girl up on the bet.

"That's five students, five action verbs, and my work here is finished," the clerk declared. "Those of you who spoke today qualify for a free meal in the cafeteria, just keep it under five creds. The rest of you can take the day off, go to work, do what you want, but do it somewhere else. I have another group coming in right after lunch."

Several of the co-ops complained loudly that they would have shared stories about work if they had known about the free lunch, but their protests fell on deaf ears. Samuel and his friends waited for the rest of the classroom to empty out while Aabina shared contact information with the admin clerk, and then they rose as a group and made their way to the Open University cafeteria.

"It seems like ages since I stood in this line," Vivian said. "The other students all look so young."

"It's only been two cycles," Wrylenth observed. "Not even three and a half months on your calendar."

"You have to remember that she's only eighteen," Aabina told the Verlock. "Three months seems like forever to young Humans."

"I'm not that young," Vivian said, winking at the Drazen behind the counter who was taking a large baking tray of some sort of seaweed concoction out of the oven. He shook his head in the negative. "No pizza today," she reported to the others. "We'll have to order off the menu."

"I was going to do that anyway," Marilla said. "Don't forget that we're getting a free lunch. The Drazen's smuggled-in pizza is cash-and-carry."

34

"Why is there a line at the old Vergallian vegan section?" Samuel asked. "I thought they pretty much gave up carrying that stuff after I stopped buying it."

"It's something new," Aabina said, wrinkling her nose. "Smells deep-fried. Jorb could have told us if he was still here."

"Falafel?" Marilla sounded out after the crowd shifted and she could see the sign. "It's written in Humanese, but I've never heard of it."

"They have falafel?" Samuel said. "Let's get in line. I've had it at a place in the Little Apple near Pub Haggis that started selling it less than a year ago and it's good. I hear it's popular with the Frunge because it's made from chickpeas."

"Are they meat or vegetable?"

"Chickpeas are a type of legume," Wrylenth informed the others as they all got into the queue for falafel. "I've been studying the etymology of Earth product names in my free time and Humans have a marked tendency for misnaming foods. If there is any relation between chicks and peas, it's that the former eat the latter. Have you ever heard of peanuts?"

"Sure, we eat them all the time," Samuel said.

"Another legume, not nuts at all."

"I've never seen so many different species ordering the same thing in the cafeteria before," Aabina said. "It must be really good."

"It's as much about the fixings as the falafel balls," Samuel told her. "I've seen Drazens smother theirs with zhug, which is some kind of hot sauce. If the server asks whether you want zhug or harif, just say no," he added for Vivian's benefit.

"What do you suggest?" Marilla asked the Horten behind the counter.

"The falafel plate, with hummus and olive oil," the server replied immediately, and then added in a lower voice, "I can't vouch for the pita bread because it comes from a Human subcontractor and you know their hygiene isn't up to par."

"Give me a falafel in a pita," Marilla declared loyally. "I work for Humans and there's nothing wrong with their hygiene, if you don't mind a little dog hair. I'll add my own fixings."

The Horten server turned bright red, but she slit open a pita, added a smear of hummus and six balls of falafel, and placed it in a sort of envelope before passing it across the counter. "I hope you haven't forgotten how to use utensils," she added snidely as Marilla stepped towards the salad bar. "Next."

"The plate," Wrylenth said. "And give me those dark-colored balls in the basket to the side. They look crunchier."

"Those are overcooked," the server told him. "I forgot them in the deep fryer while I was dicing cucumbers and tomatoes. We weren't quite prepared for the demand."

"I like overcooked," the Verlock said. "And don't give me any of the hummus stuff, it looks creamy."

"Next," the Horten called, after handing the Verlock a plate with ten rock-hard balls of falafel.

"I'm on a diet," Aabina said. "Could I get a single ball with just enough of the hummus to keep it from rolling around?"

"No olive oil?"

"What's the fat content?"

"I don't have the numbers handy but the Humans say it's the good kind."

"Just a dollop then."

"Next," the server said, handing Aabina her lunch on a small dessert plate.

"In a pita, with hummus and harif," Samuel said.

"Chips?" the server inquired, indicating another basket with her tongs.

"Do you mean French fries? Sure, stuff them in there."

"Didn't you just say not to order harif?" Vivian asked.

"For you, not me," Samuel said, accepting his stuffed pita pocket. "I'm going to have trouble getting any salad in here."

"I'll have the hummus plate," Vivian told the server. "Without any hot stuff."

The Horten spooned a giant dollop of hummus onto a plate and spread it around with an outward spiraling movement using the bottom of the serving spoon. Then she grabbed a bottle of olive oil with a top that was reminiscent of the kind used in bars that poured measured shots and added an artistic dash, moving the bottle around as the stream of oil flowed out. Finally, she placed three balls of falafel in a triangle at the center of the plate, sprinkled little green leaves over the top, and handed it over.

"Are you sure this is all Horten-safe?" Marilla asked the Frunge tending the salad bar. "I've never seen so many fixings."

"You might want to go easy on the purple stuff and the green olives, but all of it is technically edible," the cafeteria worker replied. "Hey, what are you doing?" he shouted at Wrylenth.

"Adding salad to my falafel dish," the Verlock replied imperturbably. "Isn't it included in the price?"

"But it's only what you can fit on the plate, and you're taking all of the radish slices."

"Try cutting them into a different shape next time so they don't stack so well," Wrylenth advised him. "Do these olives have pits?"

"Yes,'" the Frunge replied. "Great big ones."

"Excellent," the Verlock said, expertly wielding the tongs to place olives in the few gaps left on his plate between stacks of radish slices. "Love pits. Very crunchy."

"This is perfect," Aabina said to Samuel, loading her small plate with Mediterranean salad. "I've suggested to the ambassador that you market cucumbers and tomatoes to Vergallian women who are watching their weight."

"That would be all of them," Vivian muttered in his other ear. "You're eating standing in line?"

Samuel swallowed. "Making room," he said, and then transferred several more French fries to his mouth. He quickly filled up the newly available space in his over-stuffed pita with salad.

The five friends got their drinks and proceeded to the register where a bored-looking Grenouthian was waiting to ring them up. "Will that be together?"

"The admin said we could all get a free lunch," Marilla said. "There's five of us."

"Don't play games," the bunny replied. "Two of you already came through and they took lunches for the other three."

"Let it go, Sam," Vivian said, knowing that if he started to argue their falafels would all be cold by the time they sat down to eat. "I'll just pay," she added, handing over a programmable cred.

"I wonder who it was," Samuel grumbled, looking around the cafeteria with a scowl. It didn't take long to spot Grynlan and his Grenouthian co-conspirator feasting on falafel in wraps that were at least twice as large as a pita pocket. "I didn't know we could order in a flatbread!"

Four

"So the last editors of the cookbook before the Hortens were the Drazens?" Kelly asked Bork.

"That's right," the Drazen ambassador replied grimly. "We're talking about over a hundred thousand years ago, but our historians have demonstrated again and again that we didn't mean anything by it."

"Mean anything by what?"

"You don't know about the Great Falling Out?"

"Between the Drazens and the Hortens? I thought that was all because of an argument over some planet that you both claimed."

"Do you think we'd really let something like a little real estate dispute fester all these years? You know that the Hortens were once our greatest allies and we fought together in the Battle of Scort Woods. Did I ever tell you—"

"Yes, you would have been great in the part," Kelly interrupted Bork before he could change the subject to his amateur acting career. "I'm meeting Ortha in fifteen minutes and I really need to know the scoop about the All Species Cookbook."

"There's really nothing to know," Bork said, spreading his hands and letting his tentacle droop. "When the current editors decide to move on, the Stryx put the rights up for bid, and whoever wins brings out the next edition. The cookbook is always published in a different indecipherable version of Universal, and nobody but an AI would dream of actually making any of the recipes. It's more of a diplomatic statement."

"How can a cookbook be a diplomatic statement?"

"It's a symbol of unity. Editing the cookbook means that you're willing to look for points of commonality connecting the species rather than dwelling on our differences. It should have been a walk in the park for us since we can eat pretty much anything, but we invited the Hortens to give their input on the draft version and it all went sideways."

"You're telling me that the details of editing a cookbook over a hundred thousand years ago are still fresh in the collective memory of Drazens even though all of the records were lost in a fire?"

"It was a flood," Bork objected. "Completely unexpected on a desert world."

"Flood, fire, asteroid impact, what does it matter?"

"It wouldn't have mattered if the Hortens hadn't ended up boycotting the publication and not buying a single copy, the first time in tunnel network history that a species ever went that far."

Kelly began to ask another question and then thought better of it, instead forcing herself to count to ten while letting her eyes wander over the familiar display of medieval weapons mounted on the walls of Bork's office. "Was there something in particular that set the Hortens off?" she finally asked.

"They claimed we used the cookbook to make fun of them for being germophobes," the ambassador said. "Just because the recipe for Gamer's Goulash went through washing the vegetables six times and disinfecting all of the cookware and preparation surfaces with a high dose of radiation. A leading Drazen historian proved beyond a doubt that the recipe was adapted from the bestselling Horten cookbook of that period."

"The Hortens wash their vegetables six times? Marilla might be a little picky, but she eats with us at least once a week."

"All of the individuals living on Stryx stations are more cosmopolitan than the populations of their species living on closed worlds," Bork reminded her. "But it's not even about the recipes we published, it's about what the Hortens did when they took over the editorship from us."

"Don't tell me," Kelly said, guessing what was coming. "They put out a revenge cookbook?"

"They insulted us to our faces!" Bork exclaimed, and then continued on in an unnatural voice that sounded not unlike a Horten speaking. "Save the peelings for a Drazen friend. If it falls on the floor, don't throw it out—somebody with a tentacle is sure to appreciate it. If you get called away while the soup is cooking, an acquaintance with extra thumbs will enjoy those pot scrapings." He went back to his regular voice. "It went on and on, every recipe had a line like that. If it wasn't for the Stryx rules we would have declared war."

"But it's just words," Kelly said. "Surely nobody goes to war over—forget I said that."

"We invoked the Cultural Attack clause of the tunnel network treaty and requested a Stryx investigation of the editorial process. The Hortens claimed they had moved all of the records into space for safekeeping where they were obliterated by a rogue comet."

"That's original."

"The Stryx must have thought so too because they refused to get involved. Did you know that the Cultural Attack clause has an exemption for satire?"

"I didn't even know there was a Cultural Attack clause. Could we use it to stop the Grenouthians from making all of those insulting documentaries about us?"

"You would have to prove that they're lying with the intent to cause harm," Bork said doubtfully.

"Never mind. Do you know how much the Hortens bid to take over the cookbook from the Drazens?"

"The Stryx conduct the auction and they don't publish the bid information, they just announce a winner. Some people believe that they're picking tunnel network species in order of when they joined."

"That sounds easy enough to prove."

"Correlation doesn't imply causality," Bork replied with a shrug. "It could just as easily be coincidence. Besides, once a species wins, they're disqualified from bidding again."

"But you and the Hortens were the last two oxygen-breathing species to join the tunnel network before us. If I add up all of the previous species," Kelly said, doing the mental math, "is there even anybody left to bid against us?"

"You know that not all of the tunnel network species maintain a diplomatic presence on Union Station, and EarthCent only opens embassies on the Stryx stations where you have a large population. Your intelligence people probably have all the oxygen-breathing species sorted by now if you're curious."

"So you don't have any advice about the bid amount at all?"

"Not beyond what's written in the bid document," the Drazen ambassador said.

"Didn't read it," Kelly admitted without hesitation. "I had Donna send it to her daughters since Blythe and

Chastity will be the ones paying and the Galactic Free Press will be the publisher if we win. I also submitted a request to our president for a special budget to produce the cookbook and got back a reply that he's out of the office until after the auction."

"An effective diplomatic tactic," Bork said, nodding his head in approval. "Listen. The Stryx methodology for auctioning tunnel network monopolies is rather unique, so it's worth giving the bid document a read just for the flavor of the thing. To summarize, the Stryx deliver the funds from the winning bid to the head of the newly formed authority, which in the case of the All Species Cookbook, would be the managing editor."

"You mean the species that wins any of these monopolies gets to keep the money?"

"These aren't business monopolies that are expected to earn a profit, they're more like public works projects. Most new tunnel network members overbid for their first monopoly because they see it as a matter of prestige for their species."

"So you're saying that if Chastity wins the cookbook monopoly for the Galactic Free Press she'll actually be paying herself?"

"That's pretty much the way it works, but the Stryx require that the publisher spend the bid money producing the cookbook. I would guess that the most expensive parts are hiring the linguists to create a new language for plausible deniability and arranging for whatever natural disaster is required to destroy any legal evidence."

"I certainly hope it doesn't come down to that," Kelly said, rising from her chair. "I have to get to the Horten embassy, but thank you for your time, Bork, and I'll see you at our regular meeting."

"Give my best to Donna's girls when you see them," the Drazen ambassador called after her, pointedly ignoring the opportunity to send his greetings to Ortha.

When Kelly entered the lift tube, she was surprised to find the Frunge ambassador waiting in the capsule. It was rare for a lift tube trip to be broken up by stops, and she wondered if Czeros was on his way to see Bork, but had failed to notice the capsule's arrival because he was crouched down studying the dense text near the bottom of a display ad.

"Ambassador?" she asked uncertainly. "We're on the Drazen deck."

"Yes, I asked the station librarian to help me intercept you," the Frunge diplomat said, straightening up with a frown. "You can't trust anything you read these days. I thought that two hundred creds was a suspiciously low price for a five-day ship rental with no restriction on destinations, but it turns out that the cost doesn't cover consumables."

"Joe's never mentioned anything about consumables for the Tunnel Trips rental business."

"And hopefully he never does, but the Sharf charge for everything from fuel to air. Do you see the little comet-shaped symbol next to the two hundred?" Czeros asked, pointing towards the alien script, which meant nothing to Kelly. "Whenever there's a superscript near a price, you have to check the fine print at the bottom to see what you're really getting for your money."

"Thank you for bringing it to my attention. Do you mind if I tell the capsule to get started? I have a meeting with Ortha in a few minutes."

"That's why I intercepted you," Czeros said. "It's about the All Species Cookbook. We can talk on the way."

"Horten deck, ambassador's residence," Kelly instructed the lift tube. "Do the Frunge have a stake in this, Czeros?"

"Was that an attempt at a pun?" the Frunge demanded indignantly. "If so, I'm very disappointed in you, Ambassador."

"What? No, not steak, stake. Oh, I can see how the context could be confusing given that we're talking about a cookbook."

"And did Bork tell you about their cookbook regrets?"

"He said that the Horten recipes they offered were taken from—"

"Regrets about us," Czeros clarified, tapping his own chest. "He didn't tell you about the special section on our famous barbeque techniques?"

"But the Frunge prefer their meat raw," Kelly said. "Why would—oh."

"Exactly. Somebody thought it would be funny to tease a new section about barbeque in the advance advertising, but when the cookbook was published, it only offered a single sentence on Frunge meat preparation."

"What was it?"

"Cut into bite-sized pieces," Czeros said. "We couldn't even complain under the Cultural Attack clause since technically, it's true, but they were obviously making fun of us."

"So you were pleased when the Hortens took over the editorship?"

"Pleased?" Czeros snorted. "Their version of the All Species Cookbook is subtitled, 'In praise of grains.' They did it specifically to get on our nerves."

"Doesn't anybody publish the cookbook to share recipes that everybody can eat?"

"The last few editions included a Vergallian vegan section, but those recipes are a last resort, even for Vergallians."

The lift tube capsule came to a halt on the Horten deck and the doors opened, but Kelly said, "Hold, please," and put her hand on the Frunge ambassador's forearm. "What are you trying to tell me, Czeros?"

"If you can win the auction and never bring out another edition it would be a coup for galactic diplomacy," he told her. "We Frunge have an excellent sense of humor, so we got past the insults with little more than a few trade wars, but some species have thinner skins than us, and Humans really aren't in a position to make enemies."

"We weren't planning to make enemies," Kelly reassured Czeros. "I'm sure Donna will come up with recipes that everybody can enjoy together. We've even talked about asking the ambassadors on the station if they have any Earth-derived favorites."

Kelly thought the Frunge ambassador looked a bit taken aback as the doors closed between them, but checking the replacement for her ornamental wristwatch, she realized that she would have to hurry if she didn't want to be late for her meeting with Ortha. To her surprise, the Horten ambassador was waiting outside his embassy.

"Right on time," he pronounced, implying that the EarthCent ambassador had arrived too late for good manners. "I've made a reservation for us at a coffee shop down the corridor that welcomes clean aliens."

"Are you doing renovations or something?" Kelly asked, inclining her head towards the embassy's doors.

"Not at all. To tell you the truth, I've begun to wonder if you might take our decontamination procedures the wrong way, but our union for embassy employees is too powerful to buck."

Kelly stared at Ortha as the skin on his face began turning darker, and taking notice, the Horten ambassador glanced down at the backs of his hands, which were already black with the lie.

"Stupid polygraph skin," he muttered. "All right, already. My son Mornich told me that it's rude to keep running you through decontamination when his girlfriend practically lives in your hold and he visits her there almost every day. Satisfied?"

"I never even opened my mouth," Kelly said, watching as Ortha's skin color faded into light yellow with pink patches. "You're not nervous about something, are you?"

"The only thing that could make me nervous would be if you told me you changed your mind about bidding on the All Species Cookbook. Have you?"

"No," Kelly replied, following her colleague into a small café that happened to be empty. A suspicious blast of air hit her as she crossed the threshold, and for a moment, all of her hair stood up as some sort of electrostatic field came into play. On the whole, it was much less intrusive than the decontamination procedure for aliens at the Horten embassy.

"The usual, plus whatever my colleague is having," Ortha said to the counterperson.

"On the embassy tab?" the middle-aged Horten woman asked.

"Of course. And you may as well add one of those decorative jars of candy if you have any left. My receptionist can't get enough of them."

"Do you have any tea that would be safe for me?" Kelly asked.

The counterwoman, who apparently lacked an implant, didn't even seem to realize that she was being addressed until Ortha said, "A cup of Human Gentility for my friend, and if you have any Gem chocolate?"

"Oh, no. I'm on a diet," the EarthCent ambassador protested, but only after a strategic pause that allowed the plate of chocolates to be placed on the counter. "Since you insist…"

Ortha shrugged and accepted a tall glass of a bubbly purple concoction and a mug of hot water with a teabag still in its wrapper. "Will this do?" he asked.

"Earl Grey," Kelly read the packaging. "I was wondering what you meant by Human Gentility."

"That's what my son calls it. He has my wife and daughters drinking it by the kettleful, and then they complain they can't sleep at night."

"How old are your daughters?"

"Old enough to know better," the ambassador grumbled, leading Kelly to a table. "Did your meetings with Bork and Czeros go well?"

"You know about that? But I just met Czeros by chance in the lift tube on the way here. "

"A little bird told me. Don't be surprised if Crute and the Grenouthian ambassador get in touch."

"Because of the cookbook? But they've already had their turns editing."

"The cookbook is a known friction point and they'll get grief at home if they don't at least make an effort to get their licks in. What did Bork ask you to write about us?"

"Nothing. He expressed his sorrow that a small matter like a few words in a cookbook had contributed to such a bone of contention between your peoples."

Ortha glanced down at the backs of Kelly's hands to see if her skin color was changing before recalling that humans could lie with impunity.

"Be that as it may, it's traditional for the outgoing editors to provide a preface for the next edition of the cookbook explaining what they learned from the experience."

"Nobody mentioned that to me."

"It's been the case for at least the last fifty thousand years."

Kelly nibbled on a chocolate to buy time while her teabag steeped, and she spotted the flaw in Ortha's argument. "Nobody has brought out a new edition in longer than that. You're trying to take advantage of our short time horizon to put one over on me."

"Wasn't my idea. The truth is, there's a government faction that works to keep our feud with the Drazens alive any way they can for political purposes. Unfortunately, they're the ones who originally appointed me. Now I can tell them that I tried my best and failed."

"I'm not sure if we'll win the bid, Ortha, but if we do, the one thing I know is that we won't be taking an idea that was intended to bring the tunnel network species closer together and turn it into a weapon, propaganda or otherwise. Our goal will be to create a cookbook that honors everybody's culinary traditions with recipes we can all enjoy."

"Did Bork tell you that their cookbook implied that Hortens feel we need to irradiate the whole kitchen before cooking?"

"He mentioned something about utensils. I thought it was a low blow."

"It was the whole kitchen. Everybody sterilizes their utensils. It takes just a second and a quality countertop radiation source only costs—" Ortha noticed that Kelly was gaping at him and moved on. "Did he and Czeros explain why cookbook editors feel the need to include such insulting content?"

"I thought it was just tit-for-tat."

"There's a bit of that too, but the real motivation is financial."

"I don't understand," Kelly said. "Somebody pays the cookbook editorial staff to insult the other species?"

"Producing an All Species Cookbook is a balancing act. On one hand, the editors need to publish recipes that won't kill any of the tunnel network species while hiding how bad it all tastes with a language nobody understands. On the other hand, if you don't sell enough copies of the initial printing, it will be judged a failure and you'll lose face as a species."

"That's the craziest thing I've heard since you all thought that humanity was trying to show you up by playing that Raider/Trader game. You're telling me that you and the Drazens and the Frunge before them—"

"And the Dollnicks and the Fillinducks," Ortha interjected.

"—all published snarky cookbooks in order to sell copies to readers who enjoy that sort of thing in bad translations."

"Don't knock it until you try marketing a cookbook that doesn't have a single recipe you would eat if you were starving."

Five

"Thank you for coming, Jonah," Dorothy greeted Vivian's twin brother as he paused on the threshold of the design room at SBJ Fashions. "Come right in and make yourself at home."

"Sorry I'm late," the young man said, threading his way through an obstacle course of clothing dummies, all of which were draped in fashionable attire. "Has Margie learned any new tricks?"

"She crawls now when she's not asleep. I'm thinking of getting a crib or a playpen for work since I can't count on her staying in one place if I take her out of the bassinet."

"Did you want my advice? I've probably seen more types of cribs and playpens than the people who make them, and I help Tinka maintain the blacklist."

"InstaSitter blacklists people for using cribs?"

"I probably said that wrong. We publish a list of un-supported equipment, mainly enclosures and apparatus that create an unsafe environment. Our sitters are trained to refuse the assignment if they see a potential hazard in the work area."

"Mom says that the first time Dring saw Samuel in a playpen he mistook it for a cage, but I've never heard of safety issues."

"Really? Babies can get into all sorts of trouble as soon as you give them something to pull themselves up on or stick their heads through. I can send you our holographic training course if you like."

"No, it would probably keep me from sleeping. How's the LARPing league you run for InstaSitter doing?"

"It sort of runs itself at this point," Jonah said. "Tinka suggested early on that we give the raid leaders perks for handling the organizational details, and since they're all InstaSitters who have gone through our training, it's worked out really well. I'm just a figurehead at this point."

"Is it still mainly girls?"

"That's the funny thing. Since we started the LARPing league, the number of guys applying to be InstaSitters has soared, but when it comes time to set their work schedules, they end up opting for the minimum number of hours."

"Do they make good babysitters?"

"We don't assign many of them to babysit. Tinka has been expanding some of our other services, like dog walking and on-call companions for the elderly to go grocery shopping. Once you have the network in place and tens of thousands of part-timers on the books, it turns out that there are plenty of employment opportunities. Mom always hires InstaSitters to make deliveries for those translated alien romance books she publishes."

"On paper? I read them on my tab."

"It's a retro thing, I guess. I stopped by her office once when they were doing a shoot for the book covers and she wouldn't let me stay and watch," he added sheepishly.

"So what are you doing with your free time these days?" Dorothy asked, crossing her fingers behind her back. "I'll bet you're pretty popular with the girls."

"Is that why you asked me here? Are you trying to set me up?"

"No, and besides, you have the greatest setup of all times. You know that any girl who passes the InstaSitter test must be nice."

"I go on some LARP dates but nothing serious," Jonah said. "Why are you asking?"

"The thing is, I'm starting a new dancing circuit to boost demand for our ballroom fashions," Dorothy said. "I remembered the other day that you were Vivian's first partner in the Vergallian competitions, and I've seen you dance enough to know you're still good."

"I'm not anywhere near Sam's level."

"I want to get away from the whole competitive aspect and create a more casual dancing experience, but with the latest fashions," Dorothy amended herself hastily. "I have a few ideas about tempting people to come, but since they won't be professionals, just getting them out onto an empty dance floor could be tricky."

"You could start with the Stryx dance," Jonah suggested. "Nobody can resist that."

"Jumping and clapping in heels and a gown just looks silly. What I was thinking is that if I could get a few males from each species to act as, I don't know what to call it—"

"Shills?"

"What's a shill?"

"Somebody who places a fake bid at an auction to start the action or increase the pricing."

"No, it's more like—"

"Gigolos?"

"No! I mean, it would be better if you bring a date, though your grandmother suggested I try singles nights where males get in free and don't pay for their first drink. And I was wondering if you could run a search through the InstaSitter employee records for any guys who list formal dance training on their resumes."

"I'd have to ask Tinka about that," Jonah said. "She'll probably refuse unless you do it as an influencer thing."

"What's that?"

"InstaSitter has all sorts of perks for current and former sitters, one of which is that they can sign up for free stuff from manufacturers who are trying to get the word out. Hey, I think it started with the giveaway you guys did for SBJ Fashions a few years ago."

"How could I forget? Great, tell her we want to do that. And can I count on you to dance?"

"If it's not too often, I guess. I'm teaching a cooking class for InstaSitters and—"

"You cook?" Dorothy interrupted. "Vivian can barely make a sandwich. I've told my brother that if he wants to eat after they're married he better move in back home or learn how to cook himself."

"She can't be good at everything," Jonah defended his twin. "Vivian was always at dance practice with Sam after school, and I sort of picked it up from mom and grandma. Last year I took the InstaSitter cooking courses because I'm the guinea pig for everything we offer, and then I started teaching because Dad says that's the best way to learn."

"So you don't plan on going to the Open University?"

"What for?" Jonah asked with a shrug. "If I get tired of working at InstaSitter it would make more sense to start my own business than to go to school to become some-body else's employee."

"My sentiments exactly," Baa announced her presence, as she weaved her way through the clothing dummies. "Are you here to see me about getting your gear enchanted? You could rule the InstaSitter LARPing league like a king."

"Dorothy invited me to talk about the new dance thing she wants to do to market her shoes and stuff," Jonah replied. "I saw a replay of the raid you led in the exhibition match, Baa. Nobody is going to want to play against your team anymore if you keep beating them so badly."

"They need to farm more mobs and level up," the Terregram mage retorted. "Kids these days don't want to put in the time."

"But your character is an infinite level goddess."

"And I've been grinding for longer than any of the tunnel network species have worn clothes. Speaking of clothes, what's your new marketing idea, Dorothy?"

"I was talking, well, complaining to Kevin about how sales have stopped growing for our shoes and gowns, and he suggested that we do something to increase demand. Since our market is concentrated on the tunnel network stations where the populations of any given species are limited, most of our potential customers just don't have enough opportunities to dress up and go dancing."

"Don't try going up against the Vergallians," Baa advised. "They've had a lock on the competitive ballroom circuit for the last million years."

"I don't want to start a league or anything. I just want to convince club owners to host formal dance nights, or maybe to organize mixers at independent venues, the way our embassy manager does for EarthCent."

"If you're talking about more than a few local dances you'll need a hook to make it work," the Terregram mage said. "Let me talk it over with Jeeves and I'll get back to you."

"Did somebody call my name?" Jeeves asked, floating into sight above the clothing dummies.

"Stop doing that," Dorothy said. "It's spooky. How long have you been eavesdropping?"

"I just arrived," the young Stryx said. "When Shaina pinged me and said that you wanted us to sit down and discuss something that didn't involve spending my creds on exotic dress materials, I hurried right over."

"I've got to get going or I won't have time to prepare the ingredients for this afternoon's class," Jonah said. "Try to let me know a few days ahead if you need me."

"Coming, Baa?" Dorothy asked as she went to pick up the bassinet with her sleeping baby.

"I've got something to work on and you've already told me about your idea," the mage said. "Leave Margie here. She hates meetings."

Shaina and Brinda were waiting in the lunch room, and as Jeeves floated to his familiar position at the head of the table, Dorothy realized that she hadn't prepared a formal presentation.

"I'm still working on this idea so you'll have to give me some leeway on numbers," she said. "Imagine that SBJ Fashions sponsored—"

"No," Jeeves interrupted.

"Excuse me?"

"No, no, no, no, no. There, I feel better. Proceed."

Dorothy looked questioningly at Shaina, who just rolled her eyes. Brinda gave the EarthCent ambassador's daughter an encouraging smile, so Dorothy took a deep breath and started over.

"When do the women who buy our fashions wear them?" she asked.

"Formal social occasions like weddings and dates," Shaina replied immediately. "We've got some really good data on this from our last customer satisfaction survey."

"And would you say that people are having weddings and going on dates more, or less."

"About the same as ever, I'd guess. Why would it change?"

"Exactly my point. If we're going to sell more on the tunnel network, we need to increase the amount of dancing."

"And I take it you have some expensive suggestions about how we can go about doing this," Jeeves said.

"Well, I talked to Chastity, and she said one way would be to bring back the Wanderers—"

"No!" Jeeves thundered, and all of the lights on his casing began to blink rapidly. "Are you trying to give me a nervous breakdown? Gryph would ban me from Union Station if I did anything to encourage the Wanderers to return."

"It's just that they had a whole ship dedicated to dancing," Dorothy continued unperturbed. "But if you won't even consider it, at least you can help co-sponsor a new series of dances. It's mainly financing for promotions, since the dances should pay for themselves through ticket prices or drink orders if they're held at nightclubs."

"That sounds worth looking into, but we're going to need more details," Brinda said. "Have you already lined up these co-sponsors you mentioned?"

"Not exactly, but I'm sure that Mom, I mean, the All Species Cookbook will go along, since it's a natural fit for cross-species promotion, and I know that Chastity will throw her weight behind anything that involves dancing. I was thinking of asking her husband to produce some holographic lessons that we could distribute to guys who are interested but who don't know how to dance."

"I don't want to hear another word about it until you can show me a budget," Jeeves said. "If that's all you have for me today, I promised Paul to help him move some of the leftover ships that Aisha bought him to the auction lot."

"Paul is selling ships? I thought that Dad and he were going to take their time working through them all and either restore them or strip the usable parts."

"They're keeping the more interesting ships, but with the new rental business, they want to get rid of the dead weight and replace it with more rental stock."

"Wouldn't it be more efficient to do that at a swap meet?" Shaina asked. "I remember seeing a couple of those on other stations back when SBJ Fashions was still SBJ Auctioneers."

"There aren't any swap meets scheduled for Union Station anytime soon. It's not worth the expense and trouble of dragging all of the ships through the tunnel and then to be stuck trading them for whatever is available to avoid having to make the return trip," Jeeves said. "You know better than most that auctions are the best mechanism for price discovery. Whatever the ships bring, that's what they're worth today."

After the young Stryx left, Dorothy discussed her ideas in more depth with the Hadad sisters, and then returned to the design room, where Affie was demonstrating a boxy new purse prototype for the mage.

"Doesn't it hurt if you get prodded in the side by a corner?" Baa asked the Vergallian girl.

"Fashion demands sacrifices," Affie replied. "Besides, I thought Flazint might come up with rubber bumpers for the corners. She's good with mechanical stuff like that."

"But it looks like a shoe box. What do you expect women to carry in it?"

"Shoes? I should have worn a dress with shoulder boards for you to get the full effect. It's all about planes and angles."

"I think it's interesting," Dorothy said, her go-to expression for Affie's creations that she didn't quite understand. "Did Baa tell you about my latest marketing idea?"

"Glass slippers?"

"What?"

"My solution to promoting your dances," Baa said triumphantly, and presented Dorothy with a glass slipper. "Try it on."

"Like Cinderella?" She took a seat on the low changing bench, removed her left shoe, and then paused. "Will I be able to stand in it?"

"Just try it on and see."

The EarthCent ambassador's daughter pulled the glass slipper over her foot and nothing happened. After rising awkwardly because the heights of her heels didn't match, she invoked the heads-up menu for the shoe that she still wore on her right foot, and manipulating the control slider with practiced eye movements, adjusted the heel to bring herself into balance. Then she took a few steps. "It's not very comfortable."

"It's not supposed to be comfortable. Take it off now, and when you get home, have Kevin put it on your foot."

Dorothy's eyes lit up. "It's enchanted? It does something? I love it." She sat back on the bench and rapidly swapped shoes, then stuck the glass slipper in her purse. "Can you two babysit for a few minutes? Something important came up."

"You're running home to get your husband to put on the glass slipper for you."

"No, it's something else."

"What?"

"Never mind, it can wait until lunch," Dorothy said. The baby began to stir. "It looks like Margie is waking up anyway."

"Hey, everybody," Flazint said, entering the design room and making a beeline for the baby. "Let's have a big smile for your Frunge aunty. There's a good girl."

"What do you think?" Affie asked, displaying her new purse concept to the Frunge girl. "Some of the Vergallian royals have been sporting Brutalist fashions lately and I thought we might want a cross-species interpretation."

"I suppose it can't get much more brutal than that," Flazint said. "I'd add some rubber bumpers on the corners as a safety precaution."

"That's exactly what I told Baa," the Vergallian girl said triumphantly.

"We better call Tzachan in for a legal opinion about our liability."

"I knew it!" Dorothy said. "You don't really like the purse, you just want an excuse to see your boyfriend before our next scheduled date."

"Oh, I almost forgot," Baa said. "Tzachan stopped by when you weren't here and left a note. Now, where did I put it?" She conducted a search of her cluttered workbench while Flazint stood by with bated breath, but eventually gave up and muttered an incantation. There was a crash from the other side of the room as something fell to the floor, and then a plastic sticky-note with a shard of glass attached to the back floated into the mage's outstretched hand. "Oops," she said apologetically. "I must have stuck it to that empty beaker on your desk. I've always said that the Dollnicks should use a weaker adhesive on these notes."

"I thought that Horten glass was unbreakable," Dorothy commented, while Flazint concentrated on reading the note without cutting herself.

"I probably shouldn't have gone with such a strong incantation," Baa said apologetically. "It might have interfered with the crystalline structure of the beaker while trying to overcome the adhesive."

"This is terrible!" the Frunge girl exclaimed. "Tzachan has a source in Hazint's legal shop who tipped him that Mizpah is planning to conduct a field inspection on our next date."

"The matchmaker?" Dorothy asked. "So what's the problem? We've been doing everything by the book."

Flazint's hair vines turned dark green. "We'll talk about it later. I better find a dustpan and clean up the glass."

"Let me guess," Affie said to Dorothy after the Frunge girl fled the room. "Whenever you have a question about what's allowed, you've been asking Flaz."

"The dating calendar with the built-in calculator I had to buy is all in Frunge so I can't even understand it without her help. You don't think—"

Baa let out a short trill of laughter. "It's always the shy ones," she said. "Back when I was in a pantheon on Mengoth Four, our worshippers carried out arranged marriages through bride-napping. If you could have seen how some of those girls dressed up for the occasion and then pretended to be surprised—it was almost worth all of the time I had to spend controlling that planet's terrible weather."

Margie finally came fully awake and voiced her objection to being stuck in the bassinet.

"That's it," Dorothy declared, grabbing it up by the double handles. "Lunch time. I'll be back."

Affie checked the time on her implant. "It's not even ten in the morning on your clock."

"I mean I promised Kevin that I'd—oh, I don't know. I'll be back."

Dorothy made it all the way to her husband's chandlery in Mac's Bones in less than five minutes. She set the bassinet on the counter, hopped up next to it, and removed the glass slipper from her purse. "Kevin?"

"You got here quick," he said. "Baa was asking for you a couple of minutes ago. She must have gone around the back."

"How did you get here before me?" Dorothy demanded when the Terragram appeared a moment later. "Are you really here, or is this some sort of mage trick?"

"I'm here," Baa said. "Did you think I would miss seeing my handiwork in action? It's the most complicated spell I've cast since coming to Union Station."

"What's with the glass slipper?" Kevin asked, coming around the front of the counter.

"You have to put it on my foot," Dorothy said, removing her left shoe and straightening her knee so she would be able to see the effect. "It's Baa's marketing idea."

Kevin took the glass slipper, ran his fingers around the inside part that he could reach checking for burrs, and then slipped it onto his wife's foot. For a moment, nothing happened, but when he pulled his hands away, the slipper was suddenly replaced with a dancing shoe.

"It's our top of the line model with height adjustment, gyroscopes, and variable heel contact area," Dorothy exclaimed. "And my other shoe transformed to match! How did you do that? Is it real or an illusion?"

"They're real," Baa said. "It's been so long since I used that particular combination of spells that I don't really remember how they work, but it has something to do with altering your frame of reference in the space-time continuum. When we get back to the office, you'll find your other shoe and the glass slipper on my workbench. I pulled the shoes that you're wearing now from stock."

"How can you do magic or whatever and not even know how it works?"

Baa shrugged. "I've seen you use regular scissors to cut a nearly perfect circle out of a bolt of cloth without a pattern. Can you explain how you do that?"

"It's just something I picked up over the years."

"Same here, and I've had a lot more years."

"The glass slipper is perfect, Baa. I may even brand the dances as Cinderella balls."

"So how is this going to work?" Kevin asked. "Are you going to have a dance contest or hold a raffle?"

"No contests," Dorothy said firmly, hopping down from the counter and grabbing the bassinet again. "Maybe a raffle, maybe something else. Come on, Baa. Let's get back to work and make this happen."

Six

"You better get out here, Eminence," the Vergallian doorman's voice came through the comm link on the ambassador's desk. "Code Yellow."

"I'll be right there," Samuel replied, not bothering to correct the doorman's intentional error. After nearly four months working as Aainda's assistant, most of the embassy staff took Samuel's presence for granted, but the doorman kept trying to bait the EarthCent ambassador's son by addressing him with inappropriate titles. He heard the yelling before he even reached the lobby.

"—to the ambassador or I'm going to file a complaint with the Stryx!" a man shouted in English.

Samuel arrived just in time to prevent the security staff from zapping the visitor, who looked like a pretty tough customer. "The ambassador isn't here at the moment. Is there anything I can do to help you?"

"Who are you?" the man demanded. "You speak decent English for a Vergallian."

"I studied Humanese in school," the EarthCent ambassador's son replied to save time. "What seems to be the problem?"

"I don't know," the man shouted, becoming irate again. "That's the problem."

"I'm afraid I don't understand."

"I was out at the Camelot with friends last night, having a few laughs and playing the table games. Then the most beautiful woman I've ever seen in my life comes up to me, and after that, it's all a blur."

"I don't see what that has to do with us," Samuel said, though he had a feeling he knew where the conversation was headed.

"When I went to practice this morning, one of the other fighters who was at the casino last night started laughing and calling me a boy-toy. He said an upper-caste Vergallian woman dosed me with pheromones and I followed her off like a love-sick puppy."

"That's a serious accusation. Do you have any proof?"

The man hesitated, but then he pulled down his collar to show a bite mark on his neck. "You going to say I did that to myself?"

"No, that would be physically impossible," Samuel acknowledged. "Are you missing anything? Money? Jewelry? It's been a long time since any high-caste criminals were reported on the station."

"Nothing is missing, that's the first thing I checked," the man said. "But she dosed me against my will."

"Are you sure you weren't just captivated by her beauty? It's been known to happen."

"I'm with the Ultimate Cage Fighting tour. I can take care of myself, but we're talking about chemical warfare here. You people can't go around enslaving us with pheromones just because you can. And I have a match today. What if I'm still under the influence?"

"I don't think it works exactly the way you're thinking," Samuel said. "Are you absolutely positive that the woman who approached you was Vergallian?"

"Listen," the man said, leaning closer. "There are plenty of drawbacks to the life of a professional cage fighter, but lack of female companionship isn't one of them. There are women from all species who make a competition of collecting us, if you know what I mean."

"I can guess. Would you mind if I consult with the station librarian?"

"How's a librarian going to help?" the fighter demanded, but he waved a hand as if he had resigned himself to dealing with bureaucracy. "Go ahead and do your worst, but I'm not going to let this drop."

"Libby?" Samuel subvoced. "Would it violate any of your rules to check the surveillance video for when our guest—"

"Dominic Ryan," the station librarian interjected.

"—Dominic was approached by an upper-caste Vergallian woman in the Camelot casino last night?"

"There were no upper-caste Vergallian women present in the casino last night. There was, however, a professional escort employed by one of your guest's companions."

"Can I get the video if he needs convincing?"

"I only provide free holographic imagery for confirming ownership of items brought to the lost-and-found. Special imaging requests are charged on a sliding scale."

"Let me check with him." Samuel cleared his throat. "Dominic?"

"Sorry, I'm still a little out of it," the fighter said. "Hey, how did you know my name?"

"The station librarian told me. She also checked the casino's surveillance video from last night and it appears that your friends played a trick on you. The woman you left with was a professional escort employed by one of them, though I don't—"

"Those dirty cheats," Dominic interrupted. "I should have known better than to go partying with a professional gambler the night before a match. Horace must have put something in that orange juice he insisted on buying me, and then the escort cut my legs out from under me for today's fight."

"Excuse me?"

"It's a human thing, I wouldn't expect you to understand," Dominic said. "Coach is going to kill me when I tell him. Sorry about all the trouble."

"No trouble at all. Here, let me walk you to the lift tube. You look a bit shaky."

When Samuel returned to the embassy a minute later, the doorman greeted him with, "Well done, Your Highness. There's an urgent conference call waiting for you in the ambassador's office."

"For me? As in, for Samuel McAllister, or for the ambassador's assistant?"

"The latter," the doorman said. "You are the senior diplomatic staffer on duty."

"I'm the only diplomatic staffer on duty because the rest of them are at a seminar."

"And you're not going to score any points with a queen by keeping her waiting."

Samuel ran to the ambassador's office, noted the live holographic projection over the desk, and took a moment to straighten his jacket before moving around to the business side where he would be visible.

"My apologies, Your Highness," he said, inclining his head. "The ambassador and her senior staff are all at a seminar and I'm the only one available to take your call."

"So you're Aainda's wonder Human," the Vergallian in the hologram pronounced in a regal tone. "We are not amused by the delay."

"My humblest apologies," Samuel repeated, and this time when he inclined his head, he held it there for a three count.

"I see that somebody has schooled you in court etiquette," the queen said. "Is it true that you are also the EarthCent ambassador's son?"

"Yes, Your Highness, but I check my species at the door."

"That's good to hear." The queen stared at Samuel as if she could read his thoughts through the Stryxnet connection, and then nodded. "Tell Aainda that you'll do. And get some sleep, you look exhausted."

"Yes, Your Highness," Samuel said, and inclined his head for the third time. When he looked up again, the holographic projection was gone. He waved his hand in front of the desk comm to disable the security lock-out and said, "Raef?"

"Present," the doorman replied.

"I'm going to grab a quick nap in the storeroom. Just wake me if anything comes up."

"I live to serve, Laird McAllister."

Samuel waved the connection shut and left the ambassador's office for his storeroom. The cot was overhung with a rack of formalwear for his use at embassy affairs, and he slid it all aside so the suits wouldn't be in his face when he woke up. Then he set his implant's alarm for thirty minutes, stretched out on the cot, and fell instantly into a dreamless sleep.

"Red alert, red alert," squawked the improvised inter-com the embassy's technician had installed in the storeroom at Samuel's request.

"What is it, Raef? Are you yanking my sword belt?"

"Scout's honor," the doorman replied. "There's a Farling diplomat here to see the ambassador."

"A Farling diplomat? I didn't know they had any. I'll be right there."

The giant beetle who was waiting in the lobby wasn't quite as large as M793qK, but its carapace showed the same emerald green highlights, and it stood with the easy self-assurance of a high-status bug. Samuel approached the Farling and noted that it wore an external translation box, so it was accustomed to traveling to places where the locals couldn't understand it otherwise.

"Human," the Farling rubbed out on its speaking legs. "Are you the ambassador's idea of a joke, or is sending the janitor to greet me an intentional insult?"

"Ambassador Aainda is at a seminar, though she'll be back at any time now. Do you have an appointment?" Samuel asked, even though he knew there was nothing entered in the calendar.

"I am G32FX," the beetle replied, as if the name should mean something. "I made an appointment three cycles ago."

"That was before I started here but let me check," the EarthCent ambassador's son said, consulting the embassy's calendar via his heads-up display. "I'm afraid there's been some sort of mistake," he reported after a few seconds. "Your appointment was scheduled for three cycles ago and you're marked as a no-show."

"I'm here now," the beetle replied. "Haven't they trained you to offer a guest something to drink?"

"Oh, sorry," Samuel said. "What can I get you?"

"Nothing. It's the offer that counts."

"Ah, G32FX," Aainda addressed the Farling as she swept into the embassy with her retinue in tow. "Fashionably late, as usual."

"Ambassador," the beetle greeted her, and motioned with a few of his legs at Samuel. "I didn't expect to find a Human working in your embassy. Is he from a community that has joined the Empire of a Hundred Worlds and accepted royal leadership?"

"Samuel is a cooperative education student assigned to my embassy by the Open University. Coincidentally, he's the son of the EarthCent ambassador."

"And where is your graceful daughter?"

"Working for Samuel's mother."

The Farling's carapace jerked convulsively, as if his wings were about to deploy in a display of mirth, but he regained control almost immediately. "I see the Stryx are busy manipulating all of you soft-skins as usual. Shall we talk in your office?"

"Yes. Come along, Samuel. You're part of this."

The ambassador led the way to her office, but rather than heading for her desk, she chose the casual seating area with the couch and the overstuffed chairs. The beetle, who had obviously been there before, pushed the recliner lever on one chair forward, and the seat cushion rose to meet the back, creating a padded surface on a forty-five-degree slant. G32FX leaned against it and rubbed out a satisfied sigh. "You're the only diplomat I know who bothers with Farling-friendly furniture."

"And how are things at Farling Seventy?" Aainda inquired politely.

"The Stryx have been giving us the usual grief about our pharmaceutical exports and threatening to close the tunnel connection," the beetle replied. "Our position has always been that if we get out of the recreational drug market, somebody else will move in, and they'll never match our quality."

"I understand that you were instrumental in returning Gem genetic samples to the clones for diversifying their population."

"I just happened to be the Farling on the spot," G32FX said modestly. "The request came in when I was doing my community service time training new controllers at Market Orbital. I understand that more genetic samples have been discovered in storage and sold to the Gem since then."

"Yes, Samuel?" the ambassador said, noticing that the young man was clenching his jaw to resist interrupting. "You have a question?"

"How do you know each other?" he asked. "I thought that the Farlings and the Vergallians were on such bad terms that they almost went to war after Baylit's raid on…"

"I see you've figured it out," Aainda said after Samuel trailed off. "I was sent to negotiate a settlement after my cousin's daughter showed up at Market Orbital with her squadron and threatened to attack if the Farlings didn't hand over certain pharmaceutical export records. I believe you know how it worked out."

"And I was her counterpart for the negotiations," G32FX said. "All's well that ends well. Is the young Human privy to the second stage of our deal?"

"He's about to be," Aainda replied. "Samuel, would you be willing to undertake a confidential mission that includes travel away from Union Station? I ask because it's clearly outside the scope of the co-op agreement you signed with the Open University."

"I would be honored, Ambassador," Samuel replied immediately.

Aainda turned to the beetle and nodded. G32FX lifted his external translation box, opened a small panel on the back, and pressed a button. The air in the office began to shimmer, and Samuel thought the small background noises suddenly sounded different, as if they were being filtered somehow.

"There," the beetle said. "I have no doubt that the Stryx can reconstruct our conversation if they care to take the trouble, but none of the tunnel network species have the computational capacity to decode speech from inside our random molecular vibration shell in a timely manner."

"Thank you," Aainda said. "I'm mainly concerned with Vergallian Intelligence, which is why I can't use my own people for this. Samuel, my reparations negotiation with the Farlings led to an opportunity for rapprochement between the expansionist Imperial faction and royal families like my own. As with all such peace-making efforts, if word gets out before the deal is complete, the firebrands of the respective factions will make it impossible for leaders to negotiate in good faith. I need a trusted courier, and the fact that you're Human is a bonus in this case."

"Because I'll be seen as a neutral party?" Samuel speculated.

"Not exactly. There is also a Human component to this deal that G32FX and I will soon be negotiating with your mother."

"A three-way treaty?"

"Think of it as a trade, like in the professional LARPing league. One faction offers a mage to a second faction, which sends a barbarian warrior to a third faction, which ships a bard back to the first faction. Everybody gets something."

"Bards aren't usually worth that much," Samuel observed. "I've heard people say that the Farlings could create drugs to extend our lives if they wanted to, but we can't afford them. Is that what you'll be offering us?"

"Actually, we want something from you, and if we were able to provide the pharmaceutical products you mention, we would already be selling them on credit," G32FX said. "Instead, we are willing to forgo the remaining reparations we're owed for the Baylit incident, and the Vergallians will complete the triangle by giving Humans something you want."

"A naval ship?" Samuel guessed.

"That would be a cheap price, but the Stryx would never allow it," Aainda said. "I'll work out the details with your mother, but the first step is getting the expansionist Imperial faction and Fleet on board, so you'll be carrying a message to each."

"I thought the deal was between Imperials and independent worlds in the Empire."

"That's the endpoint, but Fleet has a stake in this as well. The fewer who know all of the details the more likely this will work. I can't promise that you won't be intercepted by Vergallian Intelligence and interrogated."

"I won't last a minute against those pheromones unless you can do something to protect me."

"Which is why I won't be telling you any names or places. My only method of granting you immunity is to dose you myself before another royal does, but that protection only lasts a few hours."

"Does this have anything to do with—no, I'm better off not knowing."

"Smart boy," the Farling said. "This deal has been fourteen years in the making and we don't want to take any chances." He touched a control on his jammer and the shimmering field vanished. "And that, Ambassador, is why I'll never meet your price."

"We'll see about that," Aainda said in a threatening voice while winking at Samuel. "I believe you know the way out."

The Farling harrumphed and stormed out of the office without collapsing the recliner. The EarthCent ambassador's son went over and fumbled with the mechanism until he figured out how to convert the inclined plane back into a chair fit for humanoids.

"You've been working too hard and I'm beginning to worry about your health," Aainda said, though the humorous expression on her face belied her words. "Perhaps a few days off would do you good."

"A vacation? I didn't think co-op students earned any vacation days."

"We'll call it a bonus. Why don't you take your fiancée somewhere and relax? When's the last time you left Union Station?"

"I'd have to think about that," Samuel said. "Other than going out with my dad or Paul to the parking area, I guess it's been since we went with my mom to EarthCent's first convention on Earth."

"Ah, yes. When a young Imperial officer took it upon *herself*," the ambassador put an ironic stress on the pronoun, "to kidnap the three of you on your way home. What was her name again?"

"Aarinia. She really treated us well enough."

"I understand that she and her cousin are still in exile," Aainda said, and Samuel noticed that she was directing her words at a potted plant. "Maybe she was overworked as well."

"I'm not sure Vivian will be able to get time off from her, uh, job," Samuel said. "She's also a co-op."

"I imagine I can work something out with her employers. After all, what's the point of being an ambassador if you can't call in the occasional favor?"

Seven

Wrylenth entered the EarthCent embassy conference room barely a half a step behind Blythe and took the Verlock-sized chair at the table. Chastity arrived a few seconds later, deep in conversation with the paper's managing editor, Walter Dunkirk. Kelly glanced at Aabina and nodded, but the Vergallian co-op student shook her head in the negative and held up one finger, indicating that somebody was still missing. Then Daniel entered from the lobby and took the seat next to Donna.

"Welcome to the kick-off meeting for the Twelfth Edition of the All Species Cookbook," Aabina began. "Thanks to the winning bid subsidized by the founders of InstaSitter," she inclined her head in the direction of Blythe and Chastity, "and their offer of ongoing technical support, the embassy believes we will be able to handle this project without any need for additional staffing. Our embassy manager will be the official editor of the cookbook, but her preference is to concentrate on the recipes, so she's asked me to handle the administrative details."

"Decades of work," the Verlock co-op student said, and looked across the table at Donna. "Will your lifespan be adequate?"

Blythe elbowed her thick-skinned Verlock protégé, who hadn't fully adjusted to human sensitivities around the issue of longevity, but her mother took the question at face value.

"Thank you for your concern, Wrylenth. While I hope to live long enough to achieve EarthCent's ever-moving target of a retirement age, I don't see this cookbook project taking more than a couple of months. We won't be creating any new recipes, and I imagine that most of the real work will revolve around obtaining high-quality images of the finished dishes and desserts suitable for all of the publishing formats."

"I mean the time it will take to create the twelfth version of Universal," the Verlock explained. "It's not just gobbledygook. The language must be fully functional, yet impossible to translate with a high degree of accuracy."

"I've already spoken with our president and he's agreed that we'll be publishing the cookbook in Humanese, I mean, English, with translations into all of the tunnel network languages," Kelly announced. "I'll be informing the other ambassadors immediately after this meeting and soliciting favorite recipes from them. Daniel will be doing the same with members of the Conference of Sovereign Human Communities."

"I don't understand. You intend to create a cookbook without plausible deniability? What if somebody actually makes the recipes?"

"The ambassador asked me to do some historical research about the origins of the All Species Cookbook and we want to return to its original mission," Aabina informed the flabbergasted Verlock co-op student. "Thanks in part to the success of Drazen Foods in exporting Earth products, it's been proven that with the exception of the odd allergic reaction, oxygen breathing tunnel network members can ingest a broad range of Earth produce without harm, and often with some benefit. In fact, the recently formed Gem Catering Guild, which operates on the majority of Stryx Stations, has certified over a thousand Earth ingredients as all-species safe."

"But the political risk," Wrylenth protested. "Food culture is a minefield."

"That's why we're going to get all of the ambassadors on board," Kelly told him. "Even if it's fruit salad or a plain chocolate bar, everybody has some Earth food they like. Instead of publishing alien recipes with ingredient substitutions that are doomed to failure, we'll publish human recipes that aliens can enjoy."

"Don't worry, Wrylenth," Aabina added. "I checked the rules before we submitted our bid, and the original purpose of the All Species Cookbook was to promote foods that would help bring the species together."

"We could publish next week if we stuck with reader-submitted recipes from the archives of the paper's food section," Walter said. "One of the most popular Galactic Free Press features in recent years has been the weekly supplement on tribute foods developed by human populations that have gone native working on alien worlds. In fact, our *For Humans* book publishing division was already building a collection of the most popular recipes to publish their own cookbook, but that project got out of hand, and now they're planning one for each species."

"Humans can't eat alien food," Wrylenth insisted. "I recompiled the list that we give EarthCent Intelligence agents who work in the field, and when it comes to ordering in restaurants, the only recommendation is Vergallian vegan."

"I'm talking about recipes for dishes that pay tribute to the host species through their appearance, aroma, or general presentation," Walter explained. "Although there are a limited number of our people living on Verlock open worlds, the paper has published quite a few volcano-themed desserts that substitute chocolate for lava. What's your favorite Earth product?"

"Stone soup."

"I love that story," Kelly enthused. "Don't you think it would make the perfect introduction to the cookbook, Donna? The way the villagers who had nothing to offer a stranger end up contributing ingredients to make a communal meal would be an inspiring message."

"I'll see if I can find an edition with good artwork that's out of copyright," the newly appointed cookbook editor replied.

"It's a story too?" Wrylenth asked. He reached in his backpack and brought out a bottle with Verlock printing on the label. The fluid had a grainy whitish color, like poorly diluted whole milk. "Stone soup from Earth. I buy it at a health food store on our deck. It's too expensive to drink by itself, but I add a capful to my coffee."

"What's in it?" Donna asked.

"Dead Sea water," the Verlock read from the label. "Contains over 26 minerals, including magnesium, bromine, calcium, and potassium."

"Are you sure you're supposed to drink that?" Chastity asked. "I've seen something similar sold in the boutiques as a skin treatment."

"Very healthy," Wrylenth asserted. "Supports the immune system. I've never been sick."

"Better stay with no more than a capful a day if you want to keep it that way," Chastity advised, and then changed the subject. "Blythe and I agreed to split any manpower requirements you have using our own employees or contractors, but it would be good if you were able to provide us with a little notice, Aabina. My sister thinks it makes sense to use her photographers for the beauty shots since they're used to doing studio work for her book covers. Walter?"

"The Galactic Free Press publishes roughly a quarter million words a day, not counting sponsored content. Our station librarian provided me with some statistics about recently published cookbooks, and thanks to open formatting and illustrations, most of them run below fifty thousand words. So my suggestion is that rather than trying to establish a workflow with us, you assemble a rough draft and dump it on me in one shot. I'll offer everyone in the office overtime and we'll turn it around for you in less than twenty-four hours."

"That would certainly cut down on meetings," Aabina acknowledged. "Donna?"

"The less time spent on back-and-forth the better," the embassy manager said. "I'm just in it for the recipes."

"Excellent," Kelly said. "Can we agree on a total number of recipes for each species so we have a target to shoot for and don't end up short-changing somebody?"

"I don't know if giving each species the same number of recipes is the best approach," Daniel cautioned. "I'd be more comfortable sticking with featuring recipes related to the aliens we have experience with so we don't accidentally offend them. All of our CoSHC host worlds would obviously be represented, and thanks to the theme park deal, that now includes the Grenouthians, but what do we even know about the Fillinducks?"

"They like molded foods. You wouldn't believe how many duplicate molds the Fillinduck ambassador unloaded at my tag sale."

"Do you really want me to separate the recipes by species?" Donna asked. "I was planning on something more logical, like appetizers, main dishes, and desserts. Maybe we should include some non-recipe text about the culinary traditions of each species to cover all of our bases. Could EarthCent Intelligence help?" she asked her older daughter.

"Wrylenth knows more about our filing system at this point than I do," Blythe said. "I remember we assigned analysts to do that research years ago, in part for our subscribers who might want to buy gifts for alien businessmen or take them out to eat."

"EarthCent Intelligence can provide the required information," the Verlock co-op student affirmed. "Just give me a word count and tell me how many illustrations you want for each species. We can provide summaries of ingredients, cooking methodologies, and facts about food production, but you'll probably want somebody to rewrite it for a general audience."

"I have reporters who can rewrite intelligence assessments in their sleep," Walter said. "Just get us the facts and we'll flesh them out."

"How about meeting with the ambassadors?" Aabina suggested. "We could even ask them to bring something for a potluck."

"Do you think they'd go for that?" Kelly asked. "I'm not sure if Czeros or Bork have ever been in a kitchen in their lives, and I think Crute mentioned something about one of his wives doing all of the cooking for the family."

"They don't have to make the food themselves, but if we're able to include what they bring, they can hardly complain about being left out later."

"I wonder if we can't add a few recipes from outside the tunnel network," Chastity said. "It would seem odd to ignore the Sharf when more humans are flying around in their second-hand ships than any other kind, and I remember when the prospective members from the Cayl Empire were here that they were able to eat some of our food as well."

"Emperor Brynt stayed with us and he was especially fond of Aisha's cooking," Kelly said. "Is it within the rules for the bid, Aabina?"

The Vergallian co-op student stared into space for a few seconds before replying. "There's nothing specifically excluding recipes from non-tunnel network species, but we should probably check with the Stryx to be sure."

"Libby?" Kelly and Donna asked simultaneously, and then the EarthCent ambassador continued. "Do the recipes in the All Species Cookbook have to be from tunnel network members?"

"It's up to you," the Stryx librarian replied. "I'm a bit surprised that nobody has mentioned the Alts."

"The Alts, of course," Chastity said. "Remember the spread they laid out when we went to visit them with the alien ambassadors? Everybody loved it."

"If nobody needs me, I have a thing," Daniel said, rising from his chair. "I'll put the word out for recipes and give everybody a deadline of next Friday. No point in dragging it out."

"I should be going too," Blythe said. "I'm meeting with a Dollnick literary agent later and I haven't finished going through our market data yet."

"You couldn't have had an analyst abstract it for you?" Chastity asked incredulously.

"Not EarthCent Intelligence data, InstaSitter data. Some of the girls have been sharing book recommendations for after their clients go to sleep, and it's a great place to spot up-and-coming romance authors for all of the species."

"Tell them to read more news," Chastity called after her sister. Then she rose from her seat, followed by her managing editor. "Don't let Aunty Kelly overwork you, Mom, and let Walter know if you need anything."

"I'll let you know and you can tell Walter," Donna replied. "Aabina, I'm going to make sure I've added everything that's coming up to the office calendar so you can fill in for me doing day-to-day embassy management, if that's all right with you."

"Thank you, Mrs. Doogal," Aabina said. "I'm going to have the most interesting resume of all of the young royals in the empire."

"Aren't you returning to work, Wrylenth?" Kelly asked the Verlock, who hadn't moved from his chair.

"I'm concerned with the speed at which you make decisions," the bulky alien answered honestly. "How can you move ahead with such a momentous project without at least commissioning a study to determine the probabilities involved?"

"That's very sweet of you, Wrylenth, but you know that math isn't our strong suit. Would you feel better if I invited you to attend our next intelligence steering committee meeting?"

"But I'm an alien—to you, I mean."

"To be perfectly honest, many of the ambassadors were uncomfortable with the results of our new civil service exam when it turned out that the aliens who took it all passed with flying colors. But after hearing me talk about you and Aabina, I know for a fact that three of the steering committee members have signed up for the co-op program with their local branch of the Open University, and I'm sure they'd like to meet you. Besides, you've been working for EarthCent Intelligence long enough now to know that we don't have any secrets worth keeping."

"That's true." Wrylenth hesitated for a moment. "I would never violate my co-op confidentiality oath, but with your permission, I would like to seek advice from Ambassador Srythlan. He is one of the senior Verlock diplomats on the tunnel network and he might detect a pitfall in all of this that's escaping me."

"You may talk to him about our plans for the All Species Cookbook with my blessing," Kelly said. "And don't forget to tell him about the potluck meeting. Aabina will contact all of the embassy managers and work out a time."

"Could I have a minute?" the Vergallian co-op asked Kelly as soon as the Verlock exited the conference room.

"You can have the rest of my day if it will keep you here past the end of your co-op assignment."

"My mother asked me to arrange a confidential meeting with you, preferably in the Vergallian embassy. There will be a third party in attendance, but I can't tell you who for security reasons." As Aabina spoke, she brought both of her hands up under her chin, and extending her index fingers, began sliding them against each other like she was trying to start a campfire by rubbing two sticks together.

Kelly stared, and then almost blurted out "A Farling," before catching herself. "I understand," she said. "I'm available at any time."

"Now would work, if that's possible. There's something else my mother asked me to bring up, and we can talk about it on the way."

Kelly stuck her head through the opening from the conference room to the embassy reception area and called to Donna, "We'll be back."

"Don't forget to bring Aabina," the embassy manager replied, before returning to her work.

The co-op student didn't speak again until they reached the lift tube, and then she requested, "Vergallian embassy, the long way around."

"We can do that?" Kelly asked.

"The station management is very accommodating in these situations," Aabina replied. Then she let out a long breath and said, "It's about the cookbook."

"But you thought it was a great idea. I wouldn't have even known the All Species Cookbook existed if you hadn't brought it up that time."

"The thing is, Vergallians have their issues with the cookbook as well."

"Really? I thought that all of the recent editions made Vergallian vegan the largest section."

"That's just it," Aabina said. "Have you ever been to a Human Burger restaurant in alien space?"

"I haven't, but Dorothy and Kevin visited a couple of Human Burger franchises when they took a trip and accidentally got married a few years ago. They thought it was funny that the only thing they could order at the Drazen franchise was fruit salad that came from a fifty-five-gallon drum."

"In other words, it wasn't authentic Human food."

"I guess that other than the fruit salad the restaurant used local Drazen ingredients and served them Earth style. Are you saying that Vergallian vegan isn't what Vergallians eat?"

"What passes for Vergallian vegan in alien space is basically diet food that's been overcooked to kill anything that might give anybody indigestion. The problem is that now everybody thinks they know Vergallian vegan because they've had it at some point in their lives. But it's the equivalent of going to a steak house and ordering the one menu option for non-meat eaters when you want a good vegan burger."

"Do aliens cook the salad too?"

"No, but have you ever had Vergallian salad dressing?"

"I don't believe I have."

"That's because it's an art form and it has to be served fresh. Royal Vergallian households employ a—you don't have an equivalent term in English—salad dressing chef who does nothing else. And every town you visit on Vergallian worlds will have at least one bottling shop where you can choose from fresh dressings and art-glass bottles. They're universally popular gift items."

"I never knew that," Kelly admitted. "But didn't the Vergallians have a turn editing the All Species Cookbook?"

"Yes, but our version of Universal proved to be so opaque that even the AI had to guess at the recipes." Aabina paused as the capsule came to a halt and they exited on the Vergallian deck. "There were some rumors that it wasn't a true language at all, but the Stryx approved it."

"Well, I'm sure Donna will be happy to accept any guidance you can give her as to which recipes to include. You know, Joe has a way of barbecuing Vergallian vegan burgers so they don't taste that bad with enough condiments."

Aabina grimaced at Kelly's unintentional slight, nodded to Raef at the embassy entrance, and showed the way to her mother's office. "I'll wait in the lobby while you meet," she told her employer.

"You're not coming in? I trust you implicitly."

"The third party insists on absolute secrecy," Aabina said, and politely triggered the door opening sensor.

Kelly stepped into the Vergallian ambassador's office and noticed a shimmer to the air. She wasn't sure whether she should pretend to be surprised at the sight of a Farling, but the beetle saved her the trouble by immediately beginning to talk.

"Don't sit," G32FX said. "The less time you spend here the better the chance we have to keep this meeting a secret. Aainda and I have come to a tentative agreement that will benefit all of us, but it depends on a number of things going right and the agreement from major players who have yet to see the final treaty. None of this can happen if word gets out before the deal is made, so we can't fill you in on all of the details, but I can assure you that your cooperation is vital."

"I'm sorry," Kelly said. "Are you asking me to agree to something without even knowing what's at stake?"

"The future of Earth," the Farling rubbed out on his speaking legs.

"He's being melodramatic, as usual," Aainda spoke up. "I can tell you that if we can bring this business to fruition, it will be the greatest diplomatic coup in tens of thousands of years. As part of a three-way deal, the Farlings are seeking access to Earth for the purpose of scientific re-search—"

"Ambassador!" G32FX interrupted. "Remember our agreement."

"—no different from the arrangements you've already made with a number of tunnel network species. I've

88

already told him that in spite of past differences, Humans are eager to establish direct relations with alien species and to create new economic opportunities for Earth."

"I'm sure our president would be thrilled with the opportunity to negotiate with the Farlings," Kelly said.

"And the whole drug thing?" the beetle asked.

"You mean the fact that some of your businesses engineered addictive drugs for humans? Our own pharmaceutical companies operated much the same way for over a century, and my understanding is that the Farlings recently stopped supplying the pirates."

"You see?" Aainda said to G32FX. "I told you we have nothing to worry about."

The Farling peered intently at Kelly through his multifaceted eyes and reached his conclusion, "That's all for now. We'll be in touch."

Eight

Joe ambled up to the group on the holographic projection stage in the area of Mac's Bones set aside for the EarthCent Intelligence training camp. "Holding a private dance contest?" he inquired.

"Judith is helping Marcus with the 3-D motion capture system and Chance and I are helping Judith," Thomas replied. "It's all for your daughter's latest scheme."

"Dorothy does have a talent for roping in helpers," Joe observed with a chuckle. "She's already drafted my co-op student and her boyfriend to represent the Hortens at her first dance event. But how does the holographic training system for intelligence agents fit in?"

"Bob and I took ballroom lessons from Chastity's husband before Dorothy's wedding," Judith explained. "Marcus has a holographic capture system in his dance studio, but it's not as flexible as the one Thomas and Chance have engineered for immersive training simulations. Your daughter is convinced that the greatest obstacle to increasing her potential market is people who never had formal dance instruction as children and are too embarrassed to start now. So we're going to create interactive beginners lessons that will work with any home immersive system using Marcus and Chance as the one-on-one instructors for humans."

"How about the other species?"

"They're all far more likely to have had classes while they were young, so we'll get to them later."

Beowulf gave a sharp bark and motioned with his head for Joe to get a move on, but the EarthCent ambassador's husband held up his forefinger to request a delay.

"I saw on the Grenouthian news that a mystery Farling is visiting Union Station, and they showed an image of him in their notable arrivals segment. It must be M793qK stopping in to pick up medical supplies that he can't get on Flower, so I was thinking of putting together a card game in his honor."

"Different Farling," Thomas told him. "The older beetles all have unique carapace patterns and that was G32FX. It's a good thing that Lynx is still on Flower because she had a bad experience with him during our first mission together."

"I'll have to remember to mention it to Kelly," Joe said, and then gave in to the Cayl hound's head-butts. "Sergeant Beowulf says I need more exercise so I'll see you all later."

Joe took a few half-hearted jogging steps before settling back into a walk for the remainder of the circuit around the periphery of Mac's Bones. As he passed the opening in the mound of scrap that provided privacy for Dring's corner of the hold, Beowulf slowed down in expectation of a possible visit, but Joe spotted Marilla walking towards the ice harvester and changed course to intercept her.

"Good morning, Mr. McAllister," the Horten girl called as soon as she saw him.

"You look very professional," Joe complimented Marilla. Instead of her usual coveralls in garish safety colors, the co-op student wore a metallic business suit of a cut that Joe didn't recognize, but which he assumed was the current fashion for her species. He dug around in his pocket and came up with a thin silver case. "That suit reminds me that I have something for you."

Marilla's skin turned a brownish-orange as she accepted the gift, a color Joe had come to associate with anticipation. She opened the cover and her face instantly flushed with pure brown joy. "Marilla, Vice President of Engineering, Tunnel Trips," she read out from the business card. "Vice President?"

"Turn it over and read the other side."

"It says the same thing in Horten," she marveled. "But I'm too young, nobody will believe it. Is this one of those weird Human jokes?"

"I'll let Paul explain the rest to you. Here he comes now, and it looks like he talked Jeeves into attending the auction."

"Somebody looks like a happy Horten," the Stryx observed. "I take it you've given her the news?"

"Just the business cards," Joe said. "She's worried that nobody will believe her."

"They will when you show them this," Paul said, pulling the tab from his belt holster and swiping it to life. A few taps and he handed it to the Horten girl.

"This is the Stryx business registration for Tunnel Trips," she said, studying the document. "It's—you've made me a ten percent owner!" The Horten girl's voice went so high that Joe missed the last couple words despite the fact she was speaking in English.

"I talked it over with Aisha and we both agreed that it's the right thing to do," Paul said. "The stake reverts to the business treasury if you quit in less than ten cycles. That wasn't our idea, it's just the way the Horten lawyer your ambassador recommended drew it up."

"Ten cycles is the absolute minimum," Marilla told them. "I don't know what to say. Thank you, thank you so much."

"Are you sure this won't get you in trouble with future in-laws?" Joe teased the girl.

"The opposite," she said. "Hortens have a saying that equity knows no species. An ownership stake changes everything because now I'm working for myself."

"Great," Paul said. "Let's get out to the auction lot and see what we want to bid on, partner."

"Did you and Jeeves finish culling out the ships you want to sell?" Joe asked.

"Yes, and I mainly stuck with the list we've been working on for years. We'll keep everything that has potential as a family trader, but we're getting rid of the barges and the bigger stuff."

"And the yachts," Jeeves added. "Nothing goes obsolete faster than fashionable spaceships because they're no good for anything other than showing off that you're in fashion."

"Coming from an AI who owns a fashion business, I guess we'll have to take that as gospel truth," Joe said.

"Part-owns a fashion business," the Stryx reminded them. "You can't spell SBJ without the Shaina and the Brinda."

Samuel caught up with the group just as they reached the tug that Paul had bought for Mac's Bones over twenty years prior using his winnings from gaming as a teen. "Hey, guys. Taking the Nova out?" he asked.

"I was sure you'd stay in bed this morning," his father said. "I was asleep before you got home last night and it's the first day of your surprise vacation."

"There's no point trying to change my sleep schedule for just a few days and I've gotten used to napping," Samuel said. "Where are we going?"

"There's a Sharf ship-carrier parked in the auction lot and we're looking for anything we can convert into rentals," Paul said.

"Great, I've never been on a ship-carrier. They're supposed to be huge."

"And Zero-G, so you'll have to grab one of the spare sets of magnetic cleats from the Nova," Joe said, as they ascended the ramp to the tug's technical deck. "Why don't you co-pilot with Paul, Marilla? I'll stay down here and catch up with my prodigal son."

The Horten girl didn't need to be asked twice, and she followed Paul up the companionway to the bridge. Samuel dug a pair of spare cleats out of a supply locker and strapped them over his boots as the Nova came to life.

"Not going to get in trouble with your elders for giving us auction advice?" Joe asked Jeeves.

"I would never do anything that interfered with the competitive balance between the species," the Stryx replied disingenuously. "It just happens that I'm in the market for a small ship myself."

"But you can travel in space without a ship," Samuel said. He took his place on the acceleration couch next to his father.

"They come in handy for carrying things. Besides, my partners have been planning on visiting a few of the stations where our fashions aren't selling well to investigate trying some pop-up boutiques. It means hiring locals who are capable of sales and management."

"You mean factory direct, to cut out the middlemen? Wouldn't it make more sense to open stores on the stations where sales are strongest?"

"The boutiques that are our biggest customers wouldn't be happy if we went into direct competition with them. It's a balancing act," Jeeves explained, maintaining the exact same floating height above the deck as the Nova got underway and Samuel felt his weight increase. "It may be time to procure a small ship for business use."

"That's crazy," Joe said. "You should rent from us."

"That's the other option," Jeeves acknowledged. "I'll have to see what the prices are like."

"What would a round trip rental for overnight cost me, Dad?" Samuel asked. "I'm thinking of asking Vivian to go on a short hop to one of the other stations to look around."

The corners of Joe's mouth twitched up, and he said, "So it's a working vacation after all."

"What do you mean?" his son replied, trying and failing to meet his father's eyes. "I'm officially off the clock until Tuesday at two fourteen in the morning."

"It sounds to me like the Vergallians are sending you on a mission and you're inviting Vivian along for cover. Have you forgotten that I ran the EarthCent Intelligence training camp for over a decade?"

Samuel hesitated, unable to choose between lying outright to his father and keeping his oath to Aainda. He compromised by saying nothing.

"Interesting," Jeeves said. "Do you have a destination in mind or is that an Imperial secret as well?"

"Just one of the stations on the network," the young man replied sullenly. "I want it to be a surprise."

"Did Baa have a chance to do that thing for me, Jeeves?" Joe asked.

"Now who's keeping secrets," Samuel complained. "What could you want from a Terregram mage?"

"I have it right here," the Stryx said. A small panel in his casing slid open, and reaching inside with his pincer, he brought out a sheathed boot knife. "She says you'll be hearing from her about the bill."

"As long as it works," Joe said, accepting the knife from the Stryx and handing it to his son. "The day that Baylit came and took Ailia she asked me to keep this for you until you came of age. The crest on the hilt belongs to Ailia's father's family and it will serve as a passport in Vergallian space."

Samuel inspected the hilt and then drew the knife partway out of the sheath. "It's a throwing dagger," he identified the weapon. "Thomas tried to teach me how to throw one but the balance is way off compared to regular throwing knives."

"My greatest hope is that you never need to use it as a weapon," his father said.

"So why did Jeeves have it?"

"You know that I spent some time on Vergallian worlds and I've had a few bad experiences with high caste females exerting control with their pheromones. If Baa did her work correctly, as long as you have the sheath on your person, you'll be immune to those games."

"Thanks, Dad, Jeeves. This could be a real life-saver. I can't wait to tell Viv. She worries about me being around Vergallians."

"Don't forget who she works for now," his father cautioned.

"Would you keep a secret like that from Mom?"

"If she was an alien intelligence agent, I might," Joe said with a laugh. "Can you show us a hologram of that ship-carrier Jeeves? It's been a long time since I've seen one, and they're more impressive from a distance than up close."

"We're already too close to see the whole vessel unless I employ some imaging tricks," the Stryx replied. An enormous hologram appeared, filling all of the empty space on the technical deck, and for a moment the humans couldn't even tell what they were looking at. Then the view pulled back and the mega-structure became identifiable.

"That's incredible," Samuel said. "It must be half the width of Union Station."

"Sharf ship-carriers have just enough structural integrity to maintain the crew quarters and handle the low acceleration needed for course changes. The bulk of what you see is little more than open latticework with air lines and power. When they require access to a given section, they turn on the atmosphere retention fields and pump in air."

"I hope the latticework includes catwalks," Joe said.

The hologram zoomed in on a section of the Sharf megastructure until a segment of lattice with several individuals shuffling through it appeared at actual size. The Dollnick in the holographic projection towered over Joe and Samuel, who were sitting on the couch.

"At least the catwalk is fully enclosed so we can't float off," Samuel said. "Why are they shuffling along instead of giving a good push and floating through twice as fast?"

"I'll take the control of my feet sticking to something over speed any day of the week," Joe said. "When you're floating down the middle of what amounts to a tube and you can't reach the walls to change course, what are you going to do if a giant mouth appears at the end?"

"Get eaten, I guess," Samuel replied. "Okay, I see your point. Hey, I can feel us slowing down."

"Because we've arrived," Jeeves said, and the hologram was replaced by a view of a large docking bay, though again, it consisted of a latticework of light structural members and catwalks with no solid bulkheads in sight. "We're within an atmosphere retention field, so as soon as the Nova stops moving and Paul gives the word, you can drop the ramp."

Samuel and Joe found themselves again weightless, meaning that the ship was no longer decelerating. They unstrapped the safety restraints and pushed off the couch gently, arriving at the main hatch that doubled as a ramp at the same time. A few seconds later Marilla joined them, followed by Paul.

"I'm surprised Beowulf didn't insist on coming along," Samuel said. "He usually enjoys these short trips."

"But he hates being left behind, and the Sharf don't allow dogs on the carrier," Joe said. "Ready, Paul?"

"Lower away," the acting captain said.

Joe hit the button, and the main hatch, which was hinged at the bottom, descended with a faint hydraulic sigh. Since there was no deck in the docking bay, Joe hit the button a second time to stop the descent when the hatch was basically parallel with the Nova's technical deck, making it a ramp to nowhere. There was a curtain of cargo netting not far off that was anchored to a catwalk, and Paul shuffled off the end of the ramp, letting his momentum carry him across the gap.

"Did he turn off his magnetic cleats so they wouldn't pull him off course?" Marilla asked.

"They aren't strong enough to have much effect over a short distance," Joe replied. "If we were shooting for a small target and it was going to take a minute or more to get there, it would make sense to cut the magnetic field, but in this case, you can't miss."

The Horten girl nodded and walked right off the ramp, followed by Joe, who chose a slightly different angle so he wouldn't land on top of her. Samuel wasn't thinking that far ahead, but fortunately, Marilla had already pulled herself out of the way by the time he arrived. The four of them climbed down the net to the catwalk where Jeeves was already waiting.

"I can see Union Station through the lattice," Samuel said. "Is the station's mass exerting enough gravity that we'd eventually be pulled over there if we weren't standing on the catwalk?"

"The whole carrier would move with us," Marilla pointed out. "We're part of the same system."

"Not if we turned off our cleats," Samuel argued. "This reminds me of one of those homework problems from first year Space Engineering at the Open University."

"You're falling behind," Joe called over his shoulder. "Talk while you walk."

"Or shuffle," Samuel said, sliding one foot in front of the other without ever completely losing contact with the catwalk. "How do you know where we're going?"

"Just following everybody else," Paul said, pointing at the figures on other catwalks who were all moving in more or less the same direction. "My guess is that the auction lots will be right on the other side of the next cargo net. There wouldn't be any point in having us all dock an hour's walk from the merchandise, and the only thing the Sharf have to do to create a docking bay is to make room and stretch nets."

"I can't thank you enough for getting your dad to take a co-op student," Marilla said to Samuel. "Have you seen my card?"

"Tunnel Trips has cards?"

"Brand new." The Horten girl fished out the silver case Joe had given her and carefully extracted a single card without letting any others float loose. She gave it a little push in his direction and put the case back in her suit pocket, buttoning the flap just to be safe.

"Vice President," Samuel read after he snatched the free-floating card. "Wow! And I was beginning to feel bad about seeing you cleaning rentals when the rest of us all got government jobs."

"Cleaning rentals is just as important as installing propulsion systems—it's all part of the same business," Marilla said philosophically. She pointed ahead to where Paul was just ducking through a break in the netting to a different catwalk that was partially enclosed in screening. "Look, those must be the ships up for auction. There have to be thousands of them."

"They're the right size," Samuel said, running his eye over the neat rows of short-distance, single-cabin craft. "I bet the Sharf auction off the similar ones in big lots to save time or we'll be out here all day. Dad told me that most of these big auctions offer a couple of typical sample craft for inspection. Not random samples, but chosen to represent the average condition."

"Wouldn't that be something if Paul could buy a hundred or so? It would quadruple the size of our fleet, or we could resell them to the franchises."

"Look at those moving symbols. I'll bet they're numbers and it's a countdown to the start of the auction."

"Twenty-two minutes," Marilla said. "Where did everybody go?"

Samuel turned all the way around before it occurred to him to tilt his head back. "There they are, directly above us. We walked right past the turn they took."

"It's funny how in Zero-G a turn can go up or down as well as side-to-side. Hey, do you want to cheat?"

The EarthCent ambassador's son checked that his father wasn't looking, then he winked at Marilla. Clicking his heels to turn off his magnetic cleats, he pushed off the catwalk and launched himself up the vertical segment. The Horten girl followed too closely, and Samuel hadn't managed to get completely out of the way at the other end before she sailed into him and they got tangled up.

"Enjoy it while you're young," Joe called, though his voice lost force in the cavernous space that was cluttered with latticework and ships. By the time the two got themselves reoriented with their magnetic cleats stuck to the right surface, Samuel had to admit to himself that it probably would have been faster to just shuffle up to the next level.

"So, it's between these two lots, Jeeves," Paul was saying when the youngsters finally caught up. "I like the Drazen daytrippers, and even though they're a few thousand years old, they look like they're in great shape. But we have no way of knowing whether they were stored away from damaging radiation or if the hulls have lost half of their strength. On the other hand, those Dollnick taxis look pretty beat, but the maintenance records were in the bid package, and paint is cheap. It doesn't matter that the upholstery is shot because we'd have to replace the chairs anyway. People don't like it when their feet can't reach the deck."

"It wouldn't be right for me to provide technical insight that isn't available to the other bidders, but since I'm shopping for SBJ Fashions, I think the taxis are worth a closer look," Jeeves said.

Marilla put a hand on Samuel's arm to hold him back as the other three entered one of the Dollnick taxis that had been chosen as a representative sample.

"How was what Jeeves just did different than cheating for Paul?" she whispered. "He probably x-rayed those Drazen ships, or did magnetic resonance imaging or something."

"You never know," the EarthCent ambassador's son replied. "Jeeves might be cheating, or the Stryx may have some reason that they want us to build a bigger rental fleet using the Dollnick taxis instead of the Drazen Daytrippers. I went to the station librarian's experimental school and grew up with young Stryx, and all I can tell you for certain is that it's impossible to know what they're thinking."

Nine

"Are you sure you got the time right?" Kevin asked. "Tzachan and Flazint have never been late to a date before."

"This is the first time we're chaperoning on their clock so I rounded off a bit," Dorothy admitted. "It might have worked out to six or seven minutes past the hour, but who can remember that?"

"Maybe we're waiting in the wrong place."

"How many botanical gardens could there be on the Frunge deck? Libby?"

"Fourteen, but I had the lift tube bring you to the right one," the station librarian replied. "Flazint is just arriving."

A few seconds later the Frunge girl appeared, wearing a long dress and walking with mincing steps as if there was a rope tied between her ankles.

"Flaz?" Dorothy asked as if she didn't believe her eyes. "What are you wearing?"

"It's a first-year dating dress and you wouldn't believe how much I had to pay for it," Flazint replied angrily. "I feel like I'm trapped in a sack, and it took forever to weave my hair vines through this low-rise trellis I borrowed from my grandmother."

"But when I asked you about all of those dating apparel rules I read about in *Frunge for Humans,* you told me that they don't apply on Stryx stations."

"They don't, unless the matchmaker is doing a site inspection. Where's Margie?"

"It's too early in the morning for her, she would have cried the whole time," Dorothy explained. "We tried to get Alexander to come, but he did this big growling act like he had to stay and protect the baby, even though I know he went right back to sleep after we left. You never realize how big those Cayl hounds really are until you try to get them to do something they don't want to do."

"I brought the chaperoning contract," Kevin said, displaying the carrier bag for the stone tablet. "I've got the calendar in here too."

"Let me see the calendar, quick," Flazint hissed. She accepted the device from Kevin and scrolled through a series of Frunge menus before finding what she was looking for. "Grains," she swore. "Keep a lookout for Mizpah. I have to fix this."

"Something's wrong?" Dorothy asked.

"I wanted everything to look symmetrical for you when I translated to the Human calendar, so I substituted units rather than reworking all of the math. Grains," she cursed again. "There's a password."

"But after adjusting for the length of the day and the days in our respective weeks, wouldn't that have doubled your number of permissible dates?" Kevin asked.

Flazint turned the calendar over, spotted a plastic peel-off strip on the back, and gently pulled it off. Then she studied the underside of the strip and breathed a sigh of relief. "You were supposed to remove this sticker and keep it in a safe place," she lectured Dorothy while entering the password. "It's so nobody can tamper with the calendar other than the chaperone."

"Like you're tampering now?"

Flazint thrust the strip with the printed password into Dorothy's hand. "Don't lose that, but if Mizpah asks, say you left it at home."

"You want me to lie to your matchmaker?"

"This is important. Did you even read your chaperoning contract?"

"It's in Frunge, and you said it was all standard legalese."

Flazint gave the calendar a final tap and invoked the safety override. The device let out a loud beep of protest and the screen began flashing bright red, but after she powered it down and then on again, everything looked normal. "Here," she said, returning the calendar to Kevin. "If Mizpah asks, just hand it over as if nothing happened."

"Did you just make us accessories to some sort of Frunge dating felony?" Dorothy asked suspiciously. "I mean, you know I'd do anything for you, but it would have been nice if you asked first."

"No time for that, we're almost late. Just act normal and don't volunteer any information."

"I hope you know what you're doing. How come Tzachan didn't arrive with you? At least we could have gotten his legal opinion."

"How could two Frunge who only meet on chaperoned dates show up together?" Flazint asked innocently. "He's waiting inside."

"Shall we?" Kevin said, offering his arm to Dorothy. She looked at him in surprise, and then realized they were supposed to be on their best behavior for the date inspector, who might be lurking behind any bush in the garden.

"Shoulders back," Flazint whispered to the EarthCent ambassador's daughter. "Posture is an important part of the grading process."

"Mizpah will be giving us grades?"

"Remember, we aren't supposed to know she's watching us, so act natural. And smile."

"There's Tzachan," Kevin said, easily spotting the Frunge attorney, who was standing next to a metal picnic table surrounded by a low privacy hedge and waving some sort of banner on a long pole. "What's with the flag?"

"We always carry a flag on chaperoned dates," Flazint said quickly. "Don't you remember?"

"Uh, right. Got it. Is there a special reason he's just standing there rather than coming to greet us?"

"This garden is very popular and he's staked out a good spot. They don't accept reservations."

"It's a restaurant too?"

"Juice bar," Flazint explained. "Don't worry, I called ahead and they have some Human-safe options on the menu. Listen, Dorothy. The best thing is for you to talk with Tzachan about work."

"Really? You're not going to get mad at me for monopolizing him?"

"Of course not," the Frunge girl replied, and managed a smile that wouldn't have looked out of place on a corpse. "Try to remember what we're doing here today."

"Sorry, I'm still waking up," Dorothy said as they reached the picnic table. "Good morning, Tzachan. Nice banner."

"They're my family colors," the Frunge attorney told her. He planted the pole in a socket at the center of the picnic table before continuing formally. "Mr. Crick. Mrs. Crick. Thank you for your supervision."

"You're welcome, Attorney Tzachan," Kevin said, trying to match the Frunge's official manner. He wracked his brain for the bits that Dorothy that insisted on reading to him from *Frunge for Humans* and recalled something about seating procedures on dates. "Aren't you going to sit, my dear?" he asked his wife.

"What? I mean, yes, thank you," Dorothy said, taking her place. "Flazint?"

The Frunge girl slid in next to her friend, and seeing no other option, Kevin went around to the other side of the table and sat across from Dorothy. Both girls began jerking their heads to the right as if they wanted him to do something, so he slid over to be across from Flazint, trying to make it look like that's what he intended the whole time. Tzachan took his place on the bench across from Dorothy.

"What would you like to drink?" the Frunge attorney inquired.

"I haven't had breakfast yet, so orange juice if they have it," Dorothy said.

"Any chance of coffee?" Kevin asked.

"Cold drinks only," Tzachan replied. "Let me check the menu." He stared off into space for a moment consulting his heads-up display. "They have iced coffee."

"Works for me."

Dorothy felt somebody kick her under the table and turned to see her friend staring at her significantly.

"Uh, aren't you having anything, Flaz?"

"Thank you for asking, Chaperone," the Frunge girl said. "If a small Feechee Nut juice could be arranged, I would be ever so grateful."

"The waitress will be out in less than five minutes," Tzachan informed them, and then fell silent. The two Frunge seemed content to sit straight-backed and stare at the humans across from them, but Dorothy felt another kick on the side of her ankle.

"So I've been hoping for a chance to talk to you about work," the EarthCent ambassador's daughter said to the Frunge attorney. "SBJ Fashions is planning to launch a dance series on the tunnel network stations. I've been thinking of naming them after Cinderella, but I'm afraid we won't have any legal protection."

"Who is Cinderella?"

"A fairytale heroine who loses a glass slipper at a ball because she has to rush off before her carriage turns into a pumpkin. The only way the prince can find her is to fit the slipper on her foot."

"Like Perzinna?" Flazint asked. "But it was a sandal."

"Fairy tales are often based on universal themes that recur across species that have never been in contact," Tzachan told them. "We have a story about a young woman, Perzinna, who loses her mother but is brought to the attention of the king by a magical flying lizard that takes her under its protection. When the girl finishes her housework and is out riding the lizard, her sandal comes off and falls out of the clouds into the king's lap. He takes this to be an omen from the gods, and when his agents find the girl, the king marries her and they live happily ever after."

"Do you mean that Perzinna went around with just one sandal until she was noticed?" Dorothy asked.

"I don't know if the story was clear on that part," Tzachan admitted. "I was never a big fairytale fan."

"Enough!" Mizpah shouted, stepping out of the hedge where she had blended in so well that nobody had spotted her. "Perzinna was at the harvest festival where she danced all night with the young king who was in disguise, and when she flew off in the morning on her magical lizard, the sandal fell in the king's lap. The king had his sorcerer enchant the sandal with a seeking spell, and then he followed it back to the girl's home with his royal troop. How can you not know that?"

"I guess it was never on a test," Tzachan replied, displaying remarkable composure considering the surprise interruption. "How nice to run into you while—"

"Oh, drop it," the matchmaker said, sliding onto the end of the bench next to Flazint, who was frozen in fear. "I know perfectly well that you were tipped off to my inspection because nobody carries banners on dates anymore, at least not after the first couple of meetings. Hand over the calendar."

"A seeking spell," Dorothy mused, while Kevin dug in the contract carrier bag for the device and delivered it to the tiny Frunge woman. "I bet Baa could cast one of those with her eyes closed."

Mizpah powered on the dating calendar and shook her head. "Reset to the factory defaults. I wonder how that happened?"

"I must have hit the wrong button when a prompt came up," Kevin said, his ears turning red. "I've been meaning to learn more Frunge."

"Right, a prompt that required a twenty character password," Mizpah snorted, flipping the calendar over and inspecting the back. "I don't suppose any of you would know why the area where the password sticker was attached is so squeaky clean, like it was just removed."

"It was all me," Flazint cried, scrambling off the bench backward and dropping to her knees. "I took advantage of my chaperone to see Tzachan more often than we should have. But we mainly went bowling or ice skating, and we never entered a theatre or a nightclub. I swear it."

"Get up, you silly girl," Mizpah said. "Do you think that it's my job to make you miserable? Look at you in that ridiculous dress, and with a trellis on your head that went out of fashion back when I was a young shrub with dirt in my boots. Now tell me. Since when is there an ice skating rink on Union Station?"

"It's on the Vergallian deck, in one of their old ballrooms that got replaced by the new complex," Flazint said, slipping back into her place on the bench between Dorothy and Mizpah. "Our friend Affie told us about it, so we've been going a lot before everybody finds out and it gets too crowded."

"I'll have to pay it a visit myself," Mizpah said. "I haven't been on the ice in hundreds of years. And you," she continued, pointing a twiggy finger at Kevin. "Protecting your friends is an admirable goal, but lying is a bad habit to get into." Then she turned to Tzachan and her glare rekindled. "The Foundational Tales of Frunge, it's in every bookshop on the deck. Buy it, read it, know it. There *will* be a test."

"Yes, Mizpah," the attorney said, bowing his head.

A waitress whose hair vines towered on a trellis at least five times the height of the low-riser Flazint was wearing arrived with their drinks.

"Orange juice must be you," she said, handing the beer-mug sized glass to Dorothy.

"I'm the iced coffee," Kevin said.

"Of course," the waitress replied, handing him a glass filled with black coffee and clinking with ice. "And three small Feechee Nut juices."

"I told them to put mine on your tab," Mizpah informed Tzachan.

"You really surprised us coming out of the shrubbery like that," Dorothy said, after taking a sip of her orange juice. "I must have looked right past you."

"Give me a little credit for something," the matchmaker replied. "The day an old Frunge can't hide in the bushes is the day petrifaction sets in. Now tell me more about your dance idea."

"Seriously? You're not just asking to be polite?"

"When have I ever been polite? And although this may come as a shock to you, the job of a matchmaker is to make matches, and dancing plays an important part in the later stages of most courtships. Now how do you plan to commercialize poor Perzinna?"

"Cinderella, though if we do sandals, Perzinna could work too. SBJ Fashions employs a Terragram mage to enchant items for the professional LARPing league. The other day she gave me a glass slipper that was ensorcelled so that if my husband put it on my foot, it turned into a pair of our best dance shoes."

"Both on the same foot?"

"No, my other shoe vanished and was replaced at the same time. Baa said it was some kind of—I don't remember."

"She probably doesn't either," Mizpah grumbled. "Magic users make terrible witnesses because they can't be bothered with details."

"Our enchanted fashions for LARPing have been doing really well, especially the bags of holding that Flazint designs."

"Baa's Bags. I bought one."

"You role-play?" Flazint asked, surprise overcoming caution.

"All of the time, but not in the sense that you mean. No, I'm too old to fool around trying to stab hologram-wrapped bots with a sword, but I visited a LARPing fair while I was doing my research on you, and I happened to need a new purse. I couldn't believe how inexpensive it was, and the metal clasp is a testament to your skill."

Flazint's hair vines flushed dark green, but something the matchmaker had said troubled Dorothy. "Did you say it was a bargain?" the EarthCent ambassador's daughter asked.

"Fifteen creds for a designer purse? I'm surprised it covered the materials and the hand-made clasp."

"It couldn't. Would you happen to have it with you?"

"How could she have it with her?" Kevin asked, but Mizpah undid the neck of the molted green and brown cloak that had allowed her to blend in with the shrubbery so effectively, and brought out a cherry-red handbag.

"Oh, no," Flazint said, pointing at the small black lightning bolt embroidered over the four feathers. "Your purse is cursed!"

"Obviously," the matchmaker said, "considering I bought it from the cursed goods table. The man assured me that the contents would be safe as long as I didn't enter a LARP studio."

"If you want more cursed clothes or accessories, we usually have a few odds and ends around awaiting destruction," Dorothy said. "Baa claims she makes mistakes when she gets tired, but I think she does it on purpose to keep Jeeves from overworking her. Tzachan, can you look into who's selling our cursed products at LARPing fairs? I know we pay a Drazen disposal service that's supposed to destroy them."

"So how is your Cinderella going to help you sell more ball gowns and shoes?" Mizpah asked.

"I'm still working out the details, but I was thinking that we'd host singles dances, and Baa would enchant a glass slipper so that it would only turn into our shoes if placed on a girl's foot by her preordained love."

The Frunge matchmaker choked and sprayed her mouthful of Feechee Nut juice all over the shrubs. "Are you begging to be sued?" Mizpah demanded when she recovered from a fit of coughing. "Are you trying to put yourselves out of business?"

"I respect the monopoly position of the Matchmakers Guild on the Frunge deck, but I don't believe you have any grounds to bring suit against my clients for poaching," Tzachan said, his professional ethics winning over his desire to please Mizpah.

"Not me, you idiot. The poor couple who get glued together by your client's cockamamie promotion." The matchmaker got up from her place so she could move to the end of the picnic table and address Dorothy without having to lean around Flazint. "There are two possible outcomes to a promotion like that. One, your mage gets the spell right, in which case you could hold dances until entropy freezes the universe without the glass slipper ever transforming. Two, your mage gets the spell wrong and you find yourselves in court."

"But Baa did a prototype glass slipper and when my husband put it on my foot, it transformed."

"Remind me again how the two of you met?"

"As children," Kevin said. "Years later, after I was captured by pirates and escaped through the old Verlock emergency rescue system, it turned out that the Stryx had taken it over, and they dumped me out at Union Station."

"Sounds like somebody's love was pre-ordained by the Stryx," Mizpah cackled. "Unless you have a deal with the station librarian's dating service to send you matches made by AI, I'd ease up on the grand ambitions and use the glass slipper for something fun."

"This coming from a matchmaker whose species doesn't let courting couples hold hands," Dorothy objected. "What kind of fun could Frunge singles possibly have at a dance?"

"Now you're beginning to get it. Cursed items aside, who can afford your fancy shoes?"

"The question *we* like to ask is can you afford *not* to own a pair. At least, that was our most successful promotion to date."

"Do I have to spell it out? You should be marketing to married women if you want to find more non-Human buyers, and you should, since Humans are a tiny part of the tunnel network population. Didn't you list the founders of InstaSitter as references on your chaperone application?"

"Yes, they used to babysit for me before they started the business," Dorothy said. "Chastity is already our biggest customer, though, and I wouldn't feel right using the glass slipper to trick her into buying more shoes when she already has a closet full."

"Is your wife playing dumb just to irritate me?" Mizpah demanded of Kevin. "You're in business. You see it, don't you?"

"InstaSitter has unique access to parents who like to get out of the house from time to time," Kevin said slowly. "You're thinking about a combined promotion, like giving them free babysitting if they go out dancing."

Dorothy jumped up so fast that she banged her knee on the picnic table and cried out. "Ow, that hurt. It's so brilliant that Jeeves will have to go along with it."

"How will you keep track of who actually goes to the dances?" Tzachan asked.

"You can validate tickets," Kevin suggested. "Back when I was a trader, I visited plenty of orbitals and habitats where parking cost an arm and a leg, but if you ate in enough restaurants or stayed in a hotel, you would get a discount on the docking arm fees."

"Not free?" Dorothy asked.

"You'd have to eat in a lot of restaurants for that. Parking isn't cheap when you're actually connected to an airlock. There are only so many to go around."

Ten

The assistant director hopped down from the stage, glared at a few Drazens in the studio audience who were whispering, and then looked up at the control booth for the giant timer counting down to the end of the commercial break. At five ticks remaining, he began stamping his foot in sync with the countdown to prepare the cast. The children were still scrambling for their marks as the status lights on the immersive cameras went hot and Aisha began to speak.

"Welcome back to Let's Make Friends. I want to thank you all again for sending in your recipe suggestions for the All Species Cookbook. I hope you've been enjoying our first cooking special as much as I know the children have enjoyed mixing the ingredients and licking off the spoons. Now, who wants to show everybody how their desserts turned out? Plynth?" she prompted, since the Verlock children were usually a sure bet to do everything right, if slowly.

"Five more minutes," Plynth replied sadly. "So hungry."

"Brule?"

"I'm only up to the sixth layer," the Dollnick child reported. "Ask me later."

"Our cookies only have one layer," Grace said in dismay.

116

"Brule wants to be a professional baker when he grows up," Aisha reminded Shaina and Daniel's daughter. "Are your cookies ready?"

"I think so." Grace ran for the row of multi-purpose kitchen appliances that one of the show's sponsors had supplied for free, but her little Stryx friend beat her there.

"Where's your baking mitt?" Twitchy demanded.

"I had it a minute ago."

"I'll take the tray out."

"But where's *your* baking mitt?"

"I don't need one. My pincer is rated for—really hot," the little Stryx concluded, having taken to heart Aisha's request not to use too much scientific vocabulary above the children's grade level.

"What's that funny odor?" Gzera asked, sniffing the air.

"That's what baking with wheat flour usually smells like," Aisha told the Frunge boy. "Your species doesn't eat grains so you aren't used to it."

"Is that what the powdery stuff was? Gross."

"I'll try one of your cookies as soon as they cool down," Binka offered, watching carefully as Grace used a spatula to move the cookies from the baking sheet to a plate. "I don't want to burn my mouth."

"I'll take one now," the Verlock boy said, shuffling over to Grace and Twitchy. He put a steaming hot cookie in his mouth and chewed thoughtfully. "It's kind of sweet and squishy. Maybe if you added salt and left them in longer?"

"My cookies should be ready to eat," Gzera said. "I hope I followed the formula right."

"Don't forget your oven mitt," Grace called to him.

"I froze mine," the Frunge boy replied. "Baking is for girls."

"Now that's not true," Aisha protested. "Just look at Brule and Plynth. Do they look like girls to you?"

"Aliens are weird," Gzera said, his go-to explanation for everything that didn't match his Frunge upbringing, and he opened the freezer unit and pulled out the plastic tray. "They look yummy."

"Do you remember what you put in them?"

"No, it was all Human ingredients because that's what the bunnies let us have. I grated lots of orange sticks and added a cup of grainy brown stuff."

"Sounds like carrots and brown sugar," Aisha said, accepting one of the cookies from the Frunge child and nibbling on the edge. "Ooh, it's cold, but I like it."

"Cold is better than lukewarm," the Verlock said, popping one in his mouth. "Crunchy."

"Pietro?"

"I made campaign biscuits," the Vergallian boy said. "It takes hours for them to bake fully."

"All right, we can try yours on the next show. Binka?"

"These are ready to eat," the Drazen girl said, carrying around a tray. "I set the oven to cool them after the bake cycle."

"Excellent," Plynth declared. "Crunchy, and with a bite."

"Edible," the Dollnick allowed,

"Water!" Grace begged. "They're too hot."

"But they're room temperature," the Drazen girl protested. "Hey, you're turning red like a Horten."

Twitchy, who had vanished in a blur a few seconds earlier, reappeared with a metal cup of water. Grace filled her mouth and swished the water around, apparently trying to cool her tongue.

118

The host sampled one of the Drazen's cookies herself and smiled. "They are a bit peppery, but I think they're very nice."

"I'm ready," Brule announced, and brought out a creation that reminded Aisha of a famous leaning tower on Earth that had featured large in a humorous Grenouthian documentary about human construction practices of the Middle Ages. "I layered organic acorn butter to even out the irregularities in the walnut cookies while controlling the bitterness of the oak tannin with chocolate chips. The frosting is made with a non-dairy milk-powder substitute in case anybody is lactose intolerant."

"What does that mean?" Grace asked her little Stryx friend.

"It means that somebody with four arms has been watching cooking shows," Twitchy replied.

"Your dessert is lovely," Aisha said. "It would almost be a shame to break it up and eat it."

"That's okay, I'll just put it on the mantle," Brule told her. He carried his wobbly creation over to the fake fireplace and placed it on the mantel where various awards given to the host over the years were displayed.

"Plynth? Is five minutes up?"

"Close enough," the Verlock said, and opening the oven, pulled the baking tray out bare-handed. "I made brownies from an Earth recipe."

"They certainly smell delicious," Aisha said. "I didn't think you went in for sweets."

"Substituted salt for sugar," Plynth told her proudly. "They're both white."

"I think you better let those brownies cool before you slice them for serving," the host said, waving back the children. "You know, I don't want complaints from all of your parents that I ruined your dinners with desserts, so maybe you could just take the brownies home, Plynth."

The Verlock shrugged. "More for me."

Aisha caught the frantic waving of the assistant director out of the corner of her eye and wondered where the time had gone. "Twitchy told me that while you were learning about the kitchen appliances before the show, you came up with new lyrics to our theme song," she said to the cast. "Do you want to sing them for our audience?"

The children formed a double chorus line, with Plynth, Brule and Pietro in the back, and Grace, Binka, Gzera, and Twitchy in the front. The theme music started to play and they came in at the regular point.

Don't be a stranger because my egg's runny,
Your food's weird too, but let's make friends.
If that apple's bitter, I'll give you some honey,
Everyone likes chocolate, so let's make friends.

"I only eat the bitter chocolate," Plynth added, right before the status lights on the immersive cameras went dark.

"Cut. That's a wrap," the excitable assistant director shouted. "Aisha, the director requests that you stay after the show for a quick discussion."

"Am I in trouble?" the host asked, watching as the parents of the children came on stage to collect their offspring and the desserts they had created.

"I suspect not, given that you've got the highest ratings for a children's show in the galaxy," the bunny replied laconically. "Besides, he's coming out of the booth now. If he was planning on yelling at you, he would have asked you to go up there instead. It's soundproof."

120

"You don't have to wait around for me," Aisha said to Grace's parents, who were busy munching on the cookies their daughter had made with her little Stryx friend. "I know you have to go back to Mac's Bones anyway to pick up Mike, but this could take more than a few minutes."

"Are you sure you don't want me here?" Daniel asked in an undertone. "You know how obsessed the Grenouthians are with rank, and they probably think an associate ambassador is on par with an associate producer."

"I don't know if that's good or bad, but if you don't mind waiting, the truth is the director intimidates me a little," Aisha admitted. "He always seems so angry about something."

"I wonder if Mike and Fenna have put poor Kevin out of business yet," Shaina said. "I think it's great that he's willing to give them so much responsibility, but I'm not sure that ten-year-olds have a clear sense of barter value."

"I didn't see any independent traders in the hold when I left this morning so they're probably just dealing with rental customers looking for snack food," Aisha said. "Besides, the dogs are always hanging around, and they won't let anybody walk off with all the stock."

"Mrs. McAllister," pronounced a giant bunny with a golden sash identifying him as the director. "And I'm always happy to have the parents of a cast member show so much interest in our production, especially when one is the co-ambassador and the other employs Stryx Jeeves in her business."

Neither of Grace's parents saw fit to correct the director's minor mischaracterizations before the bunny continued.

"In fact, it's fortunate that you all happen to be together because it may save me a good deal of hopping around. To make a long story short, I was having drinks with our ambassador last night and he pitched me an idea for a new show. The truth is, ever since he brought me the concept for Let's Make Friends, he's been trying to repeat his success just to prove it wasn't a fluke. Most of his ideas have been, shall we say," the director paused and discretely coughed behind a furry paw, "noncommercial. But this time, I think he's really onto something, and we'll need EarthCent's cooperation."

"You want to do a political show?" Aisha asked.

"A cooking show," the director said. "To be more precise, an all species cooking show, but as you know, the name is reserved for the All Species Cookbook monopoly."

"You couldn't call it something else?"

"What would make you comfortable?"

"Why does it matter what I think?"

"Because we want you to be the cook," the director said, and then wiggled his ears to placate his star before she could protest. "I know, we agreed to cut back on your hours at the last contract negotiation, but I can't help noticing how efficient you've become as a professional. We could shoot a one-hour show in the same studio, just a few times a week—"

"Absolutely not," Aisha interrupted. "If anything, I'd like to spend more time with my family, and my husband and I are trying to have another child."

"Already?" the bunny asked in surprise. "I thought you put at least ten years between them."

"You must have us confused with another species. I really appreciate the offer and I do enjoy cooking, but—"

"Aisha," the director interrupted, "I want to show you something. Promise me you'll keep an open mind." Without waiting for a reply, the bunny made a windmilling gesture with his left arm, and the lights above the stage dimmed.

"Beware of aliens who ask you to keep an open mind," Daniel whispered to the host.

A catchy theme song with nonsense lyrics that were obviously intended as a placeholder for the future began to play, and then a holographic kitchen materialized, complete with mounds of Earth produce piled high on an old-fashioned pushcart. A small funnel cloud appeared and sucked up various fruits and vegetables into a swirling mass, and then there was a clap of thunder, and the flying produce suddenly spelled out "The All Species Cookbook Show." Before Aisha could protest, an exact duplicate of herself appeared dressed in a traditional sari.

"Welcome to the All Species Cookbook show," the hologram announced in Aisha's voice, with perfect lip synchronization. "I'm Aisha McAllister and I'll be showing you how to make delicious recipes from Earth ingredients that all of the tunnel network members can enjoy. Each week we'll focus on a different ingredient or culinary tradition, so let's break out our chef's knives and get down to cooking."

The music swelled again, and the whole hologram was suddenly overlaid by text in a dozen languages that translated to, "Insert commercial break here."

"I don't understand," Aisha said to the director. "You think that audiences want to watch a hologram of me cooking?"

"Drop 'a hologram of' from what you just said and you've got the general concept. We won't tell them."

"It's not ethical and it doesn't make any sense. Half of the advanced species couldn't tell the difference between me and another woman standing side-by-side if we were wearing the same clothes. I doubt even you could recognize me in a crowd."

"I memorized your markings years ago," the bunny replied with a sigh. "Listen, Holo-Aisha wasn't my idea. The studio executives insisted on preparing it as a backup plan for in case the substitute hosts bombed when you went out on maternity leave. It just seems a shame to waste all of that development effort."

"How come I didn't know anything about this?"

"Holo-Aisha? It's common practice for all of our shows to have backups available. There's nothing fraudulent about it," the director continued, anticipating his host's protest. "It's all in the fine print of your contract. If a temporary substitution needed to be made, it would be clearly stated in the show's closing credits."

"I'm sorry, I can't go along with it. Besides, if I was casting a multi-species cooking show, I'd go with a male cook."

"But we want a celebrity Human and there just aren't that many to go around. We'll give you double the points in the new production," the bunny offered, though it clearly pained him. "The promotional tie-in is too good for us to sit back and do nothing. Don't say anything now, don't even shake your head. Just sleep on it."

"My answer won't change, Director, but if it makes you happy, I'll talk it over with my family."

"Excellent, and our ambassador will be in touch with your embassy about the sponsorship."

"You're willing to help defray the costs of the cookbook?" Daniel asked.

The Grenouthian leapt backward as if Daniel had suddenly whipped out a weapon. "What? I was talking about EarthCent sponsoring the cooking show, not the other way around. It would be an invaluable promotional opportunity for you."

Aisha accompanied Grace and her parents to the lift tube with Twitchy tagging along. The girl and her little Stryx friend kept the adults busy answering questions about cooking, and by the time they reached Mac's Bones, Grace decided that her father was getting off easy by doing the dishes instead. They all headed for the chandlery where Fenna and Mike were babysitting for Margie while also manning the store for Kevin, who was out in his new bumboat.

"Did you have any customers?" Shaina asked the ten-year-olds.

"Lots and lots," Mike replied. "We ran out of change."

"So what did you do?"

"I went home and got my laundry money," Fenna said, pointing to the glass jar filled with change that she found in the pockets of the McAllister household while helping with the wash. Aisha suspected that Joe intentionally left small denomination coins in his coveralls for that very reason. "Mikey is really good at making change."

"Grandpa taught me at Kitchen Kitsch," the boy said proudly. "I want to be in retail when I grow up."

Eleven

Donna removed the lid from the elaborate tureen that must have cost more than a year of her salary as embassy manager and almost gagged. "What is this?" she asked Czeros.

"Blood pudding," the Frunge ambassador said. "My embassy chef made it special."

"But blood pudding is actually sausage and this is a soup."

"Don't let the name put you off. It's best served while it's still cold. Here, I brought a spoon."

"I—it was really thoughtful of you, Ambassador, but I don't see how this could be safe for all of the tunnel network species, let alone us."

"Ambassador McAllister and her husband love it," Czeros insisted. "Joe always asks if the chef has any prepared when we have a formal event."

"Really?" The embassy manager looked at the soup again and shuddered. "Do they eat it just like this?"

"You have to stir it a little to get the solids floating around, and Joe always adds sour cream."

"Sour cream?" Donna repeated, and gambled on a third look in the tureen. "Is this borscht?"

"You thought I meant..." the Frunge ambassador let out a gale of laughter that sounded like a wood chipper in action. "That wouldn't be Human-safe at all. No, the beetroots are fresh from the ag deck, and our chef ferments the mixture for several days to get the sour taste. Aabina," he called to the co-op student who had just emerged from Daniel's office. "Come and try this."

"Oh, that looks yummy," the Vergallian girl said. "Are you submitting the recipe to be considered for the cookbook?" As she took the spoon from Donna, the doors to the corridor slid open and Bork entered, carrying a baking dish.

"I was counting on more than consideration," Czeros whispered, and winked in the direction of the embassy manager. "I don't need the tureen back, if you know what I mean."

"I heard that," the Drazen ambassador said. "Trying to bribe the editor of the All Species Cookbook is probably a Human crime, but if it's not, you can count me in." He set the baking dish on Donna's display desk and whipped off the foil. "Try one while they're warm."

"My eyes are watering from here," Aabina said. "How much hot pepper did your wife use?"

"Hardly any at all," Bork said. "In fact, I told Minka that everybody would find the stuffing too bland. It's a mixture of rice, nuts and tomato sauce."

"We usually stuff sweet bell peppers for baking, Ambassador," Donna said. "These look like—"

"Chili peppers," Bork confirmed. "I contacted Drazen Foods over the Stryxnet as soon as you invited us to the potluck meeting and they sent me a fresh batch of their hottest variety in the diplomatic bag."

"You get a diplomatic bag from Earth? Wait, our diplomatic bag never showed up this week."

"Don't worry, there was nothing in it for you. Aren't you even going to try one?"

"I have lots of sampling to do, and I'm worried that it will be so hot that my taste buds will be burned out for the rest of the day," Donna excused herself. "Ambassadors, I already talked this over with Kelly, and when it comes to the personal favorites that will be published with your names, I only need the recipes. We aren't going to judge your taste."

"Then I'll keep the tureen and our chef will be in touch," Czeros said. He picked up the borscht and headed across the lobby for the conference room.

Bork handed Donna a handkerchief to dry her eyes, replaced the foil over the stuffed chili peppers, and followed in the Frunge ambassador's footsteps.

"Do you think I should ping the ambassador to let her know that Bork and Czeros are already here?" Aabina asked.

"Kelly just ran home to get her contribution to the potluck, so she'll be back as soon as she can whether you ping her or not," Donna replied. "She said Aisha insisted on whipping up a few things for her to bring."

"Doesn't the ambassador cook?"

"She likes baking things with chocolate in them, but other than that, cooking has never been high on her priority list. And please remember not to volunteer for any new projects while you're in the meeting," the embassy manager added. "I'm really going to need you the next couple weeks now that we're in production."

A tall alien whose skin was covered with tiny red and blue feathers entered the embassy carrying a picnic basket. "I must have come in the wrong door," he chirped. "Where's the potluck meeting?"

"In the conference room, Ambassador," Aabina told him, pointing at the opening through which they could see

Bork and Czeros enthusiastically sampling their own contributions.

"Who was that?" Donna asked the Vergallian co-op.

"The Fillinduck ambassador, Tverk. He's been here before."

"Not without an encounter suit. I thought he was allergic to us or something. Kelly is going to be surprised." The door slid open again, and the EarthCent ambassador hurried in, pushing a small catering trolley. "The Fillinduck ambassador came," Donna told her immediately.

"Did I miss him? Am I late?"

"You're early," Aabina said. "He just went into the conference room. Bork and Czeros came early as well. What's all of that?"

"You know Aisha," Kelly said. "Once she gets cooking she always makes enough for an army. The Grenouthians wanted her to do a show."

"Do you mean an episode where she cooks instead of the children?"

"A cooking show for adults. Of course, Aisha told them that she's already too busy, but you know how persistent the bunnies are when they see a market opportunity. They think that our cookbook launch is going to create a lot of free publicity and the network execs believe that she's the perfect fit." Kelly lowered her voice and added, "When Aisha gave them her final answer, the director asked her if anybody else in the family would be interested. The way I see it, the Grenouthians are projecting their nepotism on us. They figure that choosing a host with family connections to EarthCent is the surest way to gain access to the All Species Cookbook brand on favorable terms."

"How about my grandson?" Donna suggested. "Jonah is the best cook in the family, and with Samuel and Vivian engaged, he'll be your son-in-law by marriage."

"Is that really a thing?"

"With the Grenouthians it is," Aabina explained. "They consider siblings of in-laws as cousins of a sort. You should mention Jonah to their ambassador."

"Somebody should really ask Jonah if he's interested first," Kelly pointed out. "And you don't think I should have Aisha bring it up with the director instead?"

"Definitely not," the Vergallian girl told her. "The ambassador will want credit, and if Jonah is his recommendation, the director will be relieved not to have to make the decision himself." She gently removed Kelly's hands from the push-bar of the catering cart and took over. "You talk to the Fillinduck, I'll put out the food."

"Good luck," Donna added.

Kelly followed her co-op student into the conference room while trying to come up with a greeting for the Fillinduck ambassador who had been dodging her for almost three decades. When she came face-to-face with the colorfully feathered alien, she blurted out, "Why have you been avoiding me, Ambassador Tverk?"

"I brought pickles," the ambassador replied as if he hadn't heard her question. "There's a trio in our preserved foods market who sell them by the barrel. I'm not sure if mixing cider vinegar with saltwater and dropping in various vegetables to soak really counts as cooking, but I wanted to keep it simple."

"Uh, thank you," Kelly said, feeling that it would be rude to repeat her original question. "Please make yourself at home."

"I see the Frunge brought blood pudding as usual," Tverk replied. "I think I'll have a bowl."

"Ambassador," Srythlan said, shuffling across the conference room. "I baked pretzels. I hope they aren't too hard."

"I've never seen such large salt crystals." Kelly bent forward to peer at the giant white knobs on the blackened dough sticks the Verlock presented in a large glass bowl. "Is it natural sea salt?"

"I buy the Union Station brand, which as you know, is associated with the Stryx recycling system. I believe they have a method of growing sodium chloride crystals in the wastewater treatment—"

"I'll just put them on the table for you," the EarthCent ambassador interrupted her slow-spoken alien friend before he could ruin her appetite. While placing the bowl on the buffet, she found herself next to the Gem ambassador, who was just taking the wrapping off a tray of chocolates. "Are those from Chocolate Gem's store?" Kelly asked, her mouth watering.

"I feel a little guilty showing up to a potluck with a retail product, but if I had prepared something myself, everybody would assume I was the caterer," the clone said. "Besides, there's nothing better than chocolate."

"I concur wholeheartedly. Did Donna tell me that you had asked for a private meeting later today?"

"Yes, though it's really quite simple. My sisters would like to advertise catering services in the Stryx stations edition of the All Species Cookbook. I'm told that a large number of cookbook buyers never cook for themselves."

"Hey," Bork said, looking up from the vegetable platter the Grenouthian ambassador had brought. "Don't agree to anything exclusive until you hear my offer, Ambassador

McAllister. I'm authorized to negotiate ad space for Drazen Foods."

"We're in the process of seeding our latest ag world with Earth tubers," the Dollnick ambassador volunteered. He deposited a mouthwatering basket of French fries on the table while reaching with one of his upper arms for a chocolate. "Get them while they're hot."

"Tiny salt crystals," Srythlan observed. "I am also authorized to purchase ad space."

"For what?" Kelly blurted out.

"The Verlock Molecular Gastronomy Academy. They're dedicated to spreading the use of statistics and probability in cooking. The math is quite challenging."

"Please use the toothpicks," the Chert ambassador declared, as he materialized out of nowhere and set an enormous bowl of colorful fruit balls on the table. "What am I missing?"

"We were just negotiating with Ambassador McAllister for advertising space in the All Species Cookbook," Bork told him. "The Humans aren't going to use it to insult their friends."

"Unlike some aliens we know," Ortha said, pushing into the crowd around the buffet and setting a few bottles on the table. "The two purple ones are plum wine and the clear one is plum brandy, highly distilled. Nobody ever remembers to bring drinks to these things."

"Why doesn't everybody make up a plate and take a seat," Aabina's clear voice rang out, followed by, "Hi, Mom. I didn't mean to yell in your ear like that."

"I should have had more sense than to walk in front of you while you're working," the Vergallian ambassador replied. "Could you put this on the buffet for me?"

"Sure. Is that Royal Dressing?" the co-op student asked, her eyes going wide.

"I got up early and worked on it all day with our chef's help. I just hope somebody brought salad."

"A giant bowlful, Ambassador Aainda," Kelly said. "Why don't we all take Aabina's advice and fix ourselves a bite so we can sit down and eat in comfort?"

The ambassadors didn't need to be asked twice, and with less than the usual amount of snatching and grabbing, everybody found something that suited them and took their species-appropriate chairs at the conference table. Kelly waited until Srythlan served himself before settling on a salad with a liberal dash of Royal Dressing and a side plate of chocolates. Before turning away from the buffet, she couldn't resist trying one of Crute's French fries. It was so good that her knees almost buckled.

"Great salt," the Fillinduck ambassador commented to Srythlan after sampling one of the Verlock's pretzels. "The dough part is a bit overcooked."

The Grenouthian ambassador, who must have inhaled the food from his first trip to the buffet, rose from his place with the empty plate as if he were about to go for seconds. Instead, he cleared his throat to make an announcement, "I am accepting tenders of pre-production ad buys for our new All Species Cookbook show."

"You licensed the broadcast rights?" Bork asked Kelly.

"We're in discussions," she replied diplomatically, and addressed herself to the Grenouthian. "Don't you think it's a bit premature to be selling ad time, Ambassador?"

"Pre-production ad time," the giant bunny clarified. "Once our contract with you is signed, the price goes up."

"Put us down for one spot per show for the first season," Srythlan said. "The academy will be in touch."

"Are you selling ads for the show and the cookbook separately or can we get a package deal?" Ambassador Crute inquired. "I imagine a coordinated campaign would be the most effective."

"I'll have to speak to our business backers," Kelly said. "My involvement in all of this was really limited to signing the bid package for EarthCent. Nobody said anything about the previous editions of the cookbook having advertising so it never came up."

"Would you have paid to advertise in a language that nobody could read?" Ortha asked. "I was explaining your plans for the cookbook to my home office earlier today, and I discovered that we don't even have a term to describe what you're attempting."

"Cookbook diplomacy?" Kelly suggested with a smile.

The ambassadors all froze, and Aabina hastened to say, "She meant it literally, using both words in the plain sense."

"What did everybody think I said?"

"You know how translation implants have trouble with first-time usages," the co-op student explained. "When I'm in meetings, I monitor a real-time transcript of the conversation on my heads-up display to check for translation glitches. 'Cookbook diplomacy' translates into an idiom in most of the tunnel network languages that's equivalent to gunboat diplomacy."

"Oh, sorry everybody," Kelly apologized. "You know that we're in no position to go around making threats. I have to say this dressing is the best I've ever tasted, Ambassador Aainda."

"And this wine is excellent, Ortha," Czeros complimented the Horten ambassador. "Now, does anybody have any information to share about the Alts?"

"Our Alts?" Kelly asked.

"Their purchases have singlehandedly restored our bicycle manufacturing industry to a profit," the Frunge ambassador said. "Earlier today I met with one of our businessmen who just returned from the Alt homeworld, but if nobody else is interested…"

"A diabolical people," the Grenouthian ambassador complained. "Our intelligence service stopped sending agents to Alt because they come back ruined for work. The Alts treat spies like honored guests and bend over backward to cooperate."

"We just send them a list of questions every few cycles," Crute said. "The Alts are incredibly cooperative."

"Good students," the Verlock ambassador remarked. "They already outnumber Humans on our academy worlds."

"I haven't heard from Methan in over a year," Kelly said. "They still haven't reached a consensus about joining the tunnel network and I didn't want to nag."

"I received a message from his son Antha just the other day," Bork informed the others. "He was contacting me in accordance with the terms of the treaty we concluded during their visit."

"I remember reading an article about that in the Galactic Free Press," Aainda said. "He promised to ask you first if he heard of a production on Alt that required an actor with a tentacle."

"It ties in with my information," Czeros said. "But if nobody has any substantial additions, I'm going to have to ask you all to owe me one."

"What, are we back in nursery school?" Ortha groaned. "Fine, I owe you one."

The Frunge ambassador waited patiently for the others to assent to his condition, and then he spilled the beans.

"The Alts will be making an announcement about the Stryx invitation to join the tunnel network in the near future," Czeros reported. "Bork, I'm sure that your young friend contacted you because the Alts are planning an epic documentary about their first contact with alien species, an event which most of us attended. How many historical reenactors can boast about being hired to portray themselves?"

"Where are you going?" Kelly asked the Grenouthian ambassador, who headed for the exit.

"I just remembered somewhere I have to be," the bunny flung over his shoulder. "I'll tell the network team to contact your people about managing ad sales for the show and the cookbook. The sooner we work this out the better."

"You're not all running off, are you?" Kelly was unable to keep the disappointment out of her voice as more chairs began scraping back and the ambassadors rose to their feet. "Aabina and I have a whole list of questions about the cookbook."

"I'm returning for seconds," Bork told her, displaying his empty plate. "You didn't think I was going anywhere with all of that food left?"

The EarthCent ambassador relaxed when she realized that none of her guests were following the Grenouthian. She fought off the temptation to revisit the buffet, telling herself that the French fries would be cold by now, and concentrated on the subtle flavors of Aainda's Royal Dressing as she finished her salad. When the Drazen ambassador returned with a heavily laden plate, she couldn't resist helping herself to just one of his fries.

"Addictive, aren't they," Crute commented from his seat. "Even more so than the fried snacks we make from Tan Tubers. Something to do with the starch content, I suspect."

"I have trouble choosing," the Fillinduck ambassador said, holding up a French fry in one hand and one of the Verlock's pretzels in the other. "I wouldn't be offended to have either of these listed as my contribution to the All Species Cookbook."

"What did you bring?" Aainda asked him.

"The pickles. They're also high in sodium chloride, but these," Tverk continued, shaking the fry and the pretzel for emphasis, "these would likely be banned in Fillinduck space as unlicensed salt delivery systems."

"Does your species have a problem with salt?" Kelly asked, hoping she wouldn't accidentally offend the ambassador and be subjected to another three decades of the silent treatment.

"Yes, we can't get enough of it," the Fillinduck replied with a chirpy laugh. "A single one of those pickles has one hundred percent of our recommended daily consumption, which is about ten percent of what we all crave. Will you be including dietary recommendations in the cookbook?"

"EarthCent Intelligence looked into that and concluded it was too risky," Aabina said. "While nobody has fought a civil war over daily recommended values of nutrients, there have been a couple of close calls. With the exception of the Verlocks, none of the tunnel network species have come up with a universally accepted set of values."

"Have you ever met a skinny Verlock?" Srythlan asked when all of the ambassadors turned to look at him. "Bork, if you're getting up again, please bring me a couple of those pickles."

Twelve

"Name?" Marilla asked Samuel, her finger poised above her tab.

"Come on, you can fill that in without asking," the EarthCent ambassador's son replied.

"I did the programming for the rental form myself and I wanted to show you how it works," the Horten girl said.

"Sorry, I guess I'm kind of nervous. Samuel McAllister."

"I can assure you that all of our rental craft are in top-notch condition."

"It's not that. I've never taken Vivian anywhere before."

"I see. Purpose of your trip?"

"Vacation."

"And where will you be going?"

"Corner Station."

Marilla stopped typing and looked up from the tab. "Really?"

"I've always wanted to see it," Samuel mumbled, realizing just how lame his explanation sounded.

"Are you going on some kind of secret diplomatic mission?"

"Is that really on the form?"

"I just thought I'd ask since you said you're taking Vivian. I'd think that could be awkward with you working for the Vergallians and her working for the Drazens. Ah," Marilla said, "that's why you're nervous."

138

"Here she comes, don't mention anything to her."

"Hi, Marilla," Vivian greeted the Horten girl, with whom she had become much more friendly since getting engaged. "Did you pick out a nice ship for us? Sorry in advance if I get sick."

"Dorothy stopped by earlier and left this for you," Marilla said, presenting Vivian with a piece of wax paper that had two peel-off patches stuck to it. "She said to start with an eighth and never to go above half in eight hours. It's the Farling cure for Zero-G sickness in Humans, but it has some side effects."

"Thanks. Do you have any scissors?"

Marilla pulled open the sole drawer in the rental kiosk and handed Vivian the scissors. "Don't forget to bring them back."

"I was going to cut it up now."

"And have all of those tiny scraps to keep track of? It's better to just cut a bit off if you need it."

"So, are we all set?" Samuel asked.

"I need your programmable cred."

"I thought you'd give us a bill when we got back."

"Funny, I never heard that one before," Marilla said, drumming her fingers on the Stryx mini-register.

"I have my programmable cred from the Vergallian embassy, but I don't want to use that, since it's a vacation and everything," Samuel concluded awkwardly. "Let me find Dad and borrow his."

"You can pay me back later," Vivian said, handing her programmable cred over to Marilla.

"Are you sure you want to use this one?" the Horten girl asked after inserting it in the register. "It comes up with a Drazen menu."

"Oops, I gave you my expense account cred."

The girls swapped coins and Marilla inserted Vivian's personal programmable cred in the register. "So, the basic rental is seventy-nine creds a day. How long will you be gone?"

"Just overnight," Samuel said.

"You realize that if you don't return the ship within twenty-four hours I'll have to charge you for two days," Marilla told them.

"We'll be back. Is there anything else?"

"All rentals come with basic insurance in the daily fee, but we offer a Thark umbrella policy for just ten creds a day."

"No thank you."

"Not so fast," Vivian said. "What do we get for the ten creds?"

"It can't be much or they'd charge more," Samuel pointed out.

"Says the boy who was rescued from hijackers thanks to a Thark insurance policy," Vivian reminded him.

"We don't have a printed booklet because it would be too long, but I can shoot a copy to your implant if you want to skim it on your heads-up display," Marilla said apologetically. "It's basically travel insurance for if something goes wrong and the vendor you're dealing with won't pay to make it right, but most people get it for the ransom coverage."

"For ten creds the Tharks will pay a ransom to get us back from the pirates?"

"Ten creds a day."

"It's easy money for the Tharks," Samuel said. "They never have to pay a claim because they can get one of their old battleships out of stasis and go threaten the pirates with a lot more trouble than whatever the ransom is worth."

"We'll take it," Vivian said.

"Excellent. I get a commission on insurance sales," Marilla told them, making a notation on her tab. "Snack food and Zero-G safe drinks are available at the chandlery, and that takes care of everything except for the walk-through."

"I think I can manage to turn on a Stryx controller and tell it where we're going," Samuel said.

"It's not an instructional walk-through for first time pilots—that would cost extra. You need to inspect the ship in my presence and note any damage so you don't get charged for it when you return."

"Wait a second," Vivian said. "I just bought umbrella insurance on top of the basic coverage that's included in the rental. It's not like we're planning on damaging the ship, but why should it matter to us if we do?"

"The basic insurance has a five hundred cred deductible for damage," Marilla informed her apologetically. "Please follow me."

Rather than leading them directly to the parked rentals, the Horten girl made a detour past the chandlery, where it was impossible to resist stocking up on snack food.

"What's with the metal briefcase?" Kevin asked his brother-in-law as he cashed out their purchases. "Carrying valuable underwear?"

"It's a perk from work," Samuel replied. "When I told the ambassador I was going on a vacation, she asked if I had any luggage and insisted I take something from the storeroom."

"What's that chain?" Vivian asked. "Pull up your sleeve."

"It's a fashion statement," Samuel said, grabbing the bag of snacks with his free hand. "Thanks, Kevin. We better get going, Viv."

"I knew there was something suspicious about this sudden vacation. It's a handcuff, isn't it? You're acting as a courier for the Vergallian embassy and you only invited me along as cover."

"Does it make sense that I would bring a co-op for Drazen intelligence on a secret mission?"

"Your twenty-four hours started when I ran the programmable cred," Marilla warned them.

"We'll talk on the ship," Vivian said, but the tone of her voice made Samuel wince.

"Memorize the number painted on the nose in case you park somewhere with other Tunnel Trips rentals. Please walk around the outside and make a note of any dents or perforations larger than a Stryx cred and then we'll inspect the interior."

"Perforations? You're renting us a ship with holes in it?"

"Not intentionally," Marilla said. "That's the point of the walkthrough."

"It's fine," Samuel told her after a quick circuit. "Let's check the interior and get going."

"Wow, do you clean the ships yourself?" Vivian asked after they climbed through the hatch. "It's spotless."

"Thank you," the Horten girl said, and held out her tab like a microphone. "If you guys don't want to buy the navigation tutorial you have to give me voice confirmation."

"I waive the navigation tutorial," Samuel said.

"There are Zero-G sick bags under the acceleration seats just in case. If you have to use one, please make sure the sealing strip turns black after you press the edges together.

I had to clean a ship last week where somebody left a little opening, and when the ship accelerated after coming out of the tunnel, the bag flew to the back of the cabin and everything got squeezed out."

"Maybe I'll start with a quarter-patch," Vivian said, but the piece she snipped off was closer to a half. "Does it matter where I put it?"

"Dorothy said they work fastest on the neck," Marilla told her. "Please place any personal items in your chair's saddlebags or the overhead compartments before departure. Enjoy your vacation, and thank you for choosing Tunnel Trips. I'll get the hatch on my way out."

"That was more complicated than I thought it would be," Samuel said. He placed the bag of munchies from the chandlery in the large pouch strapped to the side of his chair and zipped it closed. "Are you ready to get going, or do you want to wait a few minutes for the drug to take effect."

"It's medication, not a drug," Vivian snapped. "Maybe I should use the rest of it, just in case."

"Uh, I just remembered Kevin telling me about the side-effects it had on my sister. He said she couldn't sleep and it made her kind of aggressive."

"So now you're saying I'm too aggressive? You should have thought of that before you asked me to marry you." Vivian scowled as she put the scissors in her purse with the remaining doses of Zero-G medication and placed the whole thing in her saddlebag.

"I can't believe how fast the patch worked," Samuel muttered, and turned his attention to the Stryx controller. "Ready to launch."

"Please provide a destination," the mechanical voice responded.

"Right. The tunnel. I mean, Corner Station."

"Please fasten your safety restraints, launch in ten seconds and counting.

"Why aren't we moving yet?" Vivian demanded.

"It's only been two seconds."

"Aren't you going to take off that stupid handcuff?"

"I don't have the key."

"You mean you invited me on a romantic overnight and you're going to have a stupid metal briefcase dangling from your wrist the whole time? I'm not going."

"It's too late," he said, as she reached for the buckles on her safety restraints. "We're already moving. Can't you feel it?"

"Turn on the viewscreen. I want to see."

"I'm not sure that's such a good idea with your—"

"TURN IT ON!"

"Enable viewscreen," Samuel told the controller in a resigned voice. The large display panel lit up with an advertisement for the in-voyage entertainment system. "Look, they have the Grenouthian news, Vergallian dramas, and old episodes of Aisha's show."

"External camera," Vivian barked, and the screen shifted to a forward-looking view just as the ship began a sweeping ninety degree turn into the heavy traffic in Union Station's core. "Ugh, turn it off."

"Viewscreen off. You know that Gryph handles all of the navigation with manipulator fields until we're in the tunnel. There's zero chance of an accident."

"I'm not an idiot. What's in the briefcase?"

"I, uh, I promised not to tell anyone."

"Is that what I am to you? Anyone?"

"Here, have a juice box," Samuel said, unzipping the saddlebag and pulling one out at random. "It's grapefruit, your favorite."

Vivian accepted the juice box and peeled the seal off of the mouthpiece. "Maybe I'm getting better at space travel. I don't feel sick at all."

"We're not in Zero-G yet," Samuel told her. "Gryph keeps the acceleration up until we're on a vector for the tunnel entrance, and then he eases back until we hit trip velocity."

"So why do rental ships even need thrusters?"

"In case something goes wrong or we want to go somewhere without active traffic control. If all travel was between tunnel network stations, the Stryx could just play toss-and-catch with us."

"Sometimes I think they do that anyway. We're definitely getting lighter."

"Do you want to watch something on the in-voyage system? The basic selections come with the rental so we already paid for it."

"You mean I already paid for it. Okay, let's see the news. My handler said that I need to get rid of my Human-centric view of the galaxy if I want a career with Drazen Intelligence, but I'm dead if Aunt Chastity catches me watching the Grenouthian news."

"Why don't you close your eyes for a second in case the display continues the last program," Samuel suggested, and then watched her comply. "Viewscreen on." The display went live with a long line of ships entering the dark mouth of the tunnel even as a series of incoming vessels zipped past like meteors heading towards Union Station. "Local Grenouthian news."

"—and the Farling has been seen on the Vergallian deck, which proves our thesis," the furry presenter concluded. "In other news, the alternative species of humanoids from Earth, otherwise known as the Alts, have concluded their deliberative process and will be announcing their decision when their delegation arrives on Union Station. Now some exclusive footage from a pirate attack on the Dollnick colony ship, Flower, currently in service as a circuit ship for the Conference of Sovereign Human Communities, or whatever they're calling themselves these days."

"What?" Samuel and Vivian said simultaneously. The image shifted from the Grenouthian presenter to a trio of heavily armed ships with energy weapons ablaze making a strafing run on the camera position. A bright red finger of light came from somewhere outside of the camera's field of view and made brief contact with the pirate vessels, causing them to spin away out of control.

"Sure hope those pirates have good insurance," the bunny chortled. "And that, children, is why you shouldn't attack Dollnick colony ships. Moving on to more interesting species, in Verlock news—"

"Mute," Samuel said. "I asked Woojin about Flower's defences the last time he visited my Dad. He said she could take care of herself, but I've never seen anything like that before."

"That's because you don't watch the Grenouthian news," Vivian told him. "They have stuff like that every hour, though most of it is from places that aren't on the tunnel network. The Galactic Free Press doesn't publish anything about the wars going on around the galaxy unless there's a human connection, but the bunnies will run any story that has strong visuals."

146

"The Drazens aren't going to send you anywhere dangerous, are they?"

"Look who's talking with a briefcase handcuffed to his wrist."

"Entering the tunnel in ten seconds," the controller reported.

"Strange we don't get countdowns," Samuel said, grasping at any reason to change the subject. "Maybe the last person disabled them."

"I'll bet that Marilla resets all of the controllers to the default settings when the ships are returned," Vivian said. "She's efficient like that."

"Do you realize we've been coasting for the last several minutes?"

"Do you mean…" Vivian undid her safety restraints and floated up from her seat. "I can't believe I'm not sick. This medication is great."

Samuel breathed a sigh of relief that she wouldn't need to stick another piece of the patch on her neck and undid his own four-point harness. "I'm just going to pop into the bathroom."

"Why didn't you go before we left? Do you like Zero-G plumbing? I'm beginning to have second thoughts about this engagement."

"I'll just be a minute."

"It's got something to do with that briefcase, doesn't it? Just for the record, I'm starting surveillance on you this minute."

"You're spying on me?"

"Just doing my job like you're doing yours, unless you'd rather leave the briefcase with me."

"It's chained to my wrist!"

"So don't close the door all the way and leave it outside. There's not much space in that bathroom anyway."

"You've seen the equipment in there, it takes both hands."

Vivian made a "V" out of her index and middle finger, pointed at her own eyes, and then pointed at Samuel.

"Fine," he huffed. "Spy on me all you want. I'm just a messenger."

"So you admit you dragged me along as cover for a secret mission."

"Let's not argue. I admit I don't have to go to the bathroom and that I'm supposed to activate the briefcase when we enter the tunnel. Promise not to tell?"

"What does it do?"

"I don't know, I'm not even sure why Aainda sent me. I thought the embassy security staffers were all personally loyal to her family, but she seemed to think I was the best choice."

"How do you activate it?"

"I'm serious about not telling anybody."

"Station Scouts honor," Vivian said, holding up her right hand in a pledge.

Samuel regained his seat and strapped back in again. He pulled the briefcase down on his lap and began manipulating one of the latches. "Ten turns to the right, three turns to the left, four to the right."

"It didn't open."

"I don't think it's supposed to, it's just the activation method. Have you ever seen a metal briefcase latch that turned?"

"I'm not sure I've ever seen a metal briefcase," Vivian admitted. "So now what?"

"We enjoy a few hours in the tunnel coasting to Corner Station, have a look around, and go home."

"Big date," Vivian grumbled, reaching for her own seat. "Unmute the news."

"Put your safety harness back on, just in case," the EarthCent ambassador's son said. Between Zero-G and the repetitive nature of the news, Samuel soon dozed off, but he was awakened by Vivian's frantic cry.

"What's happening? Are we being attacked by pirates?"

"In a tunnel? They could never find us, hyperspace doesn't work that way," Samuel said. "What made you—"

There was a scraping noise outside the rental ship, followed by an unmistakable rapping on the hatch.

"That," Vivian replied. "I thought I heard footsteps on the hull, but that was definitely a knock."

"Controller," Samuel said. "Switch to outside view."

The loquacious bunny on the screen was replaced by a stunningly beautiful Vergallian wearing an elaborate uniform. Members of a royal guard were arrayed behind her in a giant hangar that would have fit Mac's Bones in a corner.

"What's she saying?" Vivian asked.

"Controller. External audio on."

"...keep us waiting any longer we will not be amused," a steely voice pronounced.

Samuel ripped off his safety harness and dove for the hatch. As soon as it opened, the Vergallian royal entered, shuffling gracefully forward on her magnetic cleats. She made a hand-sign to a group of officers, one of whom detached himself from the others and came to stand just outside the hatch, his hand on his holstered weapon.

"So you are Aainda's choice for a messenger. Very interesting." The Vergallian grabbed Samuel's sleeve and dragged him closer, which wasn't difficult, as the EarthCent ambassador's son wasn't wearing magnetic cleats and was floating in Zero-G. Then she brought his wrist near her lips and blew on the handcuffs like she was trying to cool a spoonful of soup. The lock popped open and she immediately took possession of the briefcase. "I am Queen Ashiba. Deliver your messages."

"I wasn't given any instructions and Vivian isn't with me. I mean, she's my fiancée, but she doesn't work for the Vergallian embassy like I do."

"Vivian Oxford, daughter to the head of EarthCent Intelligence and the co-founder of InstaSitter." The officer at the hatch coughed discretely, and the Vergallian royal glanced in his direction before continuing, "And currently employed by Drazen Intelligence. How could we forget?"

"She's on vacation," Samuel protested. "I didn't tell her I was on a secret mission for Aainda."

"We'll see if you speak the truth," Ashiba said, and stared intently at Samuel.

"Don't you drug him with your pheromones," Vivian shouted, but her attempt to throw herself between Samuel and the older woman failed because she had forgotten about her safety harness, and now the buckles refused to cooperate.

"You're resisting us?" the Queen demanded, peering into Samuel's eyes and frowning. "Is it possible the myth about Humans is true?"

"Which myth is that, Highness?" Samuel asked, employing every ounce of his willpower not to glance down at his boot where the hilt of the dagger Baa had enchanted was secreted.

"That the presence of your true love interferes with our abilities." Ashiba appeared lost in thought for a moment.

150

"You're a very lucky young woman, Vivian Oxford, and we don't have time to separate the two of you for the sake of confirming a myth." With that, she turned on her heel and exited the rental.

"Do you have any message for Ambassador Aainda, Highness?" Samuel called after her.

"Tell our old friend that we hope she knows what she's doing," the Vergallian replied. "Aainda always had a love for complicated plots and she may have outdone herself this time. Release them into the tunnel," she told her aide, and stalked off towards her royal guard with the briefcase.

"If it wasn't for that bit about your true love, you'd be dead right now," Vivian told Samuel.

"But think of what a great story this will make to tell our grandchildren," he said weakly, redoing his safety harness.

"Who is Queen Ashiba anyway? The name sounds familiar."

"She's the head of the Imperial Council," the EarthCent ambassador's son replied. "The top queen in the Empire of a Hundred Worlds."

Thirteen

"Are you sure about this?" Flazint asked Tzachan. "I know there will be at least one reporter from the Galactic Free Press and he'll probably take pictures for an article."

"It's an official SBJ Fashions event," the Frunge attorney reminded her. "That makes it just like we're meeting at work."

"I like your new suit."

"Dorothy picked it out for me. So why is the Galactic Free Press sending a reporter? It's just a beta test for a sponsored dance series."

"You met Bob Steelforth at Dorothy's wedding," Flazint told him. "He and Judith were standing behind Kevin and Dorothy and getting married for real so the prophetess could do the ceremony. Dorothy bought the two of them dance lessons from Marcus before the wedding, and now she's amortizing the cost over more events."

"Should I know Marcus?"

"Chastity's husband, he used to be a Wanderer and he runs a dance studio. I'm sure both of them will be coming as well."

Tzachan stuck his head out of the lift tube capsule just to make sure there weren't any Frunge passing by who would see the couple arriving together, and then he ushered Flazint into the lobby of the Empire Convention

152

Center. They chatted loudly about work on their way to the Meteor Room.

"You're almost late," Dorothy greeted them nervously. "All of the magnet dancers are here already."

"What are magnet dancers?" Tzachan asked.

"That's what I've decided to call experienced dancers who get the party started."

"They came early because you announced an open bar for volunteers before the official starting time," Flazint told her. "It really looks like everybody you know is here."

"Everybody Samuel and Vivian know too. Even Tinka came to see how the co-sponsorship with InstaSitter works out. Do you think I should make a speech?"

"Do you have something you want to tell everybody?" Tzachan asked in return.

"I do, actually. I better get up and say it before the real guests start arriving."

"Real guests?" Tzachan mouthed at Flazint.

Dorothy went to find something to stand on, and when she realized the chairs were all padded, the designer of SBJ Fashions patented shoes accessed the control panel via her heads-up display and brought her heels down to nothing, as if she were about to walk on sand. Then she subvoced the station librarian and asked to be patched into the sound system.

"Ready," Libby replied.

Dorothy motioned for her husband to come over to steady her as she got up on the chair. "I want to thank everybody for coming and to remind you why you're here," the EarthCent ambassador's daughter commenced in the no-nonsense voice she had learned to project at fashion shows. "Our real guests tonight are the couples who are getting free entry in return for a minimum five-hour babysitting commitment."

"InstaSitting commitment," Tinka interrupted.

"Yes, InstaSitting," Dorothy agreed, happy to oblige the Drazen who owned a minority stake in InstaSitter and managed the business for Blythe and Chastity. "Some of our guests will be experienced dancers, others may have only milled around at weddings, so I want everybody to be helpful and not show off too much."

"Were you directing that remark at me?" Chance asked.

"I was going to ask you and Thomas to do a tango demonstration during one of the breaks," Dorothy told the artificial person. "Our main goal is to get all of the guests dancing, and they aren't going to set foot on the floor if they're intimidated. I'm not really expecting anybody to come stag, but if you do see a single parent looking for a species-appropriate partner, I hope you'll all consider making room on your dance card."

"She expects us to dance with strangers?" Tzachan whispered to Flazint.

"We're safe. No Frunge is going to come to a dance alone," the girl replied.

"I think it would be best if we're already dancing when the real guests start to show up, so tell Mornich if you have any special requests—raise your hand so people know who you are, Mornich—because he'll be acting as the DJ tonight. Once we get a better grip on the economics I hope to switch to live orchestras, but Donna does all the EarthCent mixers with recorded music, and she says nobody ever complains. Oh. Hello, Jeeves."

"Disconnect from the public address system if you're done speechifying," the Stryx responded.

Dorothy found the big red button that Libby had thoughtfully superimposed over her heads-up display and cut the connection. "What are you doing here?"

"Did you think I would let you embark on this kind of investment without seeing the results for myself? Where are the customers? Your friends and family aren't going to buy anything from us."

"They'll be here anytime now. InstaSitter did the scheduling so everybody should arrive within the next half an hour, unless they stop somewhere for drinks along the way."

"Why do you have the Horten ambassador's son managing the playlist? I've heard his band and they specialize in jumping-up-and-down music."

"Mornich's father insisted that he make a living if he's going to have a girlfriend so he plays lots of weddings now. Marilla will keep him in line."

"I'll have to talk to her," Jeeves said. "How many couples are you expecting?"

"The last time I checked with Jonah there were nearly two hundred expected, and Tinka only let him offer the promotion to parents who had signed up to hear about special offers. If we start advertising…" Dorothy left the sentence dangling.

"I know this all makes perfect sense to your artistic mind, but I've studied the best marketing practices of all the tunnel network species, and if there's one thing they agree on, it's keeping the sales funnel short."

"Sales tunnel? Is that a new Stryx thing?"

"Funnel. You expect me to allocate marketing creds to a co-branding effort with InstaSitter, but we only get sales as a secondary or tertiary effect," Jeeves complained. "InstaSitter wins right off because it gives their clients another reason to go out for the evening, but even if those clients are motivated to buy new clothes and shoes, only a percentage of them will choose SBJ Fashions."

"But they'll want to sign up for future dances, which means we'll capture their contact information," Dorothy pointed out. "Then there's the discount coupons for our products, the clothes they see our models wearing, the—"

"I'm paying for models?"

"Not tonight, and in the future, we can use InstaSitters who will come and dance in return for clothes. We could give them the returns from boutiques that we can't sell as new."

"We'll see." A Vergallian orchestral piece that was currently popular on the station began to play. "Find your husband and make sure people see you dancing in that five-hundred creds of mine that you're wearing."

"Thanks, Boss," Dorothy said, then ostentatiously checked her make-up in the reflection from the young Stryx's casing. If Jeeves could have blushed at being caught having polished his robot body for the event, he might have turned as red as his employee's lipstick. "Come on, Kevin," she told her husband. "One beer should have been enough to find your rhythm."

The guests began arriving in a stream, handing their InstaSitter vouchers to Affie and her boyfriend, Stick, who were working the door.

"How come everybody else gets to dance and we're stuck taking vouchers?" Stick complained during a brief lull.

"We agreed to split it up in shifts. You and I are first, followed by Tzachan and Flazint, and then Dorothy will work the end of the night with Kevin. That's the tough shift, where they have to close sales."

"I can close sales," the Vergallian male protested. "I've been in retail longer than Dorothy's husband has been alive."

"You sell Kraken red stick to smoke-heads," Affie said. "It's not exactly a challenge. Have you thought about what we discussed?"

"Hey, look at Tzachan and Flazint," Stick said, changing the subject. "She's actually got her head on his shoulder."

"I was watching Bob and Judith earlier. I don't remember him being such a confident dancer."

At the very instant that Affie spoke, Dorothy was saying the exact same thing to Chastity's husband, and she went on to add, "You're a fantastic teacher, Marcus."

"They haven't told you yet?" he asked. "I'm not a big fan of surprises myself."

"I love surprises. What is it? Did they start taking lessons again? I know that Judith was helping you program the free holo-training dance courses that your wife promised to make available through the Galactic Free Press." She reflexively searched the dance floor for where Chastity was taking a turn with Kevin. "I wish I could get my husband to practice."

"Then you'll like this, but I'll let Judith tell you since she, Thomas, and Chance did all of the programming," Marcus said.

Dorothy could hardly wait for the end of the current dance, and she tracked Judith and Bob like a hunter waiting to pounce on her prey. As soon as the music ended, she cut them out of the herd and dragged the smaller woman off the dance floor.

"I saw you talking with Marcus," Judith said immediately. "Did he tell you?"

"Only that there's something to tell."

"It will be much easier to show. Take off your shoes, Bob."

The senior beat reporter for Union Station complied, and standing in his socks, slid the shoes to Dorothy. She reacted without hesitation, removing her own shoes and slipping her feet into Bob's, which being approximately six sizes too big, reminded her of standing in her father's shoes when she was a little girl. "What now?"

"Access the control panel."

"Bob's shoes have a control panel? But they're just regular shoes. They don't do anything."

"Thomas embedded the basic interface module from SBJ Fashions in one of the heels and we all contributed to the programming," Judith said. "Access it the normal way, and then choose the Shadow Dancer option."

Dorothy did as she was told and didn't notice any difference. "It's not doing anything."

"Wait for the music to start," Bob said. "It takes a minute to get used to, but then—"

A waltz began to play, and to Dorothy's shock, the outlines of a pair of feet were superimposed over her vision.

"Tilt your head down a little," he advised.

As soon as Dorothy's field of view included the deck, the ghostly feet began to advance, demonstrating the pattern for the waltz in perfect synchronization with the music.

"Are you serious?" Dorothy demanded, her voice rising. She tried to follow the pattern, but was unable to move properly due to her feet being too small for the shoes. The outlines of the steps flashed red every time she missed. "I can't believe I never thought of this. You're going to put Marcus out of business."

"I don't think he's too worried about that," Judith said. "Do you think you can work it into a product?"

"I know I can," Dorothy practically shouted, and then surprised the EarthCent intelligence trainer with a hug. "I've never designed men's shoes because, well, they're kind of boring. But we can provide Shadow Dancer as a companion product that the women who buy our fashions can give to their partners. How much hardware does it take?"

"Thomas said he can put it all on a chip, and it won't even require sensors attached to the shoes," Judith said.

"I'm going to talk to him right now."

"Wait," Bob called after Dorothy as she began to shuffle off. "Can I have my shoes back?"

"Oh, sorry." Dorothy exchanged shoes and then set off to find Thomas and Chance, not noticing that Baa had arrived and was huddled with Jeeves, Tinka, and Marilla.

"I don't understand," Marilla said to Baa, unsure she had heard the Terragram mage correctly.

"Let's go out to the lobby where you can hear each other," Jeeves suggested, and not waiting for a response, led the way.

Marilla looked back to see if Mornich would swoop in and save her, but he was staring off into space searching the playlist on his heads-up display, so she gave in and followed the other three out of the room. "What did you want to talk to me about?" she asked Tinka, who was the least intimidating of the group.

"We're recruiting you," the Drazen woman replied. "Is here good, Jeeves?"

"As long as Baa doesn't mind providing us with a little privacy."

"Needy, needy, needy," the Terragram mage scolded, but she made a quick gesture with one hand and said, "That should take care of everybody other than your nosey Elders."

"Now that Paul has given you an ownership stake in Tunnel Trips, we want to invite you to join our support group," Tinka told the Frunge girl.

"What's a support group?" Flazint asked.

"It's a Human thing they do to help cope with difficult situations," the Drazen explained. "We get together once a cycle and talk about the challenges of being in business with Human partners."

"Like how fast they do everything? I want to figure out how the McAllisters make decisions so I can create an employee handbook for future management trainees, but I'm having trouble working out their underlying thought processes."

"It's mainly instinct with Humans," Jeeves told her. "Did you know that Paul was ranked a game master on the interspecies circuit by the age of seventeen?"

"Really? Why doesn't he wear the ring?"

"He's never been one to draw needless attention to himself. I used to play against him for hours so I know something about the way his mind works. Faced with complex problems, Humans can't think fast enough to consider all the options, so they train themselves to ignore unpromising paths and concentrate on a few alternatives. Occasionally it results in a colossal error, but training their subconscious minds to simplify situations allows them to compete at a higher level than their basic intellect would otherwise support."

"Do you mean they don't always know why they've made the best choice? What's the difference between that and flipping coins?"

"Some of us would say that there isn't a difference, but Jeeves has a soft spot for Humans," Baa informed her. "The most important thing that I've noticed about working with them is that they're not as terrified of making mistakes as the rest of you. Humanity's basic lack of caution and foresight makes them useful tools for the Stryx to keep things moving towards—"

"Baa," Jeeves interrupted. "We've talked about this."

"I'm just saying," the mage muttered, one of the useful expressions she'd picked up from Dorothy.

"Would I have to keep it a secret?" Marilla asked. "I couldn't lie to the McAllisters."

"Just don't tell them that she's in the group," Jeeves said, pointing his pincer at the mage. "I'll never hear the end of it if Dorothy finds out that I gave Baa an ownership share in SBJ Fashions."

"Where do we meet?"

"Usually at restaurants," Tinka told her. "I'll add you to the ping list. We also have a Verlock, a couple of Grenouthians, and a Frunge in the group, but none of them were free tonight to come to the dance and meet you."

"I better get back in before Dorothy notices I'm gone," the Horten girl said. "Thanks for recruiting me. I look forward to learning from those older and wiser than myself."

A Horten male who Marilla didn't recognize was just leaving the Meteor room as she reached the entrance. "May I beg a quick word?" he asked her in formal language that practically compelled a polite hearing.

"Yes?"

"I was told I could meet Samuel McAllister here this evening but I didn't see him or his fiancée dancing."

"They left earlier on an overnight trip," Marilla said, anxious to get back inside and find Mornich. "I rented them the ship myself."

"Thank you," the Horten said, stepping aside. "You've saved me a great deal of time."

Something about the brief encounter stuck with the girl like an error in a mathematical calculation, and when she spotted Judith and Bob taking a break, she hurried over to them.

"Did you see a Horten wandering around in here without a date?" she asked Judith.

"You mean aside from Mornich?" the EarthCent intelligence trainer teased her.

"He was middle-aged, probably three-hundred-ish, and his suit wasn't appropriate for dancing."

"Did he have a square cut?" Judith asked, referring to an old-fashioned Horten hairstyle that looked just like it sounded.

"Yes, now that you mention it, he was a total box-head."

"Sounds like the replacement for purple-face," Judith said, and then immediately apologized. "I'm sorry, Marilla. That's just what we called—"

"I know, the head of our intelligence service on Union Station. I met him once at the embassy when I was attending a party with Mornich. The full-face tattoo was to keep anybody from reading his skin color. I didn't know he had been replaced."

"Promoted actually, he's in charge of Horten agents on all of the Stryx stations now. We got an update bulletin about it a couple of weeks ago. You didn't tell the replacement anything, did you?"

Marilla's skin turned yellow. "I mentioned that I gave Samuel and Vivian an overnight rental. He was so polite."

"You have to watch out for the polite ones," Judith told her, "and that doesn't just apply to Hortens. I'll ping our control room and let them know."

Kevin ambled up to the group and asked Marilla, "Why so worried? Sorry, I shouldn't have said anything," he added, as her yellow skin tone grew mottled with other colors.

"It's my fault," the girl said. "A Horten who is probably our new head of intelligence asked me if I knew where Samuel and Vivian were. I told him about their rental without thinking."

"I wouldn't worry about it," Kevin said. "Either they're really on vacation, in which case it doesn't matter, or one of them is on a secret mission, in which case everybody on Union Station will know where they went within twenty-four hours."

"I don't understand," Marilla said.

"Since moving into Mac's Bones with Dorothy, I meet spies all the time. Our spies, spies who stop by to spy on our spies in training, allied spies who are on exchange programs to teach our spies, I've even started selling one-time pads in the chandlery."

"What are they?"

"Spy stuff for sending secret messages. Whether your guy is really interested in Sam's work for the Vergallians or Vivian's work for the Drazens, finding out that they took a rental off the station for twenty-four hours doesn't mean anything. You know that it's impossible to track ships through the tunnels."

"Not if there was a homing device on board, but I went through that ship myself right before I rented it to them. I guess I'm worried about nothing."

Fourteen

"Oops. Sorry. Excuse me," Daniel said, dodging and weaving his way through the beehive of activity in the embassy's crowded reception area. "We couldn't have done this somewhere else?" he asked Kelly, who was standing just outside the door of her own office.

"I don't think Donna realized it would be such a madhouse," the EarthCent ambassador replied. "Why do professional photographers need so much equipment when I can take perfectly good images with my implant?"

"It could have something to do with resolution or depth-of-field, or maybe they just need props to justify what they charge," Daniel said. "I should ping Shaina and ask if she wants to bring the kids in for a portrait while everything is set up."

"Check with Aabina first." Kelly inhaled deeply and sighed. "I wonder if airborne molecules count against my diet."

"They do if you inhale too many of them," Donna said, as she passed by with some kind of paella in an obsidian dish that marked it as an entry for the Verlock section of the cookbook. "Don't forget your meeting."

"I'm going to steal Aabina for part of it," Kelly called after her, but she didn't raise her voice, and the embassy manager's lack of a response testified that the message had gone unheard.

"You're getting crafty in your old age," Daniel said. "I suppose that later you'll be citing me as a witness that you told Donna you're borrowing Aabina."

"It's not for the whole meeting, and we'll just be in my office if there's an emergency. Duck!" she added, as a careless lighting assistant nearly decapitated them both with a tripod.

"I'm going in my office where it's safe," the associate ambassador said. "Three more days of this and it will all be over."

"And I need to prepare for my meeting," Kelly said, feinting towards her own office, but as soon as Daniel's door closed behind him, she turned around and let her nose lead the way.

"To the left, to the left," a photographer yelled at her young assistant, who was holding up a large circular reflector with both hands. "No, now the broccoli is casting a shadow like a tree."

"You could press it down," the assistant suggested.

"Rule number one," the older woman said. "Never touch the food. One false move and we'll spend hours waiting for the cook to make another one of whatever it is, assuming we don't have to reschedule altogether. Now try holding it a little higher. Right there!"

"Are those worms on the pizza?" Kelly asked after the photographer straightened up again, apparently satisfied with her shot.

"Maybe some kind of larvae substitute, it's listed as Dollnick Delight," the photographer said. "You're the ambassador, right?"

"Kelly McAllister, pleased to meet you, Miss?"

"Cass," the woman said. "I only use the one name. Do you mind if I ask why EarthCent is getting into the cookbook publishing business?"

"Apparently all of the species get a turn and we were next in line. Are you one of Blythe's photographers?"

"That's right. I normally shoot erotic book covers, but I used to be an agricultural photographer for the Galactic Free press." Cass checked to make sure her assistant wasn't listening in, and then added, "I thought that photographing half-naked models would be more interesting than cattle, but in the end, beefcake is beefcake. I think the main reason Blythe hired me away from the paper is that Chastity keeps stealing EarthCent Intelligence agents and making them reporters."

"Sibling rivalry. Is that Dollnick photographer one of Blythe's also? She's told me that her hottest sellers are the translations she publishes of their Trillionaire Prince romances, and I swear I blushed when Dorothy showed me one of those covers."

"I don't recognize him," Cass said. She frowned at the towering alien, who was operating an elaborate camera of some type with his lower arms, while holding a fabric reflector in each of his upper hands. "Why is he shooting the Frunge Sashimi? That's next on my list!"

"Donna," Kelly said, grabbing at the embassy manager as she hurried past in the opposite direction. "Who hired the Dollnick?"

"Don't know, too busy to care. I have thirty more entrees coming in today, and the chocolate soufflé the Gem caterer made in our kitchenette collapsed before the photographer could shoot it."

"Wait," the EarthCent ambassador called after her friend. "I like fallen soufflé."

"Then you'll have to get it out of the recycling shaft," Donna shouted back.

Kelly spotted Aabina coming out of the conference room, moving with an unearthly grace that could only be attained through years of royal training. She was carrying a cheese soufflé with her elbows out for protection, and the room went temporarily still as she deposited it on a small folding table surrounded by lights and reflectors. As soon as the co-op student stepped away, a photographer lunged forward and began capturing images from all sorts of outlandish angles. Kelly would have sworn she overheard him muttering to the soufflé, "Work it, baby! Work it!"

"Aabina," the EarthCent ambassador beckoned her co-op student.

"The meeting isn't for another six minutes," the Vergallian girl replied. "I seem to be the only one who can carry the soufflés out without collapsing them and the Gem have a backup chocolate one waiting in the oven for me."

"That's fine, you can even come in late, though you'll have to ask Libby to tell me because I'll be locking the door," Kelly said. "But I want to ask you about that Dollnick photographer. Cass doesn't know him and—"

"Ping EarthCent Intelligence," Aabina said, after looking the direction the ambassador was pointing. "He's not working for us. I have to get back to the Gem."

"Drat, I was afraid of that," Kelly muttered to herself. She started to subvoc the station librarian to ask for a connection to EarthCent Intelligence, but then changed her mind and approached the towering alien. "Excuse me. You wouldn't happen to be here spying on us, would you?"

"Ambassador," the Dollnick said, letting his camera dangle from one hand and holding the reflectors over his head with his upper arms, to keep them out of the way. He offered her the free hand to shake. "I'm Jupe, the ag world correspondent for Terraforming Today." After releasing the ambassador's hand, he reached for a holographic ID hanging on a lanyard around his neck, and did a deep knee bend so that Kelly could inspect it. "We're a trade publication and we don't usually report about finished products, but an All Species Cookbook edition that's actually useful for cooking could alter food production patterns, which is a matter of high interest for our readership."

"Really, it's okay if you're a spy," Kelly said. "It's just that this is a working embassy and we try not to—"

"A spy?" Jupe interrupted. "I've been a journalist for over two hundred years and nobody has ever mistaken me for a spy before."

"Libby?" Kelly subvoced. "Can you tell me if this Dollnick really works for Terraforming Today?"

"Yes, he does," the station librarian replied in her head.

"My apologies, though it would be best if you had checked with us ahead of time," she told Jupe. "EarthCent is always happy to get free publicity, so you're welcome to stay as long as you don't interfere with the work. And please identify yourself to our embassy manager, who is also the cookbook editor."

"I'm hoping to interview her but she's clearly too busy at the moment," the Dollnick said sympathetically. "Perhaps you have time?"

"I'm sorry, I have a meeting in—oh, I'm going to be late. You can ask if you see me later," Kelly flung over her shoulder as she headed for her office. Aabina was already there waiting for her, so the chocolate soufflé rerun must have gone smoothly. The EarthCent ambassador heard

Donna calling for the co-op student as the door slid closed behind them.

"Do you think she'll be all right?" Aabina asked.

"Donna knows where we are if she really needs you, and Daniel is available, even though he's hiding in his office," Kelly said. "This meeting is more important for your professional development and for EarthCent's hiring plans going forward."

"If you think so. I have to admit that I can't imagine my mother inviting Samuel to a meeting of this level, not to mention the secrecy implications. Didn't you say your president will be attending?"

"The first time we had an Intelligence Steering committee meeting, the oxygen-breathing ambassadors on the station were climbing over each other to present me with a transcript or a holo-recording of the whole thing. It's when we learned that our security wasn't quite up to par."

"The president's office is connected," Libby announced, and a hologram came alive over Kelly's display desk. The other ambassadors on the steering committee appeared almost simultaneously, and none of them were in their nightclothes, proving once again the wisdom of adopting Universal Human Time.

"Before any of you blurt out any of our deep, dark secrets, I'd like to point out that Ambassador McAllister's cooperative education student is participating today," the president began with a joke. "Aabina? Would you like to introduce yourself?"

"Hello Mr. President, Ambassadors. I'm honored that you've invited me to your intelligence steering committee meeting," the Vergallian girl said in her flawless English. "I'm Aabina, daughter of Aainda, grand-daughter of Akalah, and I'm sure you're not interested in hearing the rest of my family tree. I couldn't be present today if you hadn't opened your civil service exam to other species. On behalf of myself and Wrylenth, who is co-oping for EarthCent Intelligence and would have been here today if they could have spared him, I want to thank you for being so broad-minded."

"Kelly has told us all about you and we're so jealous," Ambassador White said. "If you'd consider leaving Union Station—"

"Aabina is a minor and her mother would never permit it," Kelly interrupted, thankful for once that Vergallians were so much longer lived than humans. "Perhaps you can all introduce yourselves and then we can move on to business."

"That won't be necessary, Ambassador," Aabina said. "I memorized the pictures and biographies of all the senior diplomats in the EarthCent handbook my first day on the job."

"Of course you did," the president said, and the pleased tone of his voice combined with the groan from Ambassador Oshi made Kelly suspect that the two men had a bet riding on her co-op student. "I'm sure that you're busy with the cookbook and I don't want to keep you any longer than necessary. We invited you to get your thoughts about how we can attract more high-quality co-op students to accept work at our embassies."

"Do you mean that in general, or are you specifically interested in hiring aliens?" Aabina asked.

"Aliens," the president replied bluntly. "Although we have a limited number of data points and the Stryx aren't admitting anything, it appears that the Open University cooperative education program is sending the best qualified human candidates to work for other species. I put in a question to our intelligence people about this, and a day later I received a detailed analysis from Wrylenth suggesting that the practice began just over two cycles ago, starting on Union Station."

"I'd like to see that report," Kelly said.

"It's in your inbox, marked 'Important,'" Aabina whispered in her ear.

"After our last meeting, I signed my twins up for a night course at the Open University just so they'd qualify for the co-op program," Svetlana said.

"With their permission?" Carlos Oshi, the Middle Station ambassador inquired.

"They'd never do anything if I asked them first," Ambassador Zerakova replied. "The two of them would spend all of their time live action role-playing if they didn't have to work part-time to afford the accessories. Once they were re-accepted to the Open University, I elected deferred admission and applied to the co-op program for them. Sabina is starting at the Fillinduck embassy next week, and Katya will be working for the Verlocks."

"Have you told them yet?" the president asked.

"I've been keeping it strictly on a need-to-know basis," Svetlana said. "I'll tell the twins on the morning they're starting work, and when they see the pay package, I won't get any complaints."

"And the aliens were willing to accept them without even an interview?" Ambassador Tamil inquired, receiving a shrug from Svetlana in return.

"I think I can answer that," Aabina said. "The Open University assigns co-op students, there is no interview process, though employers can request to see the candidate's academic folder before agreeing. I'm subscribed to the Open University newsletter, and there was an an-

172

nouncement in last cycle's issue that going forward, EarthCent's civil service exam will be accepted as an alternative to the ASATs."

"What are ASATs?" Ambassador Zerakova asked.

"The Advanced Species Aptitude Test. It's required for most applicants to the Open University, but the Stryx have always waived it for Humans because—" Aabina stopped in the middle of her sentence and looked embarrassed.

"We can guess," the president said wryly. "So you're saying that the advanced species also use the ASATs in hiring for their embassies?"

"Not regular hires, just cooperative education students and interns," the Vergallian girl explained. "Students rarely have extensive work histories, and when they do, it's probably not in a field relevant to diplomacy. The test results are better than nothing."

"I've got to sign up and get me one of you," Ambassador White muttered, as if making a mental note.

"Excuse me," Libby interjected over Kelly's implant. "One of the volunteers tripped over a lighting case and dumped a pot of lentil soup all over the vegetable couscous. Donna is threatening to call off the shoot if she doesn't get Aabina back."

"I'm sorry," Kelly interrupted whatever Ambassador Oshi was saying, "but we're having a cookbook emergency and Aabina is needed."

"Thank you again for having me," the Vergallian co-op said, hopping up from her chair. "Could you get the security lock, Ambassador?"

"I need to have you added," Kelly told her, following the girl to the door and waving it open. "We'll ask Libby to do it later today."

"The EarthCent Intelligence handbook for diplomatic staff categorically states that no aliens shall be granted top access to embassy locks. I'm afraid I'll have to refuse."

"I'm sure they only intended the rule for caterers and building contractors," Kelly said, as Aabina slipped out into the chaos sowed by the cookbook production. Returning to her desk, she was surprised to hear Svetlana talking about Samuel and Vivian. "What did I miss?" Kelly asked.

"Svetlana was just telling us about an odd incident the Grenouthian ambassador on Corner Station mentioned to her last night. Did you know that their shipping news coverage includes rental craft arriving and departing from Stryx stations?"

"I had no idea. I thought they just tracked large commercial vessels and important personages. They always seem to know when you show up at Union Station unannounced."

"Perhaps they've concluded that your son is more important than I am," the president said. "Why don't you tell her the story, Svetlana?"

"I was at a reception at the Dollnick embassy last night, where I was mobbed with questions about the All Species Cookbook. The Grenouthian ambassador pulled me aside for a conversation, and he claimed that your son and his fiancée departed Union Station at, I've forgotten the exact time, and that Stryx traffic control routed them to Corner Station. But their rental ship never arrived here and ended up back at Union Station without ever exiting the tunnel."

"Samuel didn't mention anything to me, but we keep such different hours these days that I rarely see him. I didn't know it was possible to turn around in a tunnel."

"The Grenouthian told me that large ships can change course in the tunnels and emerge almost anywhere, but a

174

small rental craft just coasts through and doesn't have the capacity to reverse course. And don't take this the wrong way, Kelly, but he also said that they're picking up an abnormal amount of encrypted traffic from the Vergallians on Union Station."

"Why would—you aren't suggesting that Aabina could be involved? I'd stake my life on her integrity."

"That was EarthCent Intelligence's assessment as well," the president said. "The Vergallian royals are supposed to be incapable of breaking their oaths, and that would include her co-op agreement. But I also had a visit the other day from Glunk, the head of Drazen Foods. In addition to giving me a recipe which I already sent on to Donna, he mentioned that several of their suppliers, mainly small farmers, had reported seeing a giant beetle skulking about their fields. Nobody was able to capture a picture, but that wouldn't be surprising if it was a Farling, since their interference technology is beyond any of the oxygen-breathing tunnel network members."

"Oh." Kelly hesitated. "I might know somebody who knows somebody who might know something about that, but it's all very tentative at this point. Could you give me a little time to look into it from my end, Stephen? Things are crazy around here with the cookbook."

"I'm not particularly worried by the presence of Farlings on Earth. We're still a Stryx protectorate, and I think Glunk was mainly concerned from a business standpoint, since the beetles are masters at genetic manipulation and could break his hot-pepper monopoly if they put their minds to it. But I've also noticed a marked uptick in alien businessmen dropping by my office for casual discussions since EarthCent won the cookbook bid. I get the feeling there's something going on that they aren't telling me."

"Now that you mention it, every alien ambassador that I'm on good terms with must have stopped in the embassy for a chat in the last couple weeks," Ambassador Fu said slowly. "I had the impression they were fishing for something, but they all talk so circumspectly that I have trouble figuring out what they want even when they're trying to be open with me. I do remember several of them mentioning the Vergallians, and the Horten ambassador asked a question about the Alts."

"That's it," Ambassador Enoksen spoke up for the first time. "Two of my colleagues asked me about our contingency plans if the Alts join the tunnel network and claim that the All Species Cookbook monopoly should have been granted to them."

"It sounds like the nexus of the action is on Union Station, Ambassador McAllister, so why don't you carry the ball on this?" the president said. "I'll authorize you to negotiate in my name, and if everything works out, maybe you could replace me for—"

"I'll agree to handle whatever comes up related to the cookbook, but other than that, you're out of luck," Kelly cut him off. "If I had to choose between early retirement and moving back to Earth, I'll stay right here and find work as a mediator. I know I'd earn more than the points I'd be giving up on my pension."

"It's just that Hildy found out I can apply for the sabbatical program but I need a senior diplomat to fill in for me."

"Pass," the ambassadors gathered for the holographic meeting all declared simultaneously.

Fifteen

"Why is it so dark in here?" Vivian asked. "Can you ask Libby to turn up the lights?"

"It's past midnight on Universal Human Time," Samuel said. "We're just lucky that the Drazen and Vergallian clocks are more or less aligned today so it's morning for both of us."

"Does your dad always turn down the lights in Mac's Bones before going to bed?"

"Don't your parents turn off the lights in your apartment?"

"But this isn't an apartment and I can barely see my feet."

"Your eyes will adjust to the night lighting."

"How are we going to rent a ship if everything's closed?"

"I made a reservation and repeat customers are authorized for self-checkout. The only catch is Marilla had to bill it to your programmable cred again because that's the way she set up the system. I'll pay you back."

"Don't worry about it," Vivian said. "But how are we going to do the inspection when we can barely see?"

"I'll ask Libby for a spot." Samuel homed in on the dimly lit Tunnel Trips kiosk, where he found the check-in tab that Marilla had left on the counter. When he touched the screen, it came alive with the prefilled rental application and a blinking button to start the inspection. "Looks like we're all set. Can you put a spotlight on number twenty-one, Libby?"

The designated rental craft was suddenly bathed in a pool of warm light, and the young couple quickly finished their walk-around. Samuel returned the tab to the kiosk, and the two of them clambered in through the small ship's hatch.

"So, is that the same briefcase or a different one?" Vivian asked, as they settled into their cushioned seats and fastened their safety harnesses. Before sealing her purse in the chair's saddlebag, she removed the strip with the Farling Zero-G medication and stuck a half a patch to the side of her neck. "I did some discrete asking around at work, and while the Drazens have their own hyperspace homing beacon technology, it wouldn't fit into anything you could carry with one hand."

"I don't know if that briefcase was ever returned, but my instructions are the same," Samuel said. "Maybe I'm just a decoy this time and we'll arrive right on schedule. Controller, take us to Void Station."

"I wish the Vergallians had told you they were turning us around the last time. When we came out of the tunnel and I heard the Union Station welcome message, I was afraid we had gone through a time warp or something and everybody we knew would be dead."

"Jeeves says there's no such thing as time travel, and working for Drazen Intelligence must be making you morbid. Can you close your eyes a sec while I take a quick look at where we're going?"

"Go ahead," Vivian said, "but once we're in the tunnel I get to watch the Grenouthian news."

"Controller. Display forward view," Samuel commanded, and the screen lit up just as Gryph merged the rental into the outbound traffic still in Union Station's core. "Don't even peek," he warned her. "It's a busy night."

"Day for us," she reminded him. "Did you ever wonder why Aainda is using us for these secret missions? She knows I'm co-oping for Drazen Intelligence because she got them to let me off work, and it's not like you have any training for doing spy stuff."

"I try not to think about it too much because I'm sure she'd tell me if I had a need to know."

"I suppose she could be worried that whatever upper-caste Vergallian we're going to meet is going to separate us, and then my presence wouldn't protect you from pheromones and you'd confess everything you know," Vivian said. "You're lucky you have me."

"I am lucky I have you," Samuel agreed, but he glanced down at the enchanted dagger scabbard that protruded slightly from his boot, and rationalized that not correcting an error wasn't the same as lying. "What are you going to do if the Drazens offer you a job when the co-op term is up?"

"That depends in part on you and the Vergallians. If you keep working at their embassy, I wouldn't gain anything by going back on Universal Human Time, and whatever job my dad gave me couldn't be as interesting as the work I'm doing for the Drazens. You know that my parents have focused EarthCent Intelligence on business data and building a database of cultural information about the other species. The Drazens run a real spy agency, and they have me doing all sorts of stuff that I can't talk about."

"So we're even," Samuel said, and added, "Controller. Switch to Grenouthian News Network."

"We're in the tunnel already?" Vivian asked, opening her eyes.

"No, but the view was pretty much the same as the last time. Why isn't the bunny talking?"

"The Grenouthian presenters do that from time to time when they're about to show some clip they think is really funny. See how his whiskers are twitching?"

The news anchor finally broke the silence with, "Just in from the planet previously known as Kerach Two, a report on the new Sharf system for instantaneously defrosting ice worlds that requires no explanation."

The bunny was replaced by the image of a jewel-like ball of white hanging in space with a projectile of some sort streaking toward it. There was a blinding flash and the icy shell around the planet cracked like an egg. Chunks of ice the size of small continents could be seen flying off in all directions at escape velocity, and then the screen rapidly filled with white. The video source dissolved in static before the cut back to the studio.

"Better luck next time, and for all of you out there with an ice planet that needs defrosting, stick with the Dollnicks," the Grenouthian chortled. "They charge more because they're worth more. Getting back to our top story, exclusive video from inside the EarthCent embassy on Union Station where they're baking up a storm for the upcoming edition of the All Species Cookbook. And don't forget to check your network guides for the pilot episode of our co-branded cooking show."

"I didn't know my mom agreed to a co-branded show," Samuel said. The scene shifted to the overcrowded reception area of the EarthCent embassy, where Donna was seen sampling a bowl of chowder, while Aabina gave orders to a seemingly unending stream of volunteers.

"The Grenouthians are scouting Jonah to be the host," Vivian replied. "He told me there's some kind of big meeting at the network tomorrow and my mom is going with him to help negotiate. If everything works out, my brother could be the next Aisha, and he'll be on screens and holographic projection systems all around the tunnel network. Isn't that weird?"

"No weirder than seeing your grandmother crumbling crackers in her chowder while a Vergallian princess grinds pepper over what looks like fruit salad. Isn't this a long clip for the Grenouthian news?"

"Not when they have an exclusive. I've seen them break into segments from some of their top journalists just because they have new video nobody else has broadcast yet. The Grenouthian news is definitely an acquired taste, but it's on all the time at headquarters, and some of the Drazens I work with push the feed to their heads-up displays."

"I couldn't imagine living like that," Samuel said. The Grenouthian cameraman captured the EarthCent ambassador sidling up to a plate of chocolate frosted cupcakes only to get her hand slapped by the embassy manager when she reached for one. "Being around all that food must be tough on Mom."

"Entering the tunnel in ten seconds," the controller announced.

"Mute news," Vivian instructed the ship. "Gryph got us here fast. Do you think the Vergallians will come for us right away?"

"I honestly don't know what's going to happen," Samuel said, pulling the briefcase onto his lap and counting slowly to ten before he started working the activation trick with the latch. "How long was it last time? I fell asleep and I never asked."

"Just around twenty minutes or so. Does that mean they were waiting in the tunnel for us?"

"Probably, but capital ships move really fast, and Vergallian crews are conditioned to withstand major displacements without becoming disoriented. For all I know, they may be able to use their jump engines to enter a tunnel if they have a beacon to home in on. I never got anywhere near far enough in math to understand that stuff."

"Did I tell you that Herl asked me about our trip?"

"The head of Drazen Intelligence? No, you didn't tell me. Did you talk?"

"Hey, I work for them, and they work with EarthCent. It's not like I owe the Vergallians anything. Besides, Herl said that Aainda would have assumed that he'd approach me, and she wouldn't have chosen you for the mission if me talking wasn't part of her plot."

"Plot?"

"Plot, plan, same difference."

"I think that plotting has a negative connotation," Samuel objected. "So what did Herl make of it?"

"He said that Aainda is probably trying to broker a deal between the Imperial and Fleet Vergallians, but that there must be more to it than that or she never would have gotten us involved. Herl thought—" Vivian hesitated, as if she was trying to figure out how much she could reveal without violating her co-op oath, "—he thought it might have something to do with the All Species Cookbook."

"That's crazy," Samuel said, but something tickled the back of his brain, and he found himself trying to recon-struct every instance in which he'd heard the cookbook mentioned, which turned out to be quite a few. "Did he say why?"

"It was one of those backward reductive reasoning things that the Drazens do," Vivian explained. "He began with the thesis that you and I are at these handovers for a reason, and then he started looking at the common factors we share."

"Everything about us is shared in common. The only way we could be closer would be if we were related, and then we wouldn't be engaged."

"But that's all old hat, and Herl said that when you're trying to associate cause with effect, you should always start with the most recent events. We just saw my grandmother and your mom on the Grenouthian network news, and why was that? Because your mom had the idea of bidding on the All Species Cookbook, and my mom and aunt agreed to fund it and put my grandmother in charge."

"You know, none of us had ever even heard of the cookbook before Aabina mentioned it to my mom," Samuel said slowly. "But Aabina would never try to manipulate us like that."

"But her mother could have manipulated her—royals do that to their kids all the time."

"So Herl thinks that Aainda has you and me delivering briefcases to some of the most powerful Vergallians in the galaxy because our families are involved in the All Species Cookbook? What does he think is in the briefcase? Secret recipes?"

"Herl doesn't speculate, he forms educated hypotheses, and I'm supposed to remind you to tell your dad that it's been too long since the last poker game."

"Hey, did you feel that?"

"Like we just got caught in a manipulator field," Vivian said. "Controller. Switch to forward view."

The flat end of an enormous cylindrical ship filled the viewscreen, its bright navigation beacons tracing out circles of light in the black void of the tunnel. Both of the rental ship's occupants felt their weight increase as the rental craft was pulled into a giant hangar whose opening was at the axis of the spinning cylinder. Then came a few seconds of high-G deceleration as the manipulator fields deposited them neatly at the end of a long row of fighter craft.

"Oof," Samuel said. "Sorry about that, Viv. Are you okay?"

"I think my brain may have come loose but I don't feel sick or anything. This Farling medication is great stuff. Why do you think our landing was so rough compared to last time?"

"They had to match our acceleration to their spin for the landing," Samuel said. "It's the same as when we put down at Union Station, but Gryph does it so gradually that you barely notice. At least we won't be weightless on this ship."

"They certainly grabbed us faster than the other Vergallians. We were barely in the tunnel."

"Showtime," Samuel said, unbuckling his safety harness and standing up. "Around half of our normal weight, I'd guess. Don't jump real hard or you might bang your head."

"I never jump." Vivian released her own four-point restraints and followed Samuel to the hatch. "You don't want to wait for them to come to us?"

"They'd be out there already if that's how this was supposed to play out. Fleet does things differently than the

Empire, and I don't know if they have any special protocols for messengers. Given the size of the crew, it may be that whoever we're meeting is trying to avoid drawing attention."

"After grabbing us in a Stryx tunnel?"

"You have a point," Samuel admitted, climbing out the hatch and offering his free hand to help Vivian. "Oh, I get it. See the blue shimmer?"

"Is that an atmosphere retention field just around our ship?"

"No, it's probably a security precaution of some sort. Maybe a force field."

"Actually, you're seeing the edge of the scan area," a hidden voice announced from off to the side. "I must request that Miss Oxford remove her earrings, beret, and shoes."

"Is that really necessary?" Samuel asked, trying to spot where the voice was coming from.

"It wouldn't be much of a secret meeting if we allowed your companion to retain all of her Drazen spy toys."

"It's the training," Vivian mumbled, stripping off her earrings, beret, and shoes. "You can't blame me for trying."

The blue shimmer contracted down to a small sphere that encompassed the little pile the girl had made of her contraband, and a team of officers in Fleet uniforms walked out from behind one of the tactical fighters.

A middle-aged Vergallian whose uniform identified her as a Fleet admiral strode forward. "Let's have the briefcase," she ordered Samuel.

"I don't have the key, Admiral," the EarthCent ambassador's son said, displaying the handcuff on his wrist.

"My name is Banda and I'm not happy with Aainda and her cloak-and-dagger nonsense," the Vergallian said. She grabbed Samuel's wrist and brought it up closer to her face to inspect the cuff. The admiral grimaced, shook her head, and then blew on the mechanism, which popped open. "Tell her that breath print DNA locks can be foiled by near relations and are considered a failed security technology by Fleet." As she took possession of the briefcase, she caught sight of Samuel's boot dagger in her peripheral vision. "I recognize that crest. May I inquire how that dagger came into your possession?"

"My father received it from Baylit, who told him to give it to me when I was grown up," Samuel offered the barest explanation.

Banda tossed the briefcase to one of the male officers in the group, and then beckoned to a younger woman whose unearthly beauty clearly marked her as a member of the upper caste. "Aasina will act as truthsayer," she told Samuel. "I will ask you a series of questions and you will answer without attempt at subterfuge or you and your spy-friend will be remaining with us for the foreseeable future. What are you smiling at?" she barked at Vivian.

"Sorry," the girl said, moving closer to Samuel as if she were afraid. "It just reminded me of something I saw in a Vergallian drama."

"I'll get to you in a minute." Banda frowned at the young officer, who was staring into Samuel's eyes and looking increasingly frustrated. "What is it, Aasina?"

"I don't think he's responding. I've never worked on a Human before."

"I've been present at previous interrogations, and if anything, Humans are more susceptible than average."

"My royal trainer told us something about the possibility of natural resistance coming from the intensity of young love," Aasina told the admiral. "She said it could be related to their need to rapidly consummate courtships before they age out of their childbearing years."

"I suspect more of Aainda's skullduggery," the admiral growled, dismissing the young royal with a hand gesture. "So what is it exactly that she doesn't want me knowing?"

"Are you asking me?" Samuel said, unsure if the Vergallian was speaking to herself or him.

"We'll have to do this the old-fashioned way. When I ask a question, you will answer immediately. If I sense any hesitation, I'll separate the two of you and we'll see how long your immunity lasts. Understood?"

"Yes, Admiral. I have no reason to lie."

"Why did Aainda choose a Human co-op student as courier for negotiations of such importance?"

"We were just discussing that," Samuel replied immediately. "Vivian thinks it has to do with the cookbook."

Banda turned her scowl on the girl. "I know who you work for but I'm not aware of your connection to the All Species Cookbook. Did Drazen Intelligence have something to do with the bid?"

"No, but I couldn't tell you if they did," Vivian replied honestly. "My grandmother is the cookbook editor and my mom and my aunt paid the bill for EarthCent."

"And who are they working for? The Stryx?"

"My family? Not that I know of. It was his mother's idea," she added, pointing at Samuel.

"Thanks," he muttered, as Banda shifted her glare in his direction. "Mom just thought it would be a good way to raise humanity's profile and get the species to all agree on something."

"You won't be using the cookbook to settle scores?"

"Who do we have to settle scores with? We haven't been around long enough to make any enemies."

The admiral frowned again, and motioned for her officers to retreat, then she stepped closer to the pair of young
people and touched something on her bracelet. Vivian
immediately recognized the odd static feeling of a privacy
field from her Drazen training and Samuel guessed the
same. Despite the precautions, Banda held her hand in
front of her mouth to hide her lips while speaking.

"Ashiba agreed?

"She said she hoped Aainda knows what she's doing,"
Samuel replied.

"And the Farlings?"

"A Farling came to the embassy, I don't know what they
talked about."

"Too clever by half," Banda said. "Aainda sent the two
of you to signal EarthCent's acquiescence."

"She did?"

"I want you to take a message to your mothers, both of
you," the admiral said. "Fleet will accept the arrangement
if everybody else goes along." She stepped back and
touched her bracelet, turning off the privacy field. "You
may go."

"Are you going to turn us around in the tunnel?" Vivian
asked.

"You don't want to come out at your planned destination," Banda said. "Most of the spies on the tunnel network
will be there waiting for you by now. And Samuel—"

"Yes, Admiral?"

"Give my regards to my half-sister's daughter, Affie.
And tell her to upgrade her boyfriend or her mother is
going to force her to return home. No queen's daughter is
so far removed from the throne that she can afford a bad
marriage."

Sixteen

"Mac's Bones," Blythe instructed the lift tube, and then explained to her son, "Dorothy, Jeeves, and Aisha are waiting for us."

"You want us all to arrive at the network in the same capsule so the Grenouthians read something into it," Jonah surmised. "I get that you think it's important I learn how to negotiate business deals with aliens, but it would help if you explained things rather than making me guess."

"I have faith you'll figure it out. You've become Tinka's right-hand man in the four years since you left school and started working for InstaSitter. She's told me more than once that when you're running the war room, calls from angry parents have never been followed by legal action."

"I listen to them and take the blame, just like I was trained, but a cooking show on the Grenouthian network could turn into a really big deal."

"Bigger than InstaSitter?" Blythe chided him.

"I guess not. I think it would be fun to host a show, especially if they go for the guests and stuff I worked out with Dorothy, but I won't know until I try. I just don't want to agree to something that doesn't work out and then find that I'm stuck."

"A contract is a contract with the bunnies. You can't ask them to change it later unless you're willing to give up something else that they want. Let's concentrate on getting

189

the best deal we can today, and then say you have to take it home for your father to check. The Grenouthians are a paternalistic culture so they can't argue, and that way you'll have time to sleep on it."

Jonah nodded in agreement. "That works for me, but isn't bringing Jeeves along to the negotiations kind of like cheating? They'll think I have Stryx backing."

"Jeeves is coming to keep Dorothy from over-committing in the name of SBJ Fashions. Besides, we need him to balance the numbers, though the Grenouthians will outweigh us by at least a factor of two."

"And the bunnies will all be studio executives?"

"I'm guessing Aisha's producer and director, plus a few staff attorneys. The Grenouthians originally offered to have their ambassador negotiate the deal with Aunt Kelly, but she felt it would be unethical to get involved since her son is engaged to your sister. The bunnies don't see things that way, but meeting with us directly will probably save them a little on whatever they're already paying their ambassador for bringing them the show."

The capsule doors opened and Jeeves floated in, followed by Dorothy and Aisha. The latter looked up at Jonah in surprise. "When did you get so tall?" she asked. "I thought you were the same height as Vivian."

"I had a growth spurt," Jonah told her. "I missed the last few picnics at Mac's Bones because of work so you haven't seen me."

"Vivian told me you were too busy LARPing with a bunch of your InstaSitter groupies," Dorothy teased her future brother-in-law, and then looked disappointed when the young man failed to blush. "Do we have a strategy for this meeting?"

"Let Jonah do the talking, but jump in if you have anything to add," Blythe said. "We have to think ahead to if he ends up hosting the show. It's important that the Grenouthians accept him now as his own master or they'll ignore him on the set."

"If you feel like you're being outmaneuvered, just say you're thinking of hiring the Thark agent who helped me negotiate my last deal," Aisha told Jonah. "The Grenouthians are terrified of her."

"Then why aren't we bringing her today?" he asked.

"You don't want to put their fur up if you don't have to. Oh, and do you have a cred you can give me?"

Jonah looked puzzled by this request, but he reached in his pocket and handed the wealthy hostess of "Let's Make Friends" a coin just as the doors slid open on the Grenouthian network headquarters.

Aisha confidently led the group through a warren of passages to a surprisingly small conference room where a display panel read, in English, "Cookbook Negotiations." Inside, they found a large table with four seats on one side and five seats on the other, the network's not-so-subtle way of showing that Jeeves was expected.

"Where are they?" Jonah asked.

"They never arrive first," Aisha said. "It's a basic dominance play with the Grenouthians. They'll expect you to sit near the center, so take one of the ends instead, and Dorothy, you and I will sit in the middle. Blythe, you take the opposite end to show that Jonah is independent or they'll keep trying to talk to you instead of him."

As soon as Jonah's party settled in their seats with Jeeves floating casually by the young man's side, the floor began to vibrate, and five enormous bunnies marched into the room, moving in lockstep. "False floor they installed for the effect," Jeeves informed Jonah over his implant. "It would take a lot more than five Grenouthians to make the decks rattle on Union Station."

Blythe began to say something when she saw that the last bunny to enter was the head of Grenouthian Intelligence on the station, but he appeared not to recognize her, so she decided to play her cards close to the vest. The director and executive producer of Aisha's show were easily identified by their professional sashes, and the satchels carried by the remaining two bunnies marked them as network attorneys.

"Aisha," the executive producer began, making clear he saw her as the highest ranked human of the group, "are you absolutely certain that our holographic—"

"I'm certain," Aisha interrupted, surprising both Dorothy and Blythe with her assertiveness. "Also, I should state for the record that I've been retained by Jonah Oxford to act as a paid consultant in these negotiations."

The executive producer slammed his furry fist on the table before instantly regaining his composure. "So be it," he grunted. "Director?"

"Our attorneys have prepared a standard contract—"

Aisha burst out laughing, a sound so infectious that Dorothy, Jonah, and Blythe couldn't help joining in. Even Jeeves flickered some of the lights on his casing in appreciation.

"All right, I had to try," the director said, motioning for the attorneys to keep their satchels closed. "But it doesn't change the fact that this is a high-risk endeavor that could cost us ratings if the All Species Cookbook flops or EarthCent's bizarrely optimistic production schedule is delayed. We're already paying overtime to prepare the set, buying advertising time at last-minute rates on other shows to promote the pilot, and the whole thing could go 'pop' overnight if the recipes make everybody sick."

"Creds don't grow on bushes," the executive producer chimed in. "I know that Humans think we advanced species are all made of money, but business is business, and you're asking us to pair an untested host with an untried concept that has been tied to more than one inter-species feud. If it weren't for our ambassador's unjustified enthusiasm, I wouldn't even be sitting here."

"I know you," Jonah said out of the blue. "You came to the InstaSitter office to request we reconsider the ban on your household."

"That was you?" the producer asked, squinting across the table at the young man. "You all look so alike."

"It was around three years ago," Jonah continued. "Your children kept sneaking Vergallian dramas in their room and your wife was always calling in complaints and yelling at our InstaSitters. I think we agreed to probation."

"They were great grand-nieces, not my children, and my wife has been away on a sightseeing trip ever since they moved in with us," the executive producer said, obviously justifying himself to his own colleagues rather than Jonah. "As the head of my family, I was obligated to deal with the issue, but I can assure you that the immersive systems of my direct descendants are permanently locked to our network."

The head of Grenouthian intelligence snorted and caught Blythe's eye, at which point she realized he had recognized her as well, but had done a better job of con-cealing the fact.

"Our information is that you are currently eighteen years old," the director said. "You left the Stryx station librarian's experimental school at fourteen and began training for InstaSitter management, a position attained through nepotism." The Grenouthians all looked at Blythe and nodded their approval. "Most recently, you have been in charge of creating an exclusive LARPing league for InstaSitter employees, where you have also developed a following as a heroic raid leader. What are your plans to promote the cooking show to your fan base?"

"My contract with InstaSitter prevents me from doing any outside promotions without the approval of our managing partner, Tinka," Jonah replied smoothly. "However, I do have an idea for bringing on a guest cook from InstaSitter each show, rotating through the species we employ, which includes all of the oxygen breathers on the tunnel network."

"All young females?"

"While our most active employees are predominantly females in their species-adjusted teen years, the majority of the sitters who have ever worked for us keep their profiles active and take the occasional assignment to earn spare creds and keep their hand in," Jonah explained. "If I start with co-hosts from the cooking class I teach, they're mainly my age or a little older."

"A harem show," one of the attorneys said approvingly. "Very popular these days. I like it."

This time Jonah blushed bright red and stuttered a denial, giving Dorothy an excuse to jump in. "In addition to co-hosts, we," she pointed a finger at her own chest and waggled it back and forth to cover Jonah and Jeeves as well, "have been discussing the addition of a dance segment to help pass the time while the food is cooking."

"I see you've never worked in production," the director scoffed. "We edit out the dead time for baking, boiling, and molecular resonance. It's impossible to do a live cooking show in real-time unless you stick with raw food or frying."

"Too much fried food is bad for the health," one of the Grenouthian attorneys chipped in. "Liability issue there."

"If you're going to be editing the show, fitting in a few dance sequences will be even easier," Dorothy said brightly. "The point is, we," she did the finger-pointing thing again, "are a package deal."

The executive producer leaned forward and raised his furry chin at the head of Grenouthian intelligence, as if to ask, "Do I have to put up with this Human?"

"Ambassador McAllister's daughter," the spy chief grunted. "Her mother has final say over any subsidiary rights for the All Species Cookbook because she signed the bid for EarthCent."

The executive producer tilted his head back and wasted a long-suffering look on the conference room ceiling before exhaling and starting anew. "Do you have any idea how many cameras it takes to do a professional job on dance numbers? Do you have any idea how much our cameramen are paid?"

"SBJ Fashions is willing to underwrite—"

"Half of the cost," Jeeves spoke over Dorothy. "And I have a Thark auditor on retainer for checking the books."

"Half of the staffing cost, studio rental, and all of the costumes, practice time, and music, whether live or recorded, plus liability," the executive producer countered.

"Half of the staffing cost. I'm not paying for equipment or space rental when you own it all anyway. I agree to the wardrobe, music, and practice time, but why should I underwrite liability when the most likely accident would be one of your overpaid cameramen running a floating camera into one of our dancers?"

"My daughter owns a pair of the shoes that you sell," one of the attorneys spoke up. "Every time she raises the heels and goes out dancing I wonder if she's going to fall and break a bone."

"I'd offer to put her on the show, but the Grenouthians on Union Station all dance in their birthday suits," Dorothy said. "As Jeeves is always reminding me, we're in business to sell our fashions. Still, if her partner is any good, it might be worth having them on for the shoes."

"We decided to stick with InstaSitters for now, Dorothy," Jonah reasserted himself, having recovered from the embarrassment of being accused of planning a harem. "Don't forget the cost-sharing arrangement."

"Then I think we have enough to start bandying numbers around," the executive producer said. "What sort of figure did you have in mind?"

"I'm waiting to hear your offer," Jonah said.

The bunny nodded to one of the attorneys, who produced a Dollnick writing board and a stylus. The executive producer made a big show of doing some finger math, and then shielded the Dollyboard with one furry paw while writing a number. Then he gave a pained look, like he had just stuffed a box with sharp corners into his belly pouch, and slid the Dollyboard down the table like a puck.

"I thought I could read numbers in Grenouthian script but I guess I was wrong," Jonah said, and passed the Dollyboard to his right. Aisha glanced at the figure and her eyes widened, but she didn't say anything and moved the device on to Dorothy, who like Jonah, didn't read Grenouthian script, and wasn't particularly interested in any case. The Dollyboard stopped with Blythe, whose lips took on a grim set.

"You have our apartment under surveillance," she accused the head of Grenouthian Intelligence.

"Just for the last few days," the bunny replied complacently. "It's standard practice prior to negotiations."

"The woman who came to clean the carpets. She was on your payroll?"

"A gentleman never tells. Isn't that the figure your family decided on? Surely you can't complain about the efficiency of our negotiation process."

"Live action figures," Aisha announced, trying to regain momentum for the humans. "In addition to fifty percent for his own figure, Jonah wants the same terms for all of his guests."

"Isn't that a little greedy?" the director asked. "We would have offered them ten percent and settled at twenty-five, but not if you're insisting on half."

"I want fifty percent for the guests, not for me," Jonah said. "The same thing goes for the residual split."

"It comes out of your end," the executive producer said. "Shave the fur off your own butt if it makes you happy."

"That includes the dancers," Dorothy spoke up. "We agreed that everything would be divided by live time on camera. Do you track that?"

"We track everything, including whose brother and whose sister goes where and why," the spy chief said.

"What's that supposed to mean?" Blythe demanded.

"Come now, you don't think I attended this meeting just to confirm a few facts for my network friends. We know that young Jonah's twin and her fiancé have been playing tunnel tricks. We admire the tight coordination between your families on both the diplomatic and the business fronts, but we've been at this game for longer than you can imagine. I advised the network to play along for a piece of the action, but your attempts to obfuscate the ultimate goal with throw-ins like dinner dancing are becoming a bit much."

"You've lost me," Blythe said. "It's no secret that the Open University sent my daughter to work for Drazen Intelligence, but I had to ask Herl what she's doing at work because she won't tell me herself for security reasons. Whatever the Vergallians have Samuel doing, I can't believe he's making diplomatic policy, and the fact that our various business interests all benefit from co-branding with the All Species Cookbook is because SBJ Fashions and InstaSitter both employ and market cross-species."

The Grenouthian spy chief snorted again, clearly un-moved by the denial. Then, to her surprise, he shifted to speaking heavily accented English, and said, "So your motivation in paying for the cookbook was purely alt—ruistic."

Something about the way the bunny paused after the first syllable of 'altruistic' kept Blythe from responding immediately, and the executive producer jumped back in again.

"Of course, if InstaSitter or SBJ Fashions would like to sign on as co-producers and participate in the first round of funding, I can offer you an above-market rate of return, and more importantly, a place in the opening credits when the show is watched by Human audiences."

"You want me to extend unsecured financing without giving us any points in the production?" Jeeves scoffed. "No sale."

"I'll pass as well," Blythe said, still trying to work out what the spy chief had been getting at with his odd pronunciation.

"Then let's get the legalese out of the way so we can assign some writers and start on the pilot. It would be helpful if you could supply a draft of the cookbook to our staff, unless—" he leaned forward again and raised his chin, and this time, the head of Grenouthian Intelligence responded with a wink, "—never mind."

The two network attorneys each pulled a document printed in both Grenouthian and English from their respective satchels and passed them to the executive producer. He laid them side-by-side and rapidly scanned the dense text. "Looks right to me. Director?"

"Identical," the slightly smaller bunny confirmed. He passed a copy across the table to Aisha, while the executive producer handed the other to one of the attorneys, who extended it to Jonah.

"Jeeves?" Jonah subvoced.

"It's an old Grenouthian lawyer's trick," the Stryx explained. "Those cases they're carrying are actually thermal plastic document printers and they do the necessary editing via their implants. If I had been eavesdropping, I could tell you that the contracts reflect exactly what we discussed and that the rest is boilerplate copied from Aisha's last contract, including the clause about maternity leave."

"I'll need to show this to my father," Jonah said, drawing an exasperated sigh from all five bunnies, who were hoping to avoid a close reading of the fine print.

"Then all that's left to settle is the show's title," the producer said. "We've been kicking around a number of ideas, so tell me if any of these grabs you." The Grenouthian glanced down at his tab and read, "Let's Make Recipes, Cooking with Aisha's Future Brother-in-Law by Marriage,

Let's Make Food, The Human Kitchen Comedy Hour, The All Species Cookbook Comedy Hour, The—"

"Excuse me," Aisha interrupted. "I seem to notice a trend developing. Do you have any title suggestions that aren't a blatant attempt to piggyback on Let's Make Friends or the comedy documentaries you produce about Earth?"

"Sticking with proven concepts is what makes the entertainment industry great," the director said. "If you think you can do better—"

"Cooking with Jonah, Cooking for All Species, Food Night on Union Station," Aisha rattled off.

"Stone Soup?" Jonah suggested. "You know, like the story?"

"Stone Soup," the producer repeated. "Fewer words means they can be bigger in the ads. I'll tell you what. We'll run my ideas and your ideas past a few focus groups and see what wins out."

Seventeen

"Is there something wrong with the lighting on this deck?" Kelly asked her husband. "It's not much brighter than the night lights in Mac's Bones."

"I seem to remember hearing that Fillinducks always settle systems with red dwarf stars," Joe replied. "Give your eyes a minute to adjust."

"How come you're moving so confidently?"

"My old implant has a night vision option from my mercenary days. I'd be surprised if your diplomatic implant doesn't support it in one of the menus."

"I'll pass," Kelly said. "I don't want to end up relying on cybernetic technology like those vanished species we saw during our Libbyland vacation. Give me your arm."

"You're not worried about me ending up as a cyborg?"

"I'm sure you had the proper training so you should be immune. Oh, look. There's a bright light up ahead."

"That's probably the reception, then. Have you ever been here before?"

"Me? Before we won the cookbook bid the Fillinducks wouldn't touch me with a ten-foot pole. I'm still waiting for the other shoe to drop."

"Ambassador," a voice called from behind them. Joe looked back and easily recognized Bork, thanks to the Drazen ambassador waving with his tentacle.

"It's Bork and Minka," Joe informed his wife. He halted to allow the other couple to catch up.

"That's a relief," Kelly said. "This invitation was so sudden I didn't have a chance to check if any of the other ambassadors were coming. I was worried it would just be the two of us in a room full of Fillinduck trios all wondering what we did with our better third."

"Ah, I hoped it was you, but this lighting is atrocious," Bork greeted them.

"So it's not just us for a change. Do you have any idea what this is about?"

"It's been a few years since the Fillinducks invited us to one of their surprise parties," Minka replied. "They have a cultural aversion to planning ahead for social events, something to do with the difficulty trios have coordinating a time that's good for all of them. I did see a mention on the Grenouthian shipping news earlier today that the Thark ambassador had returned to Union Station."

"The Tharks have an ambassador?" Kelly frowned. "I remember now, but I don't think I've seen him since I was crowned Carnival queen, which must have been twenty years ago."

"He came to Dring's ball, but I don't think he ever left the card room, unless it was for a quick line dance," Joe told her. "What's the relationship between the Fillinducks and the Tharks?"

"The Fillinducks were once their vassals back before either species joined the tunnel network," Bork explained. "You probably know that the Tharks nearly destroyed themselves in a civil war, which was made almost inevitable by their warrior culture and its elevation of an exaggerated form of honor to the highest value. I believe the Fillinducks have always been grateful that the Tharks were too proud to allow their vassals to participate in the fighting."

"It's hard to picture those happy little fellows as fierce warriors, though I have to admit that their reputation came in handy when they saved us from that Vergallian hijack and kidnapping," Kelly said.

"Sometimes, the fittest members of the species selected by history are the ones who don't draw a weapon at every perceived insult. Don't you have a saying about the meek inheriting the Earth?"

"We do, but we're still waiting."

"Certainly sounds like a party," Joe said, as they approached the open doors through which both light and sound spilled out into the corridor. "I wonder if I should have brought beer?"

"The Fillinducks are always excellent hosts once they make up their minds to stage an event," Minka told him. "I'm sure they'll have both food and drink that's suitable for Humans."

When they entered the reception, Kelly couldn't help wondering if the Fillinducks had taken over some sort of playground for the party. Half of the floor space was taken up by large alien apparatus that might have been gym equipment for children. There were enormous bubbles stuck to every surface, as if somebody had attempted to do a load of laundry by filling the machine with detergent.

"Welcome to our little embassy," the Fillinduck ambassador greeted the newcomers. "Make yourselves at home, but please don't pop the Rinty bubbles. Our guest of honor is around here somewhere, and I know he's looking forward to talking to you, Ambassador McAllister. I hope you can honor his request."

"Do you know what it is?" Kelly asked.

The Fillinduck gestured for her to come closer, and bending down to her height, whispered, "I believe he has a recipe he wants to get into the cookbook."

"I'll see if I can find us something to drink, Kel," Joe said, as the Fillinduck ambassador turned away to greet Czeros, who arrived stag, as usual. "Why don't you look for the Thark and get whatever it is out of the way so you can relax?"

"You know me better than I know myself," Kelly responded, and began searching for the short ambassador in a sea of taller aliens. Once her eyes adjusted to the improved, though still dim lighting, she realized that the guests at the reception seemed to be self-segregating into diplomats versus other station celebrities. She homed in on the two largest backs she recognized, those of the Grenouthian and Verlock ambassadors. As soon as she squeezed past Srythlan, she found that her bet had paid off. The Thark ambassador was standing on a chair regaling his diplomatic audience with tales of his travels.

" —and I replied, 'But I thought you *were* the emperor!'"

The circle of ambassadors exploded in laughter, foot stomping, and belly slapping, and Kelly thought that Crute was going to break his own ribs, he was hugging himself so tight.

"No more, no more," Ortha begged the Thark through tears of mirth. "You're killing us."

"That's what *she* said," the Thark rejoined, bringing about a fresh gale of laughter, during which Kelly saw Aainda holding onto a fistful of the Grenouthian ambassador's shoulder fur to keep herself upright. "Anyway, the Bungees threw me in a dungeon, and if my grandson hadn't finally broken away from his game console and come to rescue me, I'd still be in there eating sea rats and swapping jokes with the Stryx on the other side of the wall."

"With the Stryx!" Crute wailed at this final punch line, and dropped to his knees with a thud.

The Thark ambassador must have known that it was best to leave the audience begging for more. He hopped down from the chair and made a series of gestures in front of the kneeling Dollnick, as if he were giving Crute a blessing or confirming him as a knight. The other ambassadors, all of whom were themselves accomplished raconteurs, realized it would be suicide to go on next, and opted to look for food instead. The Thark walked straight up to Kelly and immediately got down to business.

"I hear you won the cookbook monopoly."

"Yes, we hope to go final at the end of this week," the EarthCent ambassador replied.

"So soon? Then it's true you won't be publishing in Universal."

"That's correct. The initial print edition will be in English, but the electronic version will be released in all of the tunnel network languages simultaneously."

"Did you include any Thark recipes?"

"I'd have to check with Aabina and I hate to contact her at home," Kelly said. "Hold on a second. Libby?" she subvoced, knowing that the other species were often put off if she spoke out loud to the Stryx in their presence.

"The draft doesn't include any recipes from the Tharks," the station librarian answered Kelly's unasked question. "Donna did send several messages to their embassy, but the Tharks don't bother staffing when the ambassador is away."

"Our cookbook editor, who is also my embassy manager, tried to reach out to you several times," Kelly said apologetically. "I don't know if the message was passed along."

"It's why I cut short my tour and returned to the station," the Thark said. He dug in the pocket of his vest and brought out a battered English catalog. "You can use any of these for our entry. Use them all if you have room."

Kelly examined the pamphlet. "This is a catalog of homemade soaps from Anne's Boutique."

"Yes, of course. I don't believe any of our foods are safe for Human consumption, so including my favorite Earth export seems like the right thing to do."

"But these are soaps, and it's a cookbook," Kelly said slowly.

"Obviously, and this catalog gives the recipes and techniques in great detail. All of the ingredients are one hundred percent natural and certified organic, whatever that means. Here," the ambassador continued, pulling a pale green bar of soap out of another pocket. "Take a lick."

"I, uh, I just ate. Can I take this catalog with me? I need to get the editor's approval—"

"The message I got stated that entries from ambassadors would be published without having to go through a vetting process," the Thark cut her off, an edge of steel entering his jolly voice.

"Yes, of course," Kelly backpedaled. "I'm just concerned there may be copyright—"

"I checked with our legal experts and recipes can't be copyrighted under Human law. Change a word here or there in the instructions and create your own illustrations if you can't get explicit permission from Anne. I've made all of these recipes myself, but I like to support the creator by buying the original product when it's available."

"You won't be offended if we put in a note that the original purpose of the soap is for washing up?" the EarthCent ambassador asked tentatively.

The Thark broke into a wide smile. "You can write whatever you want as long as the recipe gets in there with my name and a picture." He pivoted and looked up at Joe. "Is this your husband?"

"Ambassador," Joe said. He passed his wife the glass of white wine he'd found her and then moved his beer to the other hand to offer the Thark a handshake. "Long time, no see."

"Right, it would seem long in comparison to your lifespan." The Thark turned back to Kelly and inquired in a stage whisper, "Is it considered rude to compliment a Human on his wrinkles?"

"It won't bother Joe, but don't try it with me," she said, though she wasn't at all confident that her implant had properly translated the ambassador's question. The Tharks were a wrinkly species, though she supposed it was possible that the ones she had seen up close were all getting on in their years.

"That's a fine set of knowledge lines you've got there, Joe," the Thark ambassador continued in his normal voice. "I heard that my grandnephew is underwriting insurance for your rental fleet."

"Tunnel Trips," Joe said. "I only have a small ownership stake for legal reasons involving the Stryx lease for Mac's Bones."

"Just as long as you understand that all bets are off on certain encounters that take place inside Stryx tunnels when one of the passengers of the rental craft is carrying a Vergallian homing beacon."

"I didn't even know that was possible, but I'll check the small print on the policy slip when we get home." He felt Kelly's grip tighten on his arm, and realized that the Thark wasn't speaking hypothetically.

"Our off-world betting parlor has the odds on Ambassador Aainda up to even money," the Thark continued. His voice sounded quite loud in the sudden silence, since all of the diplomats in the immediate area had stopped talking as if on cue and were leaning into the conversation. "Personally, I think that my idiot son-in-law is underrating her chances, especially given the informal alliance she's pulled together."

"You're taking bets on Aainda doing something?" Kelly asked.

"She's our proxy for a larger sequence of events. I believe there are twenty or so related prop bets on the board, including a few tied to the publication of the cookbook. Ah, I see our host summoning me. I expect he'll want me to give a speech." The Thark winked at the McAllisters and scurried away.

"What was the ambassador talking about, Joe? I don't understand gambling talk."

"You know the Tharks will make book on anything. We can swing by the off-world betting parlor on the way home and see what they have up on the big board. I'm not sure what to make of his comment about Vergallians in the tunnel, though. Did Samuel say anything to you?"

"You know how closed-mouth he is about the work he's doing for Aainda. There's Blythe and Chastity. They should know something."

"Hey, future in-laws," Blythe greeted them. "Quite the shindig the Fillinducks are putting on."

"Why were you invited?" Kelly asked the sisters, and then realizing how the question sounded, clarified with, "InstaSitter? The Galactic Free Press? EarthCent Intelligence?"

"Believe it or not, Blythe and I were both invited because we underwrote the cookbook bid," Chastity replied. "We didn't realize that every alien on the station with a get-rich-quick scheme would conclude that we must be the biggest suckers of all time. Still, some of the business plans are kind of interesting. Have you seen Bob yet?"

"Bob Steelforth? Is he covering this event for the paper?"

"The Fillinduck embassy sent press credentials for a single reporter at the last minute, and Bob's our senior Union Station correspondent. He was working on a story about the Alt delegation so he may be late."

"The Alts have arrived already?" Kelly turned to Blythe. "Did I miss an update from EarthCent Intelligence?"

"They aren't here yet, but we've gotten a number of reports about their envoys showing up on the most unlikely alien worlds."

"Where are your husbands?" Joe asked the sisters. "If I can still go out past my bedtime, a couple of young bucks like Clive and Marcus can make the effort."

"Clive is attending an ISPOA conference on Horten Eight and I don't expect him back for another week," Blythe said.

"And Dorothy has stolen my husband for the foreseeable future," Chastity added. "Your daughter has Marcus choreographing routines for every possible situation that might come up on the cooking show so the bunnies will have multiple options to choose from when they're editing.

I swear I heard Marcus muttering something about a pasta dance over breakfast this morning."

"So Jonah signed the contract?" Kelly said. "Aisha didn't tell me, but I didn't see her today, and I guess that explains where Dorothy's been."

"He signed last night," Blythe confirmed. "The Grenouthians are already pushing him to start shooting so they can have a few shows ready in time for the cookbook launch. The producer even asked me if we could delay the release by a few weeks, but I told him that my mother wouldn't stand for it."

"I think that Farling is trying to catch your attention," Joe muttered in his wife's ear. She glanced in the direction he indicated and saw a giant beetle sidling towards them. When her gaze made contact with G32FX's multi-faceted eyes, he pointed to the right with all the limbs on that side of his body and changed course towards a high stack of Rinty bubbles.

"G3-something," Kelly told them with a sigh. "He seemed a bit paranoid the one time I met him. I better go see what it's all about."

"Tell your daughter I want my husband back in one piece," the publisher of the Galactic Free Press called after her.

When the EarthCent ambassador reached the mound of bubbles where the Farling had disappeared, she heard a voice say, "Don't come any closer. Just admire the Rinty bubbles and pretend to be talking to yourself."

"Do you think anybody will really fall for that?" Kelly demanded. She made a show of examining the multicolored surface of a bubble that on closer inspection, proved to be a continuous swirl of fractal patterns that made her feel like she was being sucked into a vortex.

"Trust me, you have a reputation for one-sided conversations, though the more generous interpretation would be that you're always talking with the Stryx."

"Not always, G3-uh…"

"G32FX," the Farling rubbed out on his speaking legs, which Kelly glimpsed through a temporarily transparent section of the bubble. "Has EarthCent agreed to your end of the deal?"

"I have authorization from the president to negotiate for him, but we haven't heard any details."

"That's a relief," the Farling said. "I was beginning to think that everybody knew more about my business than I do."

"I don't understand. How do you expect me to agree to some sort of multi-party deal when you've left us completely out of the process?"

"Hasn't your son kept you in the loop?" G32FX asked.

"I don't have a clue what he's up to. The Thark ambassador just dropped some hint about meetings with Vergallians in tunnels but it's the first I'm hearing of it." The fractal pattern turned clear again and Kelly thought she saw another shape behind the beetle. "Is somebody with you?"

"Abort," the Farling commanded, and by the time Kelly got back to Joe, the beetle was halfway across the room studying a different Rinty bubble. The EarthCent ambassador noticed that Aainda stood not far away, her mouth covered with her hand.

"What was that all about?" Joe asked. He proffered a small plate of cantaloupe balls pierced with toothpicks.

"I wish I knew. I think that Aainda may be using our son to get around a prohibition on sharing information with me, but Samuel is too loyal to her for it to work,"

Kelly said in frustration. "How can he not trust his own mother to keep a secret?"

"You've got me," Joe said, striving to prevent any note of sarcasm from entering his voice. "Are you sure we should be talking about this at a party?"

"Given that we must be the least informed guests in the room, I think it's safe."

Eighteen

The doorman of the Vergallian embassy bowed his head slightly and greeted the EarthCent ambassador's son with a curt, "Sam."

"Raef," Samuel acknowledged cautiously. "The conference was a bore, Aainda didn't miss anything. I'm just going to drop the recorder in the data room and then I'm done for the day. Did the ambassador send any new instructions for me?"

"You can ask her yourself."

Samuel had to resist running through the lobby to reach the ambassador's office faster. She'd vanished from the station a day after the arrival of the Thark ambassador, and other than cryptic messages relayed by the doorman, he hadn't heard from her in a week. He skidded to a halt at her open door when he heard her speaking, but she waved him in without missing a beat.

"—everybody, but getting them all to sit down and sign in blood will still be a trick," Aainda concluded. "The one thing working in our favor is that the endless speculation on the Grenouthian news is keeping all of the intelligence services on the tunnel network chasing shadows."

"And the boy?" asked the Vergallian in the hologram, who Samuel could only see from the back.

"He's a grown man by Human standards and he just walked in," the ambassador said. "Samuel will be perfect for the job."

"It's your show, Aainda. Do me a favor and try talking some sense into that crazy daughter of mine."

"I've invited them both to dinner tonight. Just an intimate gathering," the ambassador said, a wolfish grin appearing on her perfect features. "We'll talk soon." The hologram winked out, and Aainda gestured for Samuel to take the chair in front of her display desk. "I owe you several explanations."

"I'm just doing my job," Samuel hurried to say. "To tell you the truth, it's easier for me at home if I don't know what's going on. I don't want to lie to my mother."

Aainda nodded. "I understand. It's a shame you didn't have royal training growing up. We're all taught compartmentalization techniques that are very useful for separating our work lives and our family affairs."

"But Vergallian government is a family affair," Samuel protested.

"Yes, to an extent, but in the final analysis, a queen is only as strong as the loyalty of her subjects. Our entertainment industry tends to focus on royal family pageantry and rivalries for the sake of ratings, but keeping our populations gainfully employed and providing alternative paths for those who want something different is what's made the Empire of a Hundred Worlds what it is today."

"Do you know if Ailia's world is safe? Whenever I ask, she just laughs and says that Baylit has it all under control. I'm afraid that one day she'll have to marry some stranger from another royal family just to guarantee her future."

"We all marry some stranger from another royal family to guarantee our futures," Aainda replied with a laugh.

"Marrying within one's own family leads to myriad problems, and I don't just mean the medical issues. But thank you for raising the subject as I want to speak to you about a matter that falls well outside the duties of a cooperative education student."

"Is it about Aabina?"

"No. My daughter is a long way from being old enough to marry, and I already have a stranger picked out for her in any case. It's about your sister's friend, Affie. I was just chatting with her mother."

"Oh," Samuel said, recalling the message from the Fleet admiral. "So she doesn't approve of Stick."

"Exactly. You can tell by a glance that Diemro is from an upper caste family, but Imperial Intelligence draws a blank on his background, and Fleet is no wiser than we are. Affie's mother originally agreed to let her come to Union Station to attend the Open University, and she extended that freedom when your sister got Affie involved in the fashion business, but there's a difference between a harmless flirtation and throwing away years of one's youth on a drug dealer."

"Stick's real name is Diemro? I've never heard it, but he seems like a nice enough guy. I've worked with him in some of Dorothy's fashion shows, and we did a bunch of LARPs together. I don't know much about the whole Kraken Red thing, but I thought it was legal, sort of."

"Legality isn't the point here. He's been selling individual sticks at parties for the last ten years and that seems to be the limit of his ambitions. Would you want your daughter living with somebody like that?"

"I didn't know they lived together, but I guess I think it's kind of their business," Samuel said, looking down at his feet.

Aainda sighed. "Someday you'll be a parent and you'll understand. In the meantime, the pair of them will be here for dinner this evening, and if it's not too late for you to invite your fiancée, I'd like you there to set a good example."

"Now I'm confused. You want Stick, I mean, Diemro, to propose to Affie?"

"You're missing the point. She and Diemro live as if they plan to be young forever. Even though Affie works for SBJ Fashions, she doesn't put in nearly the same hours as Dorothy or their Frunge friend, not to mention Baa, who doesn't sleep. I want to hold you and Vivian up as an example of hard-working young people who have their eyes on the future. And Aabina is bringing along a fellow co-op student who works at EarthCent Intelligence."

"I don't see how it's going to change anything, but I know that Vivian has been dying for a chance to see what I do at your dinners. She thinks—" Samuel stopped and his ears turned pink.

"I can guess what she thinks. I don't expect one dinner party to alter Affie's attitude, but I've agreed to become involved and I have to begin somewhere. It wouldn't be civilized to just start right in with the threats."

"Uh, I guess not," the EarthCent ambassador's son said, recognizing a typical plot line from Vergallian dramas and realizing that he was in over his head. "I'll just go ping Vivian, then."

"Ping her? Is that how you treat a girl once you get your ring on her finger? Buy Vivian some flowers and request the honor of her attendance. And tell her informal dress is fine. I gave the musicians the night off."

Samuel wandered out of Aainda's office, somewhat confused by the sudden shift from intergalactic diplomacy to personal relationships, though on second thought, he realized that the two might not be that far apart. He stopped by the Vergallian flower shop down the corridor from the embassy and invested a day's pay in a corsage that the seller assured him would go with anything, including a jumpsuit. Then he pinged Vivian, who informed him she was on a job at the main arrivals concourse, but if he wanted to meet her there, it should wrap up within a half hour.

When Samuel exited the lift tube at the main arrivals area on Union Station's core, he reflexively glanced up at the large hologram that cycled through the major tunnel network languages providing information about commercial space liners on scheduled runs. There were only three arrivals due in the next thirty minutes. The first was a Sharf ship coming from some orbital that wasn't on the tunnel network, the next a Dollnick liner on the eleventh stop of some sort of tourist cruise. The last was a Vergallian vessel named 'Princess Akida.' He heard a ping over his implant and immediately chose to accept the call without requesting the source.

"I see you," Vivian said in his head. "I'm at Gate Eight, but keep your distance."

"Will do," Samuel replied, and seized the opportunity to finally use some of the techniques he'd learned watching EarthCent Intelligence agents train in Mac's Bones. He strolled casually towards Gate Seven and stopped along the way to buy a bottle of Union Station Springs water at a kiosk. There he intentionally fumbled a coin to the deck and used the opportunity to turn his head and check for a tail. Next, he started for Gate Nine, only to halt behind the aliens waiting to meet arrivals coming from Gate Eight. "In position," he subvoced tersely.

"Are you playing spy?"

"Maybe. I still can't see you."

"I'll scratch my ear," Vivian said.

Samuel scanned the crowd but his fiancée was nowhere to be seen. "You must be in front of one of the tall aliens."

"I'll try again."

"Is that really you?" he asked, staring at the back of a slender Drazen woman who was idly scratching an ear with her tentacle.

"If you're staring, stop it," she hissed over the implant. "And here come the arrivals, so don't distract me while I'm working."

A stream of passengers from the Sharf liner poured through the gate, waving, whistling and hooting for family members. Samuel knew from Jeeves that the Stryx station owner employed remote sensing to check off every arrival against the ship's manifest while also scanning them for contraband. Gryph did it all so unobtrusively that even the most technically advanced species couldn't identify the means employed.

Vivian began worming her way through the crowd towards the right, and Samuel shifted his own position just enough to keep her in sight. He saw her cross one of the tributaries of travelers that had branched off from the main stream just as a Farling with five or six small pieces of baggage dangling from his various limbs passed. For a moment it looked like she had lost track of her prosthetic tentacle, which whacked the beetle on his shell, but if the Farling had noticed, he didn't make any sign.

"All done," Vivian announced. "Meet me by the all-species restrooms."

"On my way," Samuel responded, but it took him a couple of minutes to reach their rendezvous through the crowded concourse. "Are you here?"

"Don't rush me, I'll be out in a sec."

Samuel took advantage of the time to ping the EarthCent embassy and asked Vivian's grandmother if he could speak with Aabina.

"She just left for EarthCent Intelligence, though I suppose I shouldn't be telling you that," Donna said. "Do you want to talk to your mother?"

"Just tell her that I'm having dinner at the Vergallian embassy with your granddaughter, assuming she agrees."

"Buy her flowers," the embassy manager advised.

"Let's go," Vivian said, emerging from the restroom without the prosthetic or the custom facial overlay that allowed her to pass for a Drazen. "Did you see me working that tentacle? A few months ago I was terrified that I'd yank out my own hair."

"Yeah, that was pretty sweet," Samuel said. "Aainda invited us to dinner. It's informal dress, no dancing. And I got you these."

"A corsage? Now I have to go home and change."

"The Vergallian florist said they go with everything."

"I don't know," Vivian said, pinning the corsage to her Drazen pantsuit. Then she pulled a small tab from her bag and swiped it to life. "Check this out."

"What is it?" Samuel looked down at the concentric rings on the screen. "One of those tilt games where you're supposed to move the blinking light to the bulls-eye?"

"Not unless you want to get caught. It's the tracking device I stuck to the beetle's shell. The Farlings are up to something."

"It doesn't seem to be moving."

"That's an old trick to foil a tail," Vivian told him. "Just wait a few minutes and you'll see. He'll go out of range in the lift tube, but we've got agents around all of the likely hotels waiting to pick him up."

"You were right, but it's moving in this direction," Samuel said, watching the screen. "He's headed straight for us."

"Kiss me," Vivian ordered him.

"What?"

"That's what field agents always do in dramas."

Samuel grinned and leaned in for a kiss, being careful not to crush the corsage. Vivian ruined the romantic interlude by holding the hand with the tab over his shoulder and keeping up a running commentary about the Farling's movements over their implants.

"He's still coming."

"Don't you close your eyes while we're kissing?"

"You're kissing, I'm working."

"I'm still on the clock too and I closed my eyes. What, you want to wrestle now?"

"Turn left, I need to—oh, fudge."

Samuel broke away and turned to see one of the teenage skycaps who hung around the concourse after school trying to pick up a few creds carrying bags for travelers. The kid was standing right in front of them with something on his open palm.

"A chitinous gentleman of the alien variety paid me five creds to remove this from his back and deliver it to you with a message," the skycap informed them, and handed the tracking device to Vivian. Then he began rubbing his forefingers together in an imitation of a Farling's speaking legs, and said, "The day I get taken in by a fake tentacle is the day I stop practicing medicine."

"Was it M793qK?" Samuel asked as the kid sauntered off, repeatedly flipping the five-cred coin in the air and catching it behind his back. "I only saw him from the side, and to tell you the truth, I doubt I could pick the beetle doctor out of a room of Farlings unless he was the oldest one there."

"I only saw the back of his carapace," Vivian said, looking utterly miserable. "My handler is going to kill me."

"Wait a sec. I have an idea. Let's stop by his old medical shop."

"That's right, it's down here somewhere, isn't it?"

"Near that lift tube," Samuel said, leading the way. They paused outside the bank of diagnostic scanners at the entrance to the walk-in clinic and heard the Farling physician buzzing away on his speaking legs at top volume.

"You obviously haven't cleaned the DNA sequencer in over a cycle! How do you expect to get meaningful readings if there are bits of a hundred different species in there? I'm only on the station until the All Species Cookbook release party, but I've got plenty of time to find a replacement doctor if you don't shape up."

Vivian drew Samuel away, looking extremely pleased with herself. "A positive identification is even better than a tracking device. All we need to do now is get one of his old patients to ping him and he'll answer."

"So you're done for the day?"

"I'm on duty for another three hours, but I just pinged my handler, and she said if I could get inside the Vergallian embassy I should go for it. Hey, I just remembered—"

"We are not stopping for you to pick up bugs, Vivian. I have to work in that embassy, and the Vergallians are way ahead of the Drazens on surveillance technology in any case. They'd catch you at the door."

"All right, all right. What time is this dinner?"

"Your grandmother said that Aabina has already left to pick up Wrylenth, so we may as well go straight there."

"She better not be dressed up," Vivian said with a scowl.

"They're both coming from their co-op jobs and you know they dress professionally," Samuel reasoned. "That pantsuit looks great on you."

"It's from the same boutique where Tinka buys hers," the girl said, somewhat mollified. "I asked her advice about dressing for the Drazen workplace."

"Mr. McAllister, Miss Oxford," the doorman greeted the couple formally when they arrived at the embassy. "The rest of your party is here. Please go in."

"Uh, thank you, Raef."

"Is that the guy you say is always trying to provoke you?" Vivian whispered as they headed for the dining room. "He seemed very polite."

"I haven't figured it out yet. Maybe the ambassador talked to him."

"Samuel, Vivian," Aainda welcomed the latecomers enthusiastically. "My daughter and Wrylenth were just sharing their co-op experiences with Affie and her companion, and Diemro made the most amusing observation."

"I was just pointing out that Humans are easy to work with because you don't have any history to speak of," Stick said, sounding slightly embarrassed. "I was on a Frunge world once and said something about a bright star you could see before the sunset. It turned out to be light from a nova on the other side of the galaxy that had destroyed a

222

Frunge colony eighty thousand years earlier. They were all in mourning and they thought I was making fun of them."

"You've traveled, Diemro?" Aainda asked.

"A little, when I was a kid," he answered vaguely.

"Stick hasn't left Union Station in ten years," Affie told them, as if it was an accomplishment. "At least I'll always know where to find him."

Aainda winced comically at Affie's defiant use of Diemro's nickname. "Yes, that is something, I suppose. Did you have any trouble finding Vivian, Sam?"

"Not really," the EarthCent ambassador's son fibbed, avoiding a potentially embarrassing discussion about his failure to penetrate the disguise that the Farling had seen through at a glance. He pulled out the chair next to Aabina for Vivian to sit, and then took the final open seat at the end of the table for himself.

"Thumbs," Aabina muttered to Vivian, who turned bright red when she realized she was still wearing the prosthetic second thumbs from her Drazen disguise.

"Oh, sorry," she mumbled, pulling off the fingerless gloves that held the sixth digit in place. "I just came from work and I'm so used to them that I forget."

"That's perfectly understandable," the ambassador said. "I think it's admirable how all of you students have committed so fully to your assignments. It shows real maturity."

There was an awkward silence while the waitstaff brought in the dinner and Affie fumed over the not-so-subtle attack on Stick. The four young co-ops were afraid to speak for fear that their host would use whatever they said as ammunition against the fashion designer and her unfortunate boyfriend.

"Has anybody else been watching the Grenouthian news lately?" Wrylenth eventually asked in the lightest tone that his heavy body and gravelly voice could muster. "It's always on at work," he added, to justify the non sequitur.

"I've never seen so many stories about Vergallians," Vivian replied, and then quickly forked some salad into her mouth to have an excuse not to continue when she remembered where they were eating.

"Yes, I expect there must be something to it," Aainda said. "Oddly enough, I was commenting to Samuel just an hour ago that it's a shame he didn't have our royal training which can be such a big help at work. Do you find that to be the case in the fashion business, Affie?"

"I'm not in management. I mainly do color schemes and accessories."

"I've heard that your purses are quite successful, though I imagine Baa's enchantments are the main draw since it's her brand on the bags," the ambassador continued mercilessly. "Of course, I suppose that you and Diemro just take it as it comes."

Affie slammed down her knife and glared at the host. "What did my mother offer you to scare Stick off?" she demanded. "She has no right to interfere with my life as long as I'm six spots removed from succession."

"There's no greater waste than idling away one's life as a queen-in-waiting," Aainda said agreeably. "Your mother is actually very proud of your progress. She's just afraid that having accomplished more on your own than so many other young royals from Fleet, you may relax before reaching your full potential."

"Mom really said that?" Affie asked,

"It's natural for a mother to be concerned about her children," the ambassador continued without answering. "She said that of all her daughters, you were the one who worked the hardest at training. But without daily application, in a few short centuries, all of that knowledge will be gone from your memory."

"So you recommend I move to the Empire and start plotting? Maybe marry into some second-rate royal family on a backwater planet and murder my way to the top like the evil daughter-in-law in a drama?"

"Affie," the ambassador's daughter spoke up sharply. "I think you owe my mother an apology."

"No, she's quite right to be upset if that's how she interpreted my guidance," Aainda said. "But Affie, what would you say if I found you an opportunity to rule willing subjects on a contract basis?"

"Substitute queening?" Affie replied. "Why, do you know an underage heir without a regent?"

"Take some time and think about it. I can only guarantee that if the opportunity arises, you'll be breaking new ground and making your family proud. Now finish your meals and I'll get the Coronation board. We have the perfect number for a game."

Nineteen

"Why are they delivering the cookbooks here?" Joe asked. "You said Aabina was going to order just enough to give away and let the Galactic Free Press print the rest on demand."

"Donna thought that a hundred would be sufficient for the embassy but I didn't want to risk running out," Kelly said. "When the printer contacted me to confirm, I doubled the order, and then he said it would be too many boxes to bring in the lift tube."

"How many boxes?"

"He didn't give me the number. All those people talk in code anyway, but I know I doubled the order from E2 to E4."

"Uh, Kel? Do you think they were using scientific notation units?"

"Who knows? What's the difference?"

"E2 would be a hundred units, and E4 would be ten thousand."

Kelly blanched. "Oh, it couldn't be that many. I had to prepay on the embassy's programmable cred and we only had six or seven thousand creds left on it. The original order was going to cost over a thousand, so the remainder couldn't have paid for ten times as many books."

"A hundred times as many books," Joe corrected her gently.

A loud beeping was heard, and the bay doors of Mac's Bones slid back, revealing a small cargo ship with "AAA Print Brokers" stenciled on the prow. The auto landing system took over and set the vessel down right at the edge of the rental lot. By the time Kelly and Joe got there, the ramp had dropped and two burly men with hand trucks were halfway down, each with four stacked boxes.

"Do I need to sign for these?" the EarthCent ambassador asked the older deliveryman, as he expertly slid the boxes off the hand truck without losing the stack.

"Just count 'em for now," the man told her. "You're getting two hundred and sixty-one cartons."

"Two hundred and sixty-one?" Kelly asked, her voice rising. "That can't be right. How many cookbooks in each box?"

"Forty," the man said. "I know, you were probably expecting two-hundred and fifty cartons, but offset printing isn't an exact science. When you order, you agree to buy up to a five percent overrun. It's been that way for hundreds of years."

"Libby!" Kelly cried out loud. "What's the balance on the embassy's programmable cred?"

"You have six creds remaining."

"You cut that pretty fine," Joe commented with a grin. "I'm going to get a few cargo floaters over here so the kids don't have to restack the boxes. The floaters should have room for a hundred cartons each, but I'm not sure about the weight."

Kelly watched hopelessly as the deliverymen made trip after trip into the hold of their ship, piling the boxes onto the large cargo floaters Joe provided. Thomas and Chance brought some recruits over from the training camp to help, and the cargo ship was soon on its way, leaving behind two hundred and sixty-one boxes of the All Species Cookbook.

"Look at the bright side," Joe said, hefting the last box delivered, which included a printed invoice in a plastic envelope. "This carton only has nine cookbooks in it, so the total is just ten thousand, four hundred and nine. They could have stuck you with ninety-one more."

"But what are we going to do with over ten thousand cookbooks?"

"Sell them at a discount?" Chance suggested. "How much did printing cost?"

"Joe?" Kelly passed the buck.

"Well, based on what you said, less than a cred each. Ink and paper must be pretty cheap, so I guess a chunk of the cost was in the setup for offset printing. And why don't you forget about hiring the Meteor room for the launch party and have it at the training camp? You could sell some books at cost without having to drag them around the station."

"Donna is going to kill me for spending all of our funds," Kelly groaned. "Can I take a couple of copies? I better go to the embassy and get this over with."

Joe used his pocketknife to slit open the box and handed Kelly three of the glossy cookbooks. "The cover came out great," he complimented her.

"I thought so too," she said, admiring the picture of children from six different species, plus Stryx Twitchy, all working at food preparation on the set of Let's Make Friends. "The Grenouthians weren't going to let us use it unless we mentioned the show in a subtitle, but we compromised on only adding that to their edition. If you want to bring a copy by Aisha's, I'm sure she'll be thrilled. And keep a copy for Dring too, and for us. And better—"

"You're not going to use up ten thousand cookbooks in the next five minutes," Joe interrupted. "Go. I'll find a place for these and we can talk about it when you get home."

"How could you let me make a mistake like that?" Kelly asked the station librarian as soon as she was out of earshot of the others. "You know I can't do scientific whatnot."

"Scientific notation, and I have no doubt your embassy will come out ahead on the deal, whereas at a hundred copies, you were locking in a loss," Libby told her. "I didn't want to say anything while you were still in production, but I have every reason to believe your cookbook is going to be a great success. It's already the number one bestseller on the Galactic Free Press list for all-species cookbooks."

"How many other cookbooks are on the list?" Kelly asked as she entered the lift tube. "Libby?"

"That's not the point. Aainda just contacted me and asked if you can stop by her embassy."

"Great. What time is it?"

"Don't worry, I'll get you back to your own embassy before Donna heads home."

"Thanks a lot," Kelly said under her breath, but looking down at the cover of the All Species Cookbook, she couldn't help smiling. "It really does put you in a good mood."

Aainda intercepted the EarthCent ambassador in the corridor outside the Vergallian embassy and led her to a small café in a side corridor.

"Tea for two," the Vergallian ambassador told the counterman. "And if you've had a delivery from Chocolate Gem, we'll try some."

"I couldn't," Kelly protested, but her face fell when the counterman shook his head to indicate that the latest batch of gourmet chocolate was already sold out. "Have you seen the cookbook?"

"I saw the cover when Pietro's mother came into the embassy to check with our legal staff before giving permission for her son's image to appear. It turns out that the cast contracts allow the show to use any video or still images for promotional purposes, so the decision was entirely up to the Grenouthians."

"I suppose some people will look on the inside of the cover for the picture attribution and see that it's from Let's Make Friends, but from what my daughter has been telling me lately, that would be considered indirect marketing at best."

"The Grenouthians always grab all the rights they can in contracts," Aainda said. "It didn't specify that the promotion has to be for the show."

"Oh," Kelly said, and nodded her thanks to the counterman who brought the tea. "You can keep the cookbook, by the way. I have plenty."

"Thank you," the ambassador said, flipping it open and rapidly locating the Vergallian vegan section, which took up more than a quarter of the page count. "You printed it exactly like the draft," she continued, and looked up at Kelly. "I'd like to buy a few thousand copies to ship home for the Human mercenaries working in honor guards on my family's worlds. Should I ask Aabina to order them?"

"Make sure she sells them to you direct from the embassy stock rather than purchasing on-demand from the Galactic Free Press. The quality is better, and I printed extra so I could give my colleagues a diplomatic discount."

"I'll do that." Aainda took a sip from her own tea and then set it aside with the cookbook. "Ambassador, are you positive that your president will go along with your committing EarthCent to a deal with the Farlings?"

"Stephen gave me full authorization to represent the president's office in this matter, and he submitted his proxy registration to the Stryx to make it official."

The Vergallian ambassador relaxed visibly and reached for her tea again. "Your son's co-op period is up soon and I want to offer him a full-time contract. Will you have any objection?"

"Do I get to keep Aabina?" Kelly countered.

"Well, that's up to her, but from what she tells me, I think she'd be thrilled to stay on at your embassy. She says it's far more interesting than anything we do, and I believe she has plans to help your associate ambassador transition the CoSHC organization toward something more like a governing body."

Kelly was so elated with the prospect of keeping her Vergallian co-op student and quickly unloading thousands of cookbooks that her feet barely touched the deck on the way back to her own embassy. When she saw a shirtless Daniel standing against the wall with his arms spread, her first thought was that he was being robbed by a Farling, but then she saw the medical bag and realized it must be M793qK.

"Is he going to live, Doctor?" the ambassador joked.

"Not as long as he would if he didn't spend so much time sitting, and that goes for the rest of you as well," the Farling rubbed out on his speaking legs. "You can put your shirt back on, and if you don't want to have a sore back the rest of your life, get more exercise."

"Do you recommend anything in particular, Doc?" Daniel asked.

"The next time you abandon your offspring at home, instead of sitting in a restaurant and adding to your waistline, I recommend taking InstaSitter up on their dance voucher promotion." M793qK turned his multi-faceted eyes on Donna. "Is anything bothering you?"

"I'm fine," the embassy manager said, shifting slightly on her roller chair to keep as much desk as possible between herself and the giant beetle. "Maybe Aabina?"

M793qK waved an appendage dismissively. "She hasn't been sick a day in her life, you can tell just by looking at her. In your office, Ambassador?"

"There's nothing wrong with me either, I mean, nothing that requires medical attention," Kelly said.

"I'm not here drumming up business. Your associate ambassador was just taking advantage of my kind nature while I waited for your return."

"Oh. Will you join us, Aabina?"

"Next time," the Farling said, waving the Vergallian girl off. "Ambassador?"

Kelly shrugged and led the giant beetle into her office, where he removed a small box from his medical bag and placed it on her desk. The room's acoustics changed, and the ambassador immediately realized that the doctor must have been drawn into Aainda's grand bargain.

"She got you too?"

"I have a document for you to sign," M793qK said, dropping a heavy sheaf of paper on the ambassador's display desk. "You can just initial each of the pages and then we'll both sign on the signature page."

"Is this encrypted?" Kelly asked, skimming the unbroken chain of letters that continued page after page. "It doesn't even use the whole alphabet."

"It's a nucleic acid sequence. Have you studied deoxyribonucleic acid?"

"The Stryx recruited me out of my sophomore year in college. What is it?"

"DNA. At the risk of oversimplifying, ancient DNA initially exhibits a decay rate like that of nuclear materials, a half-life, but eventually transitions to a power-law—are you understanding any of this?"

"Not really," Kelly admitted. "Could you give me some context?"

"Your own scientists have been studying ancient DNA for more than a century, but their analysis of samples dating from more than a hundred thousand years ago is of limited value. Our superior techniques are capable of accurately reconstructing DNA from much older samples, and unlike the tunnel network species who prefer to live in ignorance of Stryx meddling, we have a scientific interest in getting to the bottom of certain anomalies in your development that defy natural explanation."

"Maybe if you used shorter words?"

The beetle buzzed in frustration. "Did it ever strike you as odd that so many species can eat foods from your Earth?"

"Somebody explained to me that the longer a tunnel network species has been around, the more food from other members they can digest. If I remember, it has something to do with the development of microbes that live in our guts, but it takes tens or hundreds of thousands of years."

"Yes, on a genetic level your microbiome is more interesting than you are, but how long ago did Humans join the tunnel network?"

"Less than a hundred years, which is why other than Vergallian vegan, there's not much we can eat."

"But the other species can eat your food," the beetle said significantly.

"Well, yes, but they've all been around for—but not with exposure to our food!"

"The Vergallians have a theory that millions of years ago, Stryx science ships visited Earth, among other planets, and altered the DNA of existing species. According to them, the goal was to create new species that were more Vergallian-like."

"Because the Stryx want us to eat vegan?"

"Forget the cookbook, this is important. I've made Human DNA a bit of a hobby, and my own conclusions lead me in the opposite direction. If anything, the Stryx visited your world tens of millions of years ago looking for interesting sequences they could manipulate and graft onto other—the important thing you need to understand is that we want permission to conduct a scientific expedition to Earth to analyze ancient DNA," the Farling cut his explanation short.

"Why didn't you just say so?" Kelly said, flipping through the rest of the document. The long sequence of letters finally ended on the second-to-last page, followed by a single paragraph that authorized the Farlings to establish a research center on Earth, with the exact location and scale to be determined through negotiations with the EarthCent president's office. Ignoring the DNA sequence, it was the simplest and shortest contract Kelly had ever seen.

"I brought a pen," M793qK said, handing the EarthCent ambassador a heavy gold ball-point.

"All right," she said, flipping back to the beginning and initialing every page of the DNA sequence in the corner. "Aainda said that this would square things with you and the Fleet Vergallians, but do you have any idea what they're giving us?"

"You don't know? Then why are you signing?"

"EarthCent would have agreed to your request in any case. The president is always eager to bring more aliens to work on Earth, and with all the people who have emigrated, it's not like the planet is short on space. If you want dinosaur bones or something, you'll have to negotiate with the owners. But maybe you can explain to me why we can eat the produce from Dring's garden."

"Without analyzing a sample in the lab, the simplest explanation would be that he's growing stock from Earth. Perhaps he visited long ago and keeps gathering seeds from his crops."

"That's what I thought. I just can't help wondering how long ago."

When Kelly finished initialing every page, she signed and dated the contract, followed by M793qK.

"Keep the pen as a memento," the Farling told her. "I'll see you at the cookbook launch party."

"But why did you come to sign the contract rather than the G34 fellow I met at Aainda's?"

"G32FX. I'm the most senior Farling who has extensive experience dealing with Humans so it fell to me."

"But I thought you were an outcast."

"And I thought your son had won the Human mating lottery until his girlfriend stuck a bug on my back with her prosthetic tentacle."

"They're engaged now."

"Then I guess it's too late to start running psychological tests. See you next time," the giant beetle said, stuffing the contract in his medical bag and heading for the door. "Don't let Aabina take over the whole embassy."

"See you at the party," Kelly called after him. As soon as the door slid closed, she said, "Libby? Was signing that contract the right thing to do?"

"As it happens, M793qK consulted with me before writing the contract. But as a general rule, asking me for legal advice after signing is not a useful strategy. And you let the doctor get away without answering your question."

"I know, but he was going to do that anyway. Can you tell me how he went from being an outcast to some kind of senior Farling operative?"

"Their internal politics make the Vergallians look like schoolchildren," the station librarian replied. "The Grenouthian director from Aisha's show just dropped by and Aabina is looking for you."

"On my way."

When Kelly emerged from her office, she saw the Vergallian girl explaining something to the giant bunny, who appeared to be in a bad mood.

"Did you sell the Farling any ad time on our show?" the bunny demanded.

"No, he was here about something else."

"That's no reason to let a good opportunity slip. You know we've scheduled the premiere to run during your cookbook launch party."

"I know now," Kelly said. "Have you run into problems selling the ad space? Our president mentioned wanting to run an Earth tourism campaign with a focus on ethnic restaurants around the world. His public relations person is supposed to get in touch with your producer."

"Hildy Gruen, we've already come to a tentative deal. And the answer to your question is that the ad space is already triple-booked, but a buy from the Farlings would lead to improving access to their network."

"How can you sell the same ad space three times? Are we going to get sued?"

"It's all in the contracts," the director replied impatiently. "Everybody doesn't watch at the same time or see the same commercials, it depends on the species and the network affiliate."

Twenty

"There must be reporters here from every species on the tunnel network," Kelly said to Chastity. "I would have offered Methan our embassy for his press conference, but I knew we wouldn't have enough space."

"Still, it's strange that he'd turn to the Vergallians," the publisher of the Galactic Free Press replied. "I'm sure the Stryx would have given him a nice room somewhere if he asked."

"Maybe it has to do with all of the secret missions Samuel and Vivian have been running off on. Joe said if they reserve another one-day rental before the end of the cycle, they get a free piece of luggage."

Chastity scanned the crowd and nodded approvingly when she saw that Bob Steelforth and the paper's photographer had fought their way to the front. "Look, there's a Cayl reporter, and a Nangor. I must have spotted over a dozen species in encounter suits that I don't even recognize."

"The Alts finally agreeing to join the tunnel network is a big deal. They'll be the first new oxygen-breathing species since the Drazens and Hortens signed on, and that was around a half-million years ago."

"Aren't you forgetting somebody?" Walter inquired dryly.

"We never developed interstellar travel on our own so we don't count," Kelly told the paper's managing editor. "The Alts made it without help, other than the Stryx moving them from Earth to their own planet back in their Neanderthal days."

"Wine?" Czeros offered, extending a glass to the EarthCent ambassador. "No? I guess I'll just have to drink them both myself, then."

"Have you seen Bork?"

"He's over there against the wall with the other ambassadors. They delegated me to come and get you on my way back from the complimentary bar."

"I don't think I'll be able to see from there."

"We'll find you something to stand on. Haven't you noticed all of the reporters?"

"It's a little hard not to notice them when they're all crammed in between here and the stage."

"And what's that behind you?" the Frunge asked, pointing back the way they came in.

"The exit. Are you suggesting that I leave?"

"The Vergallian embassy has active jamming to prevent electronic surveillance, so the reporters will all have to go out to the corridor to file their stories. You don't want to find yourself between them and the exit if the Alt says something newsworthy."

"I suppose I am getting up in years enough to play it cautious," Kelly said, allowing Czeros to shepherd her back to the other ambassadors. "But I'm sure the announcement is just a formality."

"Then why make it in the Vergallian embassy rather than issuing a press release?" the Frunge ambassador countered. "Here they come now, so we're about to find out."

Aainda accompanied Methan into the ballroom, but the Vergallian ambassador stood back while the Alt mounted the small stage on his own. The jabbering press representatives fell silent, and feeling a poke in her side, Kelly looked over to see that Jeeves had floated in to observe.

"Fellow sentients," Methan began. "Many of you have sent delegations to our world in recent years, and I know that the experience has been mutually educational. My people have invested millions of hours considering the Stryx invitation to join the tunnel network, with discussion groups ranging from our children meeting on playgrounds, to their grandparents watching that they don't go down the slides headfirst. In light of what we have learned about the tunnel network and the galaxy at large, it is our decision to join the Vergallian Emp—"

A roar erupted from the gathered press corps, drowning out the rest of the Alt's sentence, and then one or more reporters from each species in attendance stampeded for the exit. A fleet-footed Grenouthian bounded ahead of the crowd and slyly triggered the doors to close as he passed through, creating a pile-up that bought the bunny a few more seconds for an exclusive. When Kelly got over the initial shock, she turned to Jeeves and subvoced, "What just happened?"

"I'm sure Methan will answer everybody's questions as soon as they stop shouting," the young Stryx replied. "You shouldn't be surprised, given how nice the Alts are."

"Nice? But what kind of reason is that to join the Vergallians?"

Jeeves just gestured at the stage with his pincer, and Kelly gathered that he didn't want to steal Methan's thunder.

"Please, everyone," Aainda's voice came over the embassy's public address system. "Our guest is happy to take your questions, but only if you behave yourselves and ask politely." The shouting seemed to lessen for a moment, but then it resumed in full force, and the Vergallian ambassador added, "Don't make me release the knock-out gas."

This threat did the trick, and the correspondents who had fought their way to the front of the stage all raised an appendage like school children and put on their best "Pick me" smiles.

"Yes," Methan said, pointing at the Grenouthian.

"Is this the will of your planet's population, or did she," the bunny gestured at Aainda, "drug you with pheromones and hijack your press conference?"

"Thank you for the question," the Alt responded politely. "I believe that my statement reflects the will of my people, but as you point out, I could be saying that because I'm under an external influence. Aainda?" Methan addressed the Vergallian ambassador. "Am I only saying this because you've dosed me with pheromones to control me?"

"Of course not," Aainda replied. "Your people chose to join our empire of their own free will."

"That doesn't prove anything," the Grenouthian reporter objected. "She could be lying."

The Alt flinched as if he'd been slapped, and it took him a moment to compose himself. "I must ask you not to use such objectionable language in my presence. If you don't find me trustworthy, would you be willing to listen to my wife?" Receiving a chorus of affirmations from the crowd, he gestured to the wings, and a simply dressed Alt woman carrying a baby made her way to the stage. "My wife,

Rinla, and our youngest, who isn't old enough yet to choose her name."

"I want to thank Ambassador Aainda for granting us the hospitality of her embassy and apologize on behalf of everyone present for the unfair accusation that was leveled against her," Rinla said in a dignified voice. "I assure you that our choice to join the Empire of a Hundred Worlds on a trial basis was reached through a planet-wide deliberative process. With all due respect to the Stryx, the only other option to receive serious consideration was a request to close our space to outsiders."

"You're saying that you never really considered joining the tunnel network?" a Dollnick reporter demanded, without waiting to be picked.

Rinla shot her husband a pained look at the alien's rudeness, but he shrugged as if to say, "You know that's what they're all like."

"We initially considered accepting the Stryx invitation, but it didn't take long for us to realize that our people are ill-equipped to function on our own as tunnel network members. I don't want to hurt anybody's feelings," she paused to reposition the baby in her arms, "but our society is founded on cooperation, trust, and working towards common goals. Your tunnel network turns everything into a," Rinla hesitated again, and steeled herself before uttering the objectionable word, "business."

The Dollnick gave a puzzled whistle that plainly meant, "Am I missing something here?" The other alien correspondents were equally confused by the answer, and they were all engaged in rerunning Rinla's words in their heads to check for a translation glitch when Methan pointed at the human reporter, whose hand was still raised.

"Bob Steelforth. Galactic Free Press. How can you join the Vergallian Empire when you don't have any queens?"

"Thank you for the question," Methan said. "You've identified the precise reason we decided to accept Aainda's proposal to join their empire. We wish to gain access to a highly trained cadre of professional administrators with experience in the rough-and-tumble galaxy we find ourselves in."

"Follow-up question. You're referring to Vergallian royals?"

"Exactly. Aainda has assured us of an ample supply of young princesses on attractive terms to act as our diplomats and manage our trade. By joining the Vergallian Empire, we not only gain access to the tunnel network under the favorable arrangement already negotiated with the Stryx by our new suzerain, but those of our people who choose to travel will be welcomed at Vergallian embassies, both on and off the tunnel network, in return for a modest user fee. Yes?" Methan concluded, pointing to another reporter.

"Let me get this straight," the Frunge said slowly. "You're joining the Vergallian Empire in order for them to act as a shield between your people and the rest of us because you think we're rude?"

"Thank you for the question, though I wouldn't have put it exactly that way myself," Methan replied. "It's true that we have run into some difficulties in our limited dealings with other species. For example, when we agreed to purchase the first hundred million environmentally friendly bicycles from one of your manufacturers, we thought that the price was the price. Later we learned that our new Frunge friend who represented the manufacturing concern was working on a commission basis, and that, at the risk of speaking bluntly, our loss was his gain."

"That's just business," the reporter objected. "The whole galaxy is caveat emptor."

"But we have no tradition of 'Buyer beware' on our world. We don't hold it against you," Methan hastened to add. "In fact, our experience with the bicycles helped us realize just how poorly suited we are for your competitive environment. Perhaps future generations will choose to adapt, at which point they might reconsider the Vergallian arrangement, but my wife and I intend to continue raising our children the way our parents raised us. Yes?"

"Forgive me for speaking slowly," a Verlock reporter rumbled. "Our experience with Alts attending our academies shows you to be an intellectually advanced and peace-loving people. Why didn't you request management help from our emperor?"

"Thank you for asking, and having visited a Verlock academy world myself, I would recommend your educational system to anyone. To answer your question, it never would have occurred to us to foist our problems on another species. Aainda came to us with the offer, explaining that we would actually be doing everybody a favor. Perhaps she could answer your question better than I. Ambassador?"

"Thank you, Methan," Aainda spoke up from where she stood. "I had planned to issue a separate press release after the current news cycle has a chance to digest the idea of the Alts joining our empire, but I suppose there's something to be said for getting it all out there at once. I'm sure you all know that the Vergallian body politic has experienced a growing schism between an expansionist Imperial faction that believes it is our manifest destiny to absorb the

Humans into our empire and the more independent worlds which disagree."

"The Alts offered themselves as a sacrificial exchange?" a Horten reporter blurted out.

"As the Alts are originally from Earth, the Human homeworld, the expansionist Imperial faction has agreed to accept them as substitutes for the Humans, bringing to an end a painful episode. We also expect substantial savings on Imperial intelligence efforts to undermine the Stryx-backed EarthCent and the independent Conference of Sovereign Human Communities."

"This was the deal I was involved in?" Kelly asked Jeeves. "I didn't know I was selling the Alts to the Vergallians."

"I think it worked out rather well for all involved," the young Stryx responded. "The Farlings get to establish a scientific presence on Earth, the Fleet Vergallians save on reparations for Baylit's armed incursion, the Imperial Vergallians heal one of their largest internal divisions, the Alts get a crop of professional administrators to keep the rest of you from eating their lunch, EarthCent no longer has to worry about continual harassment from Vergallian Intelligence, and of course, everybody wins with the All Species Cookbook. Think of it as our version of stone soup."

"Do you mean the Stryx were behind it the whole time? But Aainda did all the cooking."

"And we provided the pot and the stones."

"I get that the tunnel network is the pot, but—are you saying that we're the stones?"

"It would be more accurate to describe you as catalysts. I'm sure you've heard that every time a new species joins the tunnel network, there's a window of a few hundred years to shake things up before everybody settles into a new normal."

"But how about the Alts?" Kelly asked, as in the background Methan began a response to a Sharf reporter's question about shipping regulations, and the rest of the other correspondents began slipping out to file their stories. "Can't you use them to bring about change?"

"They're too nice. Hello, Aainda."

"Stryx Jeeves, Ambassador. I hope you weren't shocked by Methan's announcement, Kelly, but Vergallian Intelligence has been breathing down my neck ever since I approached the Imperial Council, which leaks like a sieve. I never would have used our children if I had seen another option."

"You mean those overnight trips Samuel took with Vivian?"

"I needed a way to convince the various factions that I had the backing of EarthCent. In negotiations between Vergallian worlds, we send a princess or a royal consort, but as EarthCent lacks royalty, I had to make substitutions."

"Just like we did with the alien ingredients in our cookbook, but what role did your daughter play?"

"None she was aware of," Aainda said. "I did encourage Aabina to take the EarthCent civil service exam when it was offered, and later I planted the idea of telling you about the All Species Cookbook. That was the final piece that made it all work."

"Getting her the job at EarthCent?"

"Making sure that Vergallian vegan was finally presented in a positive light. You wouldn't believe how frustrating it is for the most populous species on the tunnel network to receive no respect for our culinary traditions while the Drazens get by with drenching everything in hot sauce."

"My ears are burning," Bork said, joining the ambassadors and Jeeves. "As long as we're on the subject of the cookbook, Kelly, I have a bone to pick with you."

"I know we included your recipe for stuffed chili peppers. I began to sweat just looking at the picture."

"It's not about our section," the Drazen ambassador said. He took a quick look around and lowered his voice. "It's the Horten recipe for seafood chowder."

"That wasn't Ortha's, it must have come from one of our communities on their open worlds by way of the Galactic Free Press. What was the problem?"

"Don't attempt to add tentacle directly to the chowder," Bork recited from memory. "Blanch the tentacles in boiling water for thirty seconds, and then bake at a low heat in their own juices for five hours, or until tender. Add the tentacles to the chowder just before serving."

"It sounds like octopus or squid was substituted for something with tentacles on Horten worlds."

"There are no sea creatures with tentacles on Horten worlds," Bork complained. "Somebody must have put your people up to it just to get back at us."

"Get back at you for what?"

The Drazen ambassador suddenly looked embarrassed for perhaps the second time Kelly could remember. "I just received an urgent ping from Herl," he said. "Emergency meeting to discuss the Alts."

"Did that make sense to you?" Kelly asked Aainda, as Bork hurried off.

"I think we're about to hear the other half," the Vergallian ambassador said. "Thank you for coming, Ambassador Ortha."

"Quite a coup for you, my dear," the Horten said, then turned to Kelly with a scowl. "After all the effort I went to fixing it so my son's girlfriend could work for your husband, this is how you repay me!"

"I don't know what you mean, Ambassador. The only part I played in the negotiations was agreeing to let the Farlings open a research facility on Earth."

"I'm talking about the Drazen hit-job you published in the cookbook," Ortha said, and pitched his voice so that the translation from Kelly's implant sounded not unlike Bork speaking. "Drazen cocktails are too toxic for most species to imbibe without intestinal damage, but you can enjoy the aesthetics of a Divverflip by substituting for the acid. Prepare ice cubes with blue pea flower tea and watch any clear cocktail change colors before your eyes. Add sparkling juices to achieve hues from deep purple to vibrant pink, and your friends will turn green with envy."

"You don't think—"

"I don't think, I know," the Horten ambassador growled, even as his skin reddened with anger. "How could you have let such an obvious insult get past the censor? I demand you remove it."

"I'm afraid it's too late for that, Ortha. Besides, Bork was just complaining to me about a seafood recipe with chopped tentacle."

"Oh, that. It was obvious the Drazens were going to try something so we were forced to act preemptively."

"So can't we call it even and move on? I had Aabina make sure that none of the recipes in the Horten section called for washing anything more than twice."

"We'll see," Ortha said. "Our cookbook response team is still analyzing the recipes from other species to see if anything else slipped past you."

248

Twenty One

Aabina climbed onto the holo-training platform at the EarthCent intelligence training camp and gave Beowulf the sign to begin. The Cayl hound tilted back his head and howled like a moon was about to crash into the hold, causing Alexander to join in for a test of endurance. When the improvised duet came to an abrupt end, Aabina took advantage of the sudden silence to begin her speech.

"Welcome everybody to the combined launch party for the All Species Cookbook and the new, soon-to-be-a-smash-hit on the Grenouthian network, Stone Soup. The broadcast premiere will be showing on the holographic system in just a few minutes, but first, could we have a round of applause to thank Joe McAllister and EarthCent Intelligence for making this space available on short notice?"

The audience, which included several hundred InstaSitters who had taken cooking classes from Jonah or participated in the LARPing league he started, gave a hearty round of applause. Alien audience members, including a number of ambassadors and their families, added their own distinctive noises of approval.

"Next, I want to thank all of the volunteers from the EarthCent mixers who took off time from work to help prepare recipes and stage them for the photo sessions at the embassy. We couldn't have done it without you."

"We couldn't have done it without her," Donna said loudly to Kelly, as the audience applauded again. "If all of the surplus princesses turn out like Aabina, the Alts made the right decision. Did it ever occur to anybody that we would have been better off if the Stryx had let the Vergallians conquer Earth?"

"We're doing all right for ourselves," the EarthCent ambassador protested. "Jeeves even says that we're useful."

"We also have the first edition printing of the All Species Cookbook available for sale at half off the cover price," Aabina continued. "If you ask nicely, Jonah, or the editor, Donna Doogal, might be willing to sign a copy for you. Put it in your family vault for a few thousand years and who knows what it will be worth?"

"She's so good at this," Kelly murmured to Donna. The crowd shifted subtly towards the folding tables where Thomas and Chance had stacked a few hundred cookbooks. Fenna and Kevin were manning the mini-register borrowed from his chandlery.

"My hand hurts just thinking about autographs," the embassy manager said, but it was obvious that she was tickled with the idea of being asked to sign her work.

"You're all welcome to stick around for dancing after the broadcast," Aabina continued. "Don't mind the Grenouthian cameramen, they're just topping up on dance footage to fill the odd time gaps for Stone Soup."

At this announcement, the young InstaSitters in the crowd began to whisper excitedly. Many of them pointed at their ears as they pinged their friends to drop whatever they were doing and hightail it for Mac's Bones and a chance to be immortalized in a future Grenouthian broadcast.

"The Gem caterers will be setting up hot food while we watch Stone Soup, and every recipe they've prepared tonight is from the All Species Cookbook, so I don't want to hear any complaints," Aabina said. "On a more personal note, I have accepted an offer for full-time employment at the EarthCent embassy where I'll be working in the newly created position of executive assistant. Please feel free to contact me if you have any questions about humanity."

Kelly, Donna, and Daniel continued clapping loudly at this final announcement until the lights dimmed and the holographic system for immersive training lit up with the Grenouthian broadcast. A life-sized Jonah wearing a white apron appeared in a cozy kitchen, flanked by an attractive Frunge girl and a petite female Verlock.

"I guess the producer talked him into the harem concept after all," Samuel said to Vivian, whose brother had recounted the contract negotiations for them.

"And it looks like he's settling right into the celebrity role," she replied, indicating where Jonah was busily signing the cookbooks that Fenna was ringing up under Kevin's supervision. "Those girls are more interested in him than watching the show."

"They can always get it on demand later. What's wrong with the volume?"

"Sound!" dozens of voices from the audience called out, and whoever was running the holographic system made the correction almost instantly.

"—from right here on Union Station," Jonah's voice became audible mid-sentence. "We're opening with a tribute recipe for Sharf omelets contributed by workers on one of their recycling orbitals. I'll start with beating the eggs while my assistants prepare the vegetables."

"He doesn't look nervous at all," Kelly marveled.

"It's not live," Donna reminded her. "Blythe told me they had to do six takes to get through the opening scene."

"Can I help you?" the EarthCent ambassador asked a young Drazen girl, who hesitantly approached the two women.

"Could you sign this 'To my friend, Binka?'" the alien requested nervously, holding the cookbook out to Donna.

"Maybe you should go sit with your grandson," Kelly suggested to her friend, observing that a line of InstaSitters with cookbooks was queuing behind the Drazen girl.

"My public calls," Donna said, winking at the ambassador. "If you see Czeros, remind him that he forgot his borscht tureen. It's in the embassy's kitchenette."

Kelly set off to find the ambassadors who she had spotted earlier near the temporary bar Joe had set up. Working her way through the crowd, she encountered the Horten ambassador's son, who thrust a pamphlet in her direction before he recognized her.

"Sorry, Ambassador," Mornich said. "Marilla is making me hand these out."

"A recipe for travel success that won't break your budget," Kelly read from the cover of the Tunnel Trips brochure. "Who came up with the slogan?"

"Affie's boyfriend, Stick. We were all kicking ideas around at Dorothy's last dance thing. He seems to have a knack for marketing."

"Have you seen your father?"

"Pop was arm wrestling with the Drazen ambassador last I knew. I think they were up to best out of twenty-one."

Kelly paused and looked back at the holo-stage. A Drazen girl was grating some type of hard cheese while Jonah gave a detailed description of its manufacturing and aging process on Earth. The hologram was intercut with scenes from the Italian cheese factory that must have been supplied by Hildy Gruen, EarthCent's public relations director.

"Ambassador," M793qK called to her from the fringe of the crowd. "I was hoping to speak with you before heading back to Flower later this evening. Can you give me a little time?"

"I can do better than that," Kelly said. "I can give you a few things to bring Lynx for the baby. Do you mind?"

"Em is hardly a baby," the beetle doctor said. "She's already started preschool."

"In that case, I'll send her some children's books. We can talk while I pick them out."

While choosing a dozen books to send back with M793qK, Kelly learned that the other Farling she had assumed was a spy, G32FX, would be heading the scientific mission to Earth. The rest of what the doctor told her about their detailed plans for recovering ancient DNA went in one ear and out the other, but it was sufficiently distracting that it took Kelly forever to choose the titles in Em's age range. By the time she returned to the party, Stone Soup had wrapped up and the dancing was starting, though the line for cookbook signing was longer than it had been when she left. She saw Thomas guiding a cargo floater with another load of boxes into position behind the table and decided that her ordering mistake had actually been a subconscious flash of business brilliance.

The smell of freshly-baked cookies compelled her towards the tables where the Gem caterers had set up, and as she approached, the EarthCent ambassador spotted a giant paw stretch out from under the table cloth that draped to the deck, and drag back what looked like a fallen half-sandwich. Then she heard a loud yelp and saw Alexander bounding backward from a tiny Frunge woman who she didn't recognize.

"Is he bothering you?" Kelly asked.

"He tried the old bump-and-dump trick on me, but he seems to have forgotten who he's messing with," the Frunge matchmaker replied. "You must be the chaperone's mother. You have the same eyes."

"Kelly McAllister," the ambassador introduced herself. "And you are?"

"Mizpah. Your daughter hasn't mentioned me?"

"Are you the scary—I'm sorry," Kelly interrupted herself, but the old Frunge just laughed.

"I'm here undercover so don't tell her you saw me," the matchmaker said. "This sashimi is excellent, it's no wonder Alexander let his nose get the better of him."

Kelly finally made her way to where the ambassadors were lounging around the keg on chairs somebody had brought over from the ice-harvester's patio and arguing about advertising rates.

"You settle this," Crute said, the moment the EarthCent ambassador was within speaking range. "The instantaneous ratings for the premiere were above the predicted range and he," the Dollnick pointed at the Grenouthian with all three hands that weren't holding a beer, "says that they can apply a surcharge to the negotiated ad rates."

"It's in the contract," the giant bunny reiterated. "You can't believe that we wouldn't protect ourselves from an unexpected success."

"Protect yourselves from success? What kind of sense does that make?"

"Say you were a prince instead of an ambassador and you terraformed a moon for a real estate developer who told you he'd be selling a million vacation estates to retirees for a million creds each."

"An even trillion," Crute said. "Standard deal is sixty percent for terraforming, or six hundred billion."

"Correct. Now let's say the developer turned around and sold the retirees the vacation estates for a million and a half apiece. Wouldn't you want to protect yourself from that in the contract?"

"Dollnick retirees have a million creds to spend on retirement estates?" Kelly asked in amazement.

"That's not the point," the Grenouthian ambassador said. "When we sell commercial time, it's for an estimated range of viewers, and if twice as many sentients end up watching, we have to recoup our theoretical losses."

"What happens if you overestimate the number of viewers?" Crute demanded.

"Well, that's different. We do have fixed expenses."

"I'm going to talk to Aainda," the EarthCent ambassador excused herself, not having any interest in a business argument featuring numbers larger than a hundred, or millionaire alien retirees buying vacation estates. The Vergallian ambassador was standing with Jeeves and Baa, and Kelly was sure they changed the subject when she approached.

"Come join us, Ambassador," Aainda said. "The premiere was lovely. I can't wait until your future son-in-law-by-marriage cooks up some Vergallian vegan."

"Is son-in-law-by-marriage an official family relationship for Vergallians?" Kelly couldn't help asking.

"All family relationships are official with us, it makes things much easier when we have to arrange for hostage swaps during visits."

"It's all in my book, *Vergallians for Humans*," Jeeves said. "I don't see the need to mention that it's on the official EarthCent reading list for diplomats."

"I'll ask Aabina to summarize it for me," Kelly retorted. "I'm glad you could come, Baa. Dorothy told me that you've been a great help with her new promotions."

"Glass slippers are easy once you get the hang of it," the mage replied modestly. "The only problem is settling on the prize."

Not far away, a trio of teens who had been summoned late to the party by their InstaSitter girlfriends were standing as close as they dared to the keg, trying to goad each other into asking the old man to sell them a beer. Before any of them could muster up the courage to ask, they heard a quiet voice from the side say, "Psssst, over here."

"Are you talking to us?" the tallest of the young men asked the Vergallian, who was just a little too handsome to pass as human.

"I've got something that will help you relax and dance so you won't need that beer," Stick told them. "Come over here where everybody can't see."

"What is it? Some kind of alien drug? Hey, do you sell Kraken stick?"

"Better than that. Do you all have implants?"

"Yeah."

"Sure. I've jacked into stuff," the stockiest youth said boldly.

"Did you think we just fell off a pepper barge from Earth?" the youngest of the trio demanded.

"No, you guys are cool," Stick reassured them, and passed each of the young men a small black memory module that looked a bit like a poker chip. "Try jacking into this."

"I'm all in," the leader said, though his hand shook a little as he held up the memory module and squinted at it. "How does it work?"

"Activate your heads-up display and you should see a new menu option to side-load Shadow Dancer. It connects wirelessly."

"Is this for real?" the youngest kid said, his eyes going wide as the proper foot positions for the current ballroom dance appeared before him. "It's not some kind of gag to make us look bad?"

"Solid as Stryx," Stick promised. "It's the latest thing from SBJ Fashions, but your girlfriends don't have to know."

"Will this cover it?" the leader asked, pulling out a handful of creds and offering them to the Vergallian.

"Shadow Dancer is on the house tonight. Tell your friends."

"Dude!"

The three youngsters danced off in search of their girl-friends, placing their feet in the ghostly outlines. Stick checked his pockets, and finding he was fresh out of memory modules, headed back to the SBJ Fashions table to restock.

"Are you giving Shadow Dancer to guys who are using it or just dumping the memory modules in the trash?" Dorothy demanded. "I've got Tzachan, Samuel, and Wrylenth working the floor with you, but none of them have even used up their first batch yet. How many times have you been back?"

"Four," Stick said. "If you let me charge for the memory modules we'd be raking it in. You really have to ask

Thomas to program a counter to keep score of successful foot placements and get those kids competing with each other. I bet we could hook half the young gamers on the station, and then charge extra for add-ons, like special dance moves."

"Or instructions for what to do with their arms," Affie commented. "Some of the boys look like they're doing a ballroom version of—what did you call it, Dorothy?"

"Irish step dancing," the ambassador's daughter told them. "Well, we're all out of memory modules, Stick, so you're done for the night unless you want to take pity on Srythlan and distribute his share."

"I'd be happy to, but Verlocks get offended if you do anything to insinuate that they're too slow."

"Can you hold down the fort while I put together a dish to take Dring, Affie? He's babysitting for Margie at our place."

"Why didn't you hire an InstaSitter?" Stick asked.

"It's the principle of the thing."

Dorothy went to check if the Gem caterers had improved their interpretation of Vergallian vegan, and Flazint arrived, over an hour late. The Frunge girl was resplendent in an SBJ Fashions ball gown and a towering trellis. "Where's Dorothy going?" she asked.

"To feed her babysitter," Affie said. "Leave it to our friend to get a Maker to provide free babysitting with hundreds of InstaSitters milling around, not to mention the owners. You missed the premiere of Jonah's show."

"It's this new trellis, my hair vines aren't used to it yet. How did our co-sponsorship work out?"

"The Grenouthians did a good job with the dance interludes, and I caught a flicker of our SBJ logo blinking in the hologram, so Jeeves must have paid extra for a subliminal overlay."

Samuel arrived at the table and said, "Ready for another batch,"

"Stick used them all up," Affie told him. "Vivian stopped by and made me promise to have you ping her when you finished handing out your allotment."

"Is Dorothy still making us do the glass slipper thing? Vivian will have my head if the slipper doesn't transform when I put it on her foot."

"She didn't tell you? Jeeves changed the glass slipper giveaway to a raffle after Tzachan told him what Flazint's matchmaker said about the liability. It's not about love now, just some free prizes."

"Are you selling tickets?"

"No, Jeeves is going to give some random guy the slipper, and I've got to let him put it on my foot so the Grenouthian cameramen can get immersive video for an ad campaign," Affie explained. "Baa won't even tell me what the enchantment is going to do."

"You're about to find out," Jeeves said, extending his pincer to Stick with the glass slipper. "You're on."

"Me?" Stick backed away. "I told Dorothy that the whole Cinderella thing only works for Humans. If you wanted a Vergallian fairytale—I'm not sure I remember any."

"He's picking the two of you for the aesthetics," Flazint surmised. "You're both too attractive to actually be Human, but you know how their advertising focuses on the unattainable."

"Take the slipper, Stick," Affie said in a resigned voice. "Where are the Grenouthian cameramen set up?"

"Over by the bar, of course," Jeeves said. "By the way, the enchantment is binding."

"What does that mean?"

"It means that whatever the slipper delivers, you're stuck with it. And before you ask, yes, you have to participate in any SBJ Fashions promotion I request. It's in your contract."

"It better not be that green dress Dorothy is always trying to make me model," Affie said to Stick, as they followed the Stryx back to where the ambassadors were gathered. "I'll wear it, but not until I run it through the wash with some dye."

"I'm not under contract to anybody," her boyfriend pointed out.

"You'll do it, because if you don't Jeeves will give the glass slipper to some other guy to put on my foot, and then I'll have to kill you."

"You princesses are all the same," Stick muttered under his breath, but he got down on one knee where the Grenouthian cameraman indicated and managed to give the impression of an eager young lover.

"Action," the Grenouthian ambassador called, much to the chagrin of the cameramen who reflexively obeyed, even though the shot wasn't perfectly framed.

Affie had already removed her left shoe when she sat down, so Stick took a gentle hold of her heel and eased her toes into the glass slipper. For a moment nothing seemed to happen, and then both Vergallians looked around angrily.

"Binding," Jeeves reminded them. "And welcome aboard, Diemro."

"What happened?' Flazint asked. "The glass slipper didn't change."

"A signed contract was just delivered to my heads-up display," Affie told her. "I've been assigned to handle Alt business interests on Union Station. I'm just lucky they don't have much going on or I'd have to quit SBJ Fashions."

"Where I am now employed as the outside sales manager," Stick groaned. "Regular hours cramp my style."

"I'm your style and you'll take the job to get my family off our backs," Affie said. "But how can you claim there's promotional value in a slipper that doesn't transform, Jeeves?"

"We'll use a still for display panel advertising. The mystery of what the slipper will become is far more compelling than showing the actual transformation."

"But that's what I told Dorothy," Stick protested, and then realized he been hanged by his own words. Both participants in the glass slipper ceremony glared in the direction of Aainda, who gave them a friendly wave before going back to talking with Kelly and Baa.

"I do enjoy when my plans work out," the Vergallian ambassador said. "And I should thank you for your contribution as well, Baa. That enchanted dagger scabbard saved Samuel a great deal of trouble."

"About that," the Terragram mage said. "You might want to test it if you get the chance because it's been hundreds of thousands of years since I tried that one and my memory isn't what it used to be."

"What are the two of you talking about?" Kelly asked.

"Young love," Aainda eventually answered with a sigh. "If the Hortens are right about reincarnation, maybe I'll try coming back as a Human."

From the Author

Do you have a recipe suggestion for the All Species Cookbook? I'm thinking about putting together a condensed, low-bandwidth version for solo traders hosting alien friends. Living so much in Zero-G, traders have limited experience cooking and iffy access to ingredients, but all of the advanced species know it's the thought that counts. Credit will be given in modified form, so "Jane Doe from Iowa" could end up listed as "Jane, from Ooolah, a Dollnick ag world." Send your submission (or comments) to e_foner@yahoo.com.

The next EarthCent book will be Assisted Living, a sequel to the spinoff which takes place on the circuit ship Flower. If you haven't seen my AI Diaries series, the first book is **Turing Test**. For notifications of new releases, sign up for the mailing list at www.ifitbreaks.com. You can also find me on Facebook.

Also From the Author

Independent Living

Turing Test

Human Test

Magic Test

Meghan's Dragon

EarthCent Ambassador Series:

Date Night on Union Station

Alien Night on Union Station

High Priest on Union Station

Spy Night on Union Station

Carnival on Union Station

Wanderers on Union Station

Vacation on Union Station

Guest Night on Union Station

Word Night on Union Station

Party Night on Union Station

Review Night on Union Station

Family Night on Union Station

Book Night on Union Station

LARP Night on Union Station

Career Night on Union Station

Last Night on Union Station

CPSIA information can be obtained
at www.ICGtesting.com
Printed in the USA
BVHW070913250719
554325BV00002B/201/P